DEATH OF A DREAM

A BARBARA O'GRADY MYSTERY

SHARON ROWSE

THREE CEDARS PRESS

ALSO BY SHARON ROWSE

The Barbara O'Grady Series: (in order)

Death of a Secret

Death of a Threat

Death of a Promise

Death of a Shadow

Death of a Lie

Death of a Dream

Death of a Chance

The John Granville & Emily Turner Historical Mystery Series: (in order)

The Silk Train Murder

The Lost Mine Murders

The Missing Heir Murders

The Terminal City Murders

The Cannery Row Murders

The Hidden City Murders

The Dockside Murders

For details on these and upcoming books or to sign up for her mailing list, visit Sharon's website at: www.sharonrowse.com

DEATH OF A DREAM
A Barbara O'Grady Mystery
By Sharon Rowse

Copyright © 2021 by Sharon Rowse

Book cover designed by Sharon Rowse & Three Cedars Press
Published by Three Cedars Press
www.threecedarspress.com

ISBN: 978-1-988037-20-2

CHAPTER ONE

"Barbara! You're back." Marie Deslauriers, my soon-to-be-ex temporary assistant and the former bane of my existence beamed at me as I walked through the front door of my seventh floor office on a golden September afternoon. "I didn't expect you 'til next week."

I just stared. Last time I'd seen her, Marie's bright red hair had been spiked straight up, she had a ring through her right eyebrow and seven more in each ear, and she was wearing hot pink, acid green and some kind of grapey purple. Most of it spandex.

Now the hair was a pale blond, cut short and tapering neatly backwards to her nape. The eyebrow ring was gone. Her ears looked naked with only three small gold hoops apiece. And everything she wore was black.

And my office!

I glanced back at the door, checking that I'd walked into the right place. "Barbara O'Grady, P. I." the lettering said.

Yep, this was the place. What had Marie done to it?

Last time I'd seen it—all of a week and a half ago—there had been my battered oak desk with a couple of wing chairs that served as visitor's chairs, a smaller desk for Marie, a partition between our "offices" and a folding table and some chairs stuffed in a corner near the big windows that faced the parkade.

Now that same space held four desks. I think they were desks. Mostly large flat surfaces with spindly metal legs at the corners—four of them crammed into a space that had held two nicely.

And the colors Marie used to wear? Those had somehow ended up on the desks. One surface was a glaring fuchsia pink. One was citron—that yellowed green I love everywhere. Except apparently on a desk surface. Another was a sort of burnt orange. Orange! And the last desk was a deep, rich purple, almost dark enough to be black. Okay, that one wasn't so bad.

Who even makes desks like that? And more to the point—what were they doing in my office?

And where were my chairs? My favorite burgundy leather desk chair, the one that reminded me of where I'd come from in this business. The matching vintage guest chairs that clients always commented on. Gone.

In their place… I blinked. Those were chairs? How did you sit in them? And why would anyone want to sit in them?

"Marie. Where's my stuff?" I asked, my voice as level as willpower and clenched fists could make it.

"Barbara! It's good to see you," she said, springing up and racing forward. "And congratulations! Your show was—well, amazing. And did you read the reviews?"

She reached for what looked like the art section of a couple of newspapers, waving them in my face.

The one-woman show of my paintings that I'd dreamed of all my life had opened last week at the Courtland Gallery. I'd taken too much time away from my investigation business—especially in that last ten day sprint—to finish the paintings I'd promised gallery owner Margaret Courtland. Then it took more time and focus than I'd ever anticipated to get those paintings delivered and see them hung.

And the show itself…

There were no words. It was beyond my expectations.

If I'd had any expectations to start with. Which I hadn't. Just a few tattered dreams.

But how many people ever achieve their dreams? I just did. And none of it had seemed real. It still didn't.

Which was why I was here, instead of in the Bahamas. Or at home, trying to paint something inspired. I needed to get back to reality. To the familiar routine of my detective business.

I glanced around me. Not seeing a single thing that was familiar, aside from the sign on the door, the one that read Barbara O'Grady Investigations.

I did not need this. Not now.

"Yes. I saw them," I said slowly. "And thank you. But what—is—this?" And I waved my arm around what used to be my very professional office.

"You like? You have to admit it's an improvement over our previous crap," Marie said, rubbing a hand along the rounded edge of the desk nearest her—the very pink one. "And you know we needed to make changes. I just thought I'd do it as a surprise."

I stared at her, speechless, for a long moment.

"Why would I need to make changes?" I said at last. "The show is done. I'm back. And I don't need an assistant any longer. That was just until I got my paintings finished, remember? You can start taking full-time art courses, fulfill your own dream."

This new, polished version of Marie just shook her head at me, making a tsking noise with her tongue. "You've got post-show letdown, that's what it is," she said. "You're a success. Everyone wants your paintings. And you can't tell me Margaret Courtland hasn't already started talking to you about another show."

She had. I was ignoring her.

Or trying to.

And I'd come running back to the familiarity of my life where no-one valued my art, and I'd built a life and a business for myself without it. And been just fine, thank-you very much.

Well, mostly.

Of course it was also a life where I lived alone. And the man in my life wanted that to change as well.

I was trying to ignore that, too. I'm just lucky Nick is a patient man.

But just because I knew I was deluding myself right now didn't mean I was prepared to admit it to anyone else. Or accept change on this scale.

I glared at the room again. And finally noticed the once neutral grey-toned walls, which were now bright white. At least they didn't clash with the furniture. And the big whiteboards we used for brainstorming were still there. But why four desks?

Did I even want to know?

It didn't matter. Marie was about to tell me. When did she learn to read me so well?

And why didn't that thought scare me as much as it should have?

"Four desks," Marie said, holding up the requisite number of fingers, as though it wouldn't mean anything to me otherwise. "For the three of us. Plus Badger, when we need her. And you get first choice of desks."

Badger made sense, sort of. She was our sometime computer consultant. The really expensive one. The one I didn't expect to need often. But...

"The three of us," I repeated. Stupidly.

"You, me and Cory. Your nephew," Marie said. "I know he's still part-time, but he's really good. He deserves his own space. And in case you're about to start worrying about me, don't. I'm loving my evening art classes. And I think I'm good at detective work. Besides, I still owe you."

No, she didn't. As a former client, she'd paid me well. Very well. Then she'd spent six months as my underpaid assistant—despite my protests—giving me the time I needed to finish the paintings for my show.

But Marie didn't see it that way. She'd taken it personally that I'd been shot on her case. As well she should.

It was her headstrong actions that had caused it. But she'd more than compensated for it.

I'd had my show. It was her turn.

And it had been hard enough working with her enthusiastic energy when I was focused on my show... Wait a minute. "You're good at detective work? How would you know?"

"The Lang case?" Her tone said she shouldn't have to remind me.

Not this again.

"Yes, you did a stellar job on the Lang case," I said. "You proved you're very good at research. But that's just one aspect of detective work, Marie. And a small part of your current job. Mostly, your focus is handling communications when I'm not here."

She fidgeted with a small stack of papers on the pink desk. Wouldn't meet my eyes.

Oh no. I'd obviously been too focused on my show in the last few weeks. What had I missed? "Isn't it?"

"Well, yes. Except for our newest case..."

"Our newest case? What case?"

I'd closed out all my active cases just in time for my show. Barely. And Marie had been invaluable in that process, even if I hated to admit that.

"Oh, you're going to love this one," she said. "I've been working with them all week, setting things up for your return—they're great! And they gave us this amazing furniture in partial payment—at cost, of course. We could never have afforded to update your stodgy old office like this otherwise."

She'd been what? I glanced at the furniture. It felt like my head was going to explode. Marie had taken on a case? Without letting me know?

Again?

And what was with this furniture?

"Marie," I said, fighting to keep my voice level. "Who is the client?"

"Justine Grayson. The designer. She's being sued for fraud, and she wants us to prove her innocent."

She couldn't have said anything worse.

Justine Grayson is one of my least favorite people. I've known her since our university days, when we took some fine arts courses together. Just like I'd known Don James since then—and look how well that had turned out when I ran into him again on the Lang case.

And I'd actually liked Don, back then. Justine, on the other hand…

We'd always rubbed each other the wrong way. For her to even consider coming to me for help, let alone actually hiring me? Something had to be very wrong in her life. And sorting it out would not be pleasant.

Justine always had an amazing eye for design—with the arrogance to go with it. And she didn't mind sharing her opinions with everyone around her.

She was also all too vocal about other people's shortcomings. "This is a hot mess," she was fond of saying. "Have you no eyes? How can you call yourself an artist?"

I could hear that tone ringing in my memory. And I suddenly realized that she sounded exactly like Jayson Ho, a very successful abstract artist and a former boyfriend of mine.

Jayson was the first—and the last—man I'd lived with. It had been five years, now. More.

And Nick was the first man I'd actually considered sharing space with since.

Even though I suspected that I loved Nick, I hadn't quite made it past the considering stage. Living with Jayson had been that toxic. For my relationships, and for my art.

I swallowed hard, reminded myself I was no longer that person. That I'd just had a very successful show.

"So exactly what is this case we've taken on for Justine?" I asked Marie.

She shrugged one shoulder and managed to make it look

elegant. Almost as elegant as her elder sister Celeste. I wasn't used to Marie looking elegant.

I didn't recognize this new Marie.

She still had her tattoos though. And she'd added a new one, in a blue line around her right wrist. I looked a little closer—it was a variant on a Celtic knot, and it looked like one of her own designs. That too was elegant.

Then she grinned at me. Ah, there was the old Marie. She hadn't gone anywhere. I was strangely relieved.

"I've only seen parts of the case—Justine said she was waiting for you for the rest. But why don't we let her tell you," Marie said. "She'll be here in half an hour."

"She'll what?" I said. "I can't possibly be ready to talk to a new client, and especially not Justine, that quickly."

Marie just stared at me. "Why not?" she asked

For once, I didn't have the words. I couldn't even begin to explain my history with Justine. Or the difficulty I was having coming down from the high of my recent show and readjusting to the life I had built here. Which Marie had just turned upside down.

Again.

It seemed to be a specialty of hers.

————

TRUE TO HER WORD, Marie gave me my choice of desks, since there wasn't even a pseudo-office for me anymore. Considerate of her. And yes, there'd be a reckoning between us later.

After I'd got through the meeting with Justine.

I'd barely got myself settled at the eggplant desk—surprisingly, the color was growing on me—when the phone rang. I recognized Margaret Courtland's number and cringed a little, but answered it anyway. I didn't have time for this—not when my office looked like a pop art gallery, and Justine Grayson, of all people, would be here in less than half an hour.

And I suspected Margaret wanted to talk about next steps in my painting career. I wasn't sure if I even wanted next steps. Or how I was going to balance a painting career with the rest of my life if I did.

But I owed Margaret—she was the reason I was now experiencing some small measure of success in the field I'd long assumed could never be more than a hobby. I'd always take her calls. Even if she had the worst sense of timing of anyone I knew.

"Good morning, Margaret," I said, trying to force some alertness into my voice. Hoping I didn't sound as disconcerted as I felt.

"Barbara? I'm glad you're there. I have a problem, and I need to see you. Immediately. Can you come to the gallery?"

Margaret sounded upset, her usually matter-of-fact tone ragged and a bit uncertain. "Margaret? What's wrong?"

"Not over the phone. Can you come?"

There was only one answer. "I have a meeting in a few minutes, but I can be there by four-thirty at the latest." Depending how messy Justine's case turned out to be. "Will that work?"

"I'll be here," she said, and disconnected.

Leaving me with a new worry. What was going on with Margaret? I'd never even seen her ruffled, no matter how chaotic a show became. And they can get pretty bad.

For a couple of months after university, I had a temp job assisting Ian Wong of the Omega Gallery while he was putting on a particularly complex show with several well-known artists. Between temperamental artists who thought their work was the most important, misplaced artwork, incorrectly installed displays and missing paperwork, I decided it would be easier to manage a circus. My opinion hasn't changed much since then.

So what was serious enough to leave Margaret Courtland sounding like that?

CHAPTER TWO

While I was still worrying about what might be wrong with Margaret, Justine Grayson showed up at the door with two of her minions. Being Justine, she would have minions. Looking across the office, she spotted me at my desk and stopped dramatically, her eyes locked on mine.

"Barbara," she said, swinging her arms wide. "How amazing to see you again. How long has it been?"

Not long enough.

But I had to admit Justine looked good. Every inch the successful designer, from her artfully tousled ruby-toned hair, to the fluid but beautifully fitted designer outfit—and that was the only word for it—she was wearing.

Tiny and graceful, Justine was one of those women who always make me feel like a giraffe.

And five foot ten is not that tall. Especially these days, when they seem to be growing them taller and taller. I often walk down the sidewalk beside high school girls who top six feet. And, best of all, who look comfortable in their skin at that height. That never used to happen, not when I was that age.

"So I gather you want to hire my firm. What seems to be the

problem?" I hate sounding that stilted, but with Justine, it seemed the safest approach.

At least until I figured out what she'd got herself involved in.

Justine dropped her handbag, a parcel and a Nordstrom's shopping bag on the nearest desk, and sank into the chair across from me. I wondered what the minions had been doing while she'd been shopping.

"I'm being maligned," she said in dramatic tones.

"You're being what?" I asked. Who says maligned these days?

"Maligned! My name brand is being threatened. Do you know how hard I've worked to build my brand?" She pushed back the fringe that had fallen into her eyes. Even that movement looked like it had been designed.

"I'll need a few details," I said dryly.

"Details! I'm beset with details!" Justine said she waved her hands towards her entourage. "They have all the details. They'll fill you in."

"That won't help, Justine. I need to know, in your words, what is going on," I said as calmly as I could. I remembered this drama show of hers all too well.

"Oh, very well," she said.

I was pleased to see Marie take charge of the minions, getting them seated at the table by the window. Not that it made much difference since they could see and hear everything that was being said.

"It started nearly two weeks ago," Justine said, ignoring everyone else in the room in typical Justine style. "Just before your show. And congratulations, by the way."

She sounded sincere. Which surprised me. We hadn't exactly been complimentary of each other's work back then. Not the way I remembered it, anyway.

"Thank you," I said. "Go on."

"Anyway, I get this phone call, out of the blue. Some guy trying to sound threatening. And he was saying something stupid about me needing to pay, or I'd be sorry."

"That sounds like a pretty clichéd threat," I said. "Pay what?"

"Yes, exactly. And I laughed at him, and was going to hang up. But then he said…," She paused, shook her head. "No, you need to hear it."

And she pulled out her phone and tapped a couple of times on the screen.

"You recorded it?" I asked.

"I always record my calls," she said matter-of-factly.

Interesting. I wondered why.

A low, menacing voice came out of the speaker. "You are going to pay, Justine," it said. "Or I'll ruin your name and that brand you're so proud of. Or worse. Don't think I don't know what you did."

What she did? Justine wouldn't be here if there weren't some validity to that threat. So what exactly had she done?

Justine was watching me. She used to be unsettlingly good at reading people's feelings, no matter how hard they tried to hide them. It seemed she hadn't lost that skill. She gave me a tiny smile.

"I know, I know," she said. Hands brushing at her fringe again. "You think there has to be something behind a threat like that."

"No, I think you believe there is something behind it. Or you wouldn't be here. And I need to know what that something is, if I'm going to keep your case."

I uttered the words deliberately, knowing they were another kind of threat. Then I watched her closely.

Justine's face showed nothing, but she was absently rubbing her right thumb along the fingers of her left hand. It was her 'tell', and it meant she was genuinely upset, no matter what she said. And far more worried than she would ever admit.

And her chin was set. I recognized that stubborn line. Whatever Justine was being threatened with, she really didn't want to talk about it.

Maybe she'd refuse to tell me. Then I wouldn't have to work with her. And she'd have to take this ridiculous furniture back.

Justine hesitated long enough that I'd started wondering what

Marie had done with my old furniture, and how hard it would be to get it back. Finally she looked up at me, then glanced around my ridiculous office. Her glance slid to Marie and her own assistants.

"I'll tell you," Justine said. "But it's just between us. And not here."

She stood up. "Besides, I need a drink. Let's get out of here."

CHAPTER THREE

Since my current office design didn't allow for client privacy—which was utter stupidity in my book—I had to go along with Justine's request for another location. I took her to my current favorite wine bar, one with impeccable service and a killer view of Vancouver's busy harbor.

Spacious and understated, the Harbor Bar offers comfortable seating and a top-notch wine selection. Technically, it's part of the adjoining hotel, but it's the view of the harbor and the ocean beyond that brings people back.

Sitting at one of the tables, you feel like you're on the bridge of a sailing ship, looking out over the prow. The place was chichi enough to please Justine, and I never tire of looking out over Burrard Inlet.

"So Justine," I said as we sat. "What is so critical that you would ask for my help?"

"I don't understand you, Barbara," she said. "Why wouldn't I seek out your services when I needed help?"

I stared at her. Surely she wasn't serious? But I decided to leave it there. I was more interested in what had her so worried. What was it she didn't want to tell me?

The waiter came by, and Justine ordered a double Martini. Absolut dry, with a twist. I briefly considered ordering scotch, but it was two in the afternoon.

I ordered a glass of wine. Six ounce, not nine.

"Cut the crap, Justine," I said as soon as the waiter had moved out of earshot. "What's the big secret?"

"Hold that question," she said. "I need that drink first."

While we waited, I looked out over her shoulder at the panorama of working waterfront, English Bay and the North Shore with the mountains beyond.

There were a few trees starting to turn color on the far shore, but on the on the lower slopes most of the trees are evergreen, primarily spruce and fir. The sky was that incredible blue it gets in September, and the water reflected it, the color broken by the reflected wisps of cloud and decorated by the ripples kicked up in the wake of a seaplane landing. The light flickered off the ocean, reflecting a large tanker, anchored closer to the far shore than you'd usually see.

The sun was still high in the sky so the colors were in brilliant contrast. But I had no urge to pick up a paintbrush. Which told me exactly how much getting ready for my show had taken out of me. I seldom look at a view like that one without wanting to paint it.

At the moment it felt like I might never paint again.

What is it that people say about the dangers of success, especially if it's one you waited for a long time? That it's hard to follow up? Well, apparently they know what they're talking about.

Somehow, I hadn't expected that old adage to apply to me. I'd wanted my own show for too long. And it had been a success. Everyone said so.

So why did I feel like this?

Before I could take myself too seriously, the waiter came back with our drinks. Justine reached for hers like a drowning woman reaching for a life raft. She downed half of it in what looked like one swallow.

She'd been serious about needing what my father used to call Dutch courage. And he should know. He'd always needed a lot of it.

"I—I just…" Justine's voice tapered off.

Whatever it was she'd been hiding, she was having a tough time getting it out.

"Just start at the beginning," I said. "Who is doing this to you? When did they contact you? And how?"

She emptied her glass, signaled for another, then gave me a half-nod.

"He's called a few times," she said. "Mostly on my cell, but on the private line at the office, too. The first few were a nothing kind of message—need to get in touch, call me back, that kind of thing."

"That's a place to start, then," I said. "You'll need to forward all of those recordings to me. And have someone send me copies of all your phone records, too. Including the ones for your private line."

Justine looked annoyed. "If you must, you must. I'll trust you to respect my privacy."

I ignored that. "So you didn't return the calls?"

"I haven't time to answer calls from everyone who wants to talk to me."

"But this caller had your private number. That didn't worry you?"

She waved that off impatiently. "I'm very well known. Even with my security, it happens occasionally."

"So what changed?" I asked. "And when?"

"The last call—I answered it. I recognized the number, and I was getting tired of all the calls."

She'd said there'd been "a few" calls before. I wondered how many "a few" was, if she was getting tired of them. Just how persistent had this guy been?

"Well, that call—which was the first threatening one, by the way —was a week ago," she said. "That's the recording I played you. I think he called in the morning."

Her smooth brow creased just a little. "I can't remember exactly, my mind was so caught up in the new designs I'm planning. I was only half paying attention. You know how it is, Barbara."

I did know. I was just surprised to hear her acknowledge it. The Justine I remembered had been competitive enough that she rarely acknowledged even the commitment of other artists.

It had been a long time ago, but Justine had made quite an impression.

"I'll need a copy of that recording," I said.

She pulled out her phone, pressed a few keys. "You should have it now."

I glanced at my phone. I did.

"Go on," I said. "There was another call?"

"Yes."

"You didn't record that one?"

"He caught me off guard."

That wasn't a reason, not when she'd said she recorded all her calls. Had she taped that one, then erased it for some reason? "So what did he say?"

"Something annoying, like 'You've been ignoring me.' But his next words I remember very clearly indeed." She gave a harsh laugh, and gulped down some of her second martini.

Funny, I didn't remember her being a drinker. Not like this, anyway.

"He said I was a fraud, that I'd never deserved my success. And that it was time for everyone to know it." She paused, fiddled with her glass. "Then he said it was important that I admitted what I had done. Or he'd do it for me. And make sure everyone knew every single detail."

She kept dancing around whatever it was she didn't want to tell me. What was she so afraid of?

"Go on," I said.

"He's saying I stole my design for the Argyll award. You know, the one that started it all," she said in a rush.

I stared at her. "Not the first one? The one you're known for?"

"That's the one. Winning that competition had me named to

"Young Designers to Watch" lists in 17 countries. It made my name and my fortune."

She gave a broken laugh. "Well, eventually it made my fortune. After a hell of a lot of hard work."

"And is it true?" I asked her. "Did you steal it?"

She finished her martini. Thumped the glass on the table. Met my eyes. "No. I didn't. But I can't prove it. That's what I need you for."

Me? She thought I could fix this? I took a sip of my wine. "That's what we do," I said.

She gave me a slight smile. "Thanks, Barbara," she said. "You were always one of my favorite people, back then."

I was? That was news to me.

"So what did you tell him?" I asked her.

"I asked him how much. And he said he didn't want money. He wanted me to admit what I'd done. Barbara, how can I admit to something I didn't do? But now I'm afraid he'll go public, and I'll find my reputation shredded. You know how fragile an artist's reputation can be. And everything I've worked for will be gone," she said all in a rush. "Just like that."

"Calm down," I said. "If you didn't steal that design, then he can't prove something that isn't true. So he's threatening you. So what?"

"Easy for you to say, Barbara," Justine said. "It isn't your reputation on the line."

"There must be some way you can prove that his accusations have no merit," I said.

She frowned at me. "You still don't understand," she said. "I can't say anything about that design. At all. I really, really can't."

Really, really can't? That didn't sound like Justine. What was going on here?

"Why can't you?" I asked.

She stared at me, eyes wide and a little wild.

"It's a simple question," I said. "Why can't you say anything about your winning design?"

"We were sworn to secrecy," she said. She didn't sound as if she really believed what she was saying.

"Come on, Justine. That was years ago. And these are extenuating circumstances," I said.

"Well, I can't afford to say anything. Not until I know who's threatening me. And how connected they are. If it comes to my word against his, who he is going to matter. A lot."

She had a point. But she still wasn't telling me everything.

"We'll uncover him for you," I said. "That's what we do. But you need to tell me what you're afraid of."

"I can't," she said. "And I can't tell you why. Not until you tell me who's behind this."

She was protecting someone, or something. Herself? Another artist? Her award, maybe?

It would make my job a lot easier if she'd just trust me enough to tell me the truth.

I didn't expect it though. It was already obvious that she was going to try to micromanage this whole case.

I'd had some strange clients in the past, but Justine was shaping up to be one of the worst. Good thing we'd be charging her a premium.

We were going to earn it.

———

AND SPEAKING of charging her a premium.

"I gather the new look of my office is courtesy of you," I said.

She looked relieved at the change of topic. "It certainly is. It's designed around the furniture from my new line—which is all absolutely cutting edge. Don't you love it?"

"Not exactly. The stuff you've stuck in my office isn't even usable," I said. "Sure, it looks good..."

"Why thank you," she said.

I ignored her. "But mine is a working office. This stuff isn't designed for serious work."

"What do you mean? It most certainly is!" Her back straightened even more and her eyes flashed as she defended her furniture.

Now my furniture. I winced at the thought.

"This 'stuff' as you call it, is designed to be used—the way we work now," she said. "You know, in this century. Not the last one. Those desks will charge your phones and tablets wirelessly. There are hidden drawers in case you need a pen or something. The file cabinets are minimalist and streamlined—as your files should be. We don't need paper any more—or rather, we need a lot less of it. There's a reason I'm an award-winning designer, you know," Justine said.

"But it's all wrong for me, for my business. This isn't how my office should look."

She gave me a very puzzled look. "What do you mean? It fits you and your style perfectly. Marie and I both agreed on that. And between us we know you very well."

I felt like my head was going to explode. "Look, I'm a private eye. A licensed investigator. My office needs to reflect that."

"Barbara, you're an artist as well," Justine said. "Your new office reflects that. And you may be an investigator, but you're one who specializes in art-related cases. And especially art fraud."

I did?

I mentally ran through my last few big cases. And realized she might be right. Much as I hated to admit it.

But that didn't mean I needed to work in an office that looked like mine now did.

"Doesn't matter," I said. "I need a private office. My clients won't talk to me if they don't have privacy."

"It was working for you before."

"That was temporary. Just until after the show." Now it was time for my life to get back to normal.

"You didn't want to talk about your case in my new office, either," I said.

She glanced around her. "I don't know, this seems like a better choice anyway. You can hold your client meetings in locations like this one, something that suits their individual styles."

I looked at the wine in front of me. Yeah, and end up an alcoholic. "It's no way to run a business."

She laughed at me. "It's the way business is done in the real world. And it's how any successful business is run. You're thinking too small. You don't need to be operating out of a run-down one room office. Not with your reputation."

My reputation? What reputation? "What do you mean?"

She cocked her head to one side. Considered me for a moment. "Oh my. You mean you really don't know?"

"Know what?"

"You didn't think you could uncover an international art smuggling ring and nobody would notice, did you?"

I'd been too busy to think about it. But I kinda did. "That was an Interpol operation," I said firmly. "With local help."

"Barbara, Barbara, Barbara," she said, shaking her head at me. "I know you've been focusing on your show. And congratulations on that, by the way. It's long overdue."

I was floored. This was Justine? The woman who never had a good word for anyone? Much less me.

She must really need this case of hers solved.

"Thanks," I said. And waited.

There would be more. There had to be. Otherwise the world had stopped making sense in the last couple of weeks, while I wasn't paying attention.

I pictured the new Marie and the new office I'd come back to. Maybe it had, at that.

"Even on the edges of the art world, you must know it runs on gossip," she said.

True.

"And with something that big, everyone was talking," she said, and drained her martini. "Especially when the rumor started to spread that one of our own was involved."

"One of what? I left the art world years ago."

"Says the woman who just had one of the most successful one-woman shows the Courtland has seen in years," she said.

"Though your recent case might have had something to do with that, too. Come on Barbara. Face it. You're one of us, and you're ready to be a player."

I ignored the verbiage as typical Justine-speak—if I'd actually listened, my head might've exploded—and focused on the one fact buried in there. "What rumors started to spread? No-one knew what we were working on."

"Hmm," she said. "Except a few police forces."

And she waved a silencing hand at me before I could say anything. "And no, the rumors didn't come from there."

"Well?" I said, knowing full well that none of my team would have talked.

Except maybe Marie? No, not even her.

Justine had been watching me closely. Now she actually grinned at me. Not an expression I'd have ever expected to see on her face.

"You didn't really think you could ask all those questions and not have people start putting things together, did you?" she asked me.

My mind raced as I thought back. Who had I talked to? "Questions?"

"You were looking for Anna Lang, remember? And you talked to Margaret Courtland. And Ian Wong at the Omega Gallery. And Kathleen Marchant—who already sings your praises to the sky as the best P. I. ever, by the way. And to top it off, you talked to Cassandra Stone. And you didn't expect people to put it together? What kind of detective are you?"

A distracted one, it seemed. I should have known Cassandra, for one, wouldn't leave it alone.

"So?" I threw at her.

"So you're a star. And your office needs to look the part."

My office needed to look the part? Had she seen Marie? Oh, wait…

Well, at least I had an explanation for Marie's new look. It wasn't one I much liked. And I'd grown oddly fond of Marie's own particular sense of style.

After the hectic joy of my show, I badly needed to get back to normal. The old normal, the one before my show. Which included my former bike courier assistant with her wild clothes, and the—okay, possibly dated—furniture that was all I'd been able to afford when I started.

My office always felt to me like an old-style P. I. Office, which was all I aspired to. It fit me perfectly. Unlike those bright pink and green desks.

I wasn't even going to try to explain that to Justine.

"The furniture you chose is wrong for my office," I said flatly. "Just wrong."

"No," she said calmly. "Your office is wrong. It's too small for the firm you are building, and the acclaim you're receiving. You need to re-adjust your self-image here. And then do some work on your brand."

Right. So she could save herself more money on her bill by 'consulting' with me on that new brand. While I tried to solve her impossible case.

She'd been watching me with a quizzical look on her face. Now she said, "You don't understand, Barbara. You need an image update. And I'm just the one to design it for you."

I understood, all right. But an image update? Did she know how ridiculous that sounded? No, thank you.

"Let's concentrate on your issues, Justine. Not my brand."

"I find designing brands calming," she said. "It isn't real design, after all. More like a puzzle, when you need to choose the right pieces."

She was kidding, right? Whatever.

"You're getting threats, Justine. You need to be focused on those, not on puzzle pieces." Especially not on puzzle pieces that seemed to be designed to turn my professional life upside down.

Even more than it already was.

"I am focused on the threats. I find answers when I'm creating," and she gave me a sideways look, as if daring me to disagree.

She knew full well I couldn't. That happened to me, too, when I was caught up in a painting. In fact, it might be why the Lang case had been so successful—I'd made time every morning to create, because I had to have the paintings finished in time for my show.

Justine gave me a twisted grin. "It'll make your job easier if you let me work on your brand. Trust me, I'm easier to deal with if I have a really creative project on the go. And your office? The potential of what you're building there is really stirring my creative instincts to new heights."

And wasn't that a scary thought.

Now wasn't the time to get into this argument with her, though. If I could solve her case fast enough, I could put a quick end to all this ridiculousness. Maybe even get my old furniture back.

I took a deep breath, then glanced at my watch. Luckily, Margaret would be expecting me.

"Sorry, Justine. I have to run," I said briskly. "My next appointment is waiting. Can I drop you somewhere?"

"You go ahead. I'm going to make a few calls while I'm here," she said, signaling the waiter for another martini. "I'll catch a cab later."

I reached for my wallet, but she waved it away.

"I've got it. You'll be in touch?"

"As soon as we know something, you'll be hearing from me."

"Thank you, Barbara. I'd appreciate that. My reputation and my career are depending on you."

I hoped she wasn't serious, though I suspected she was. That was a pretty big expectation.

I gave her a professional smile and a quick nod, and left her sitting there.

CHAPTER FOUR

When I reached the Courtland Gallery, there was no sign of Margaret. A discreet sign on the door announced that on Mondays the gallery is open by appointment only. Visitors are politely requested to press the buzzer for assistance. I did so.

My recent experience with the gallery told me that one of the ways they stayed in business through lean times was to cut staffing costs on slow days. On Mondays, only Margaret or her husband would be working.

The locked door and polite buzzer allowed them to catch up on paperwork without losing valuable artworks from an unattended showroom. This must be one of Margaret's Mondays.

As I waited, I considered what I could see of the gallery. It looked different to me now that I knew what it felt like to have my own works on these walls. The spacious gallery was brightly lit, and through the big glass show windows at the front, I could see the bright spots of color hanging on the walls.

I noted that several walls had been repainted in different colors than they'd been for my show, in order to highlight these specific works.

Just like Justine wanting to change how my office looked?

It was an unwelcome thought. I batted it away, relieved to see someone moving in the back of the gallery. And a tall, thin silhouette heading for the front door. It had to be Margaret.

It was. She let me in, locking the door behind us and ushered me to the back, and into her spacious office. There were no windows here to give away our presence. "Thank you for coming," she said, and slid around the desk and sank into her chair.

I sat in the designer chair opposite her, which was outrageously comfortable, and waited. Whatever was wrong, I'd learn more if I left her to tell it in her own time and her own way.

Margaret was not someone you rushed. Not more than once, anyway.

Before she said anything, she reached for an insulated carafe and filled the two mugs sitting on the desk in front of her. The rich smell of good coffee filled the room.

"Here," she said, pushing the closer one and a much smaller thermos towards me. "It's fresh. And there's cream."

I accepted both with thanks, doctored my coffee and drank. It was indeed fresh. And it was good coffee, too.

Margaret drank a little of her own coffee, then put the mug down with a decided motion, and clasped her hands together on the desk in front of her.

I braced myself, expecting questions about my painting. And my next show. I wasn't ready to discuss either. And right now, I didn't know if I'd ever be.

But Margaret surprised me.

"I'm hearing rumors I don't like," she said. "And I'd like to hire you to get to the bottom of them."

That I really hadn't expected. From everything I'd ever known of Margaret, she was refreshingly oblivious to the rumors and the gossip that the rest of our local art world thrived on.

"Rumors? What kind of rumors?"

"That someone is pushing up the prices on local art. And I'm afraid it's some kind of scam."

"Why?"

"The buyers I'm seeing these days? Too young, too much attitude. Sharp suits, fancy cars—but the vibe is all wrong. They have zero interest in the art itself, it's all about the appreciation, the future value. For their collections," she added, and her face twisted a little.

"The artists I represent mostly aren't famous—not yet—and their works aren't in demand enough to use as some kind of guaranteed investment. It just doesn't make sense."

"Maybe the buyers are naive."

She gave a harsh laugh. "They're paying cash. And some of them are repeat clients."

Uh oh. "Small bills?"

"Do I look like an idiot to you? No, I'd recognize money laundering. But not whatever this is. Which is why I need you. I can't afford to get caught up in any kind of art fraud. Even if I'm innocent. My reputation would never survive it."

I watched her face, waited. There was something she wasn't saying.

She gave me a wry grin, shrugged. "Sales are good, and we've never been so profitable. I'm making too much money these days, much too easily. To be honest, I can't afford to start counting on this revenue source unless it's legitimate."

I thought about that for a moment. The art world is all about cash flow. Too little, you don't survive. Too much, and you have to expand, or die because you can't meet the demand.

But buying fine art, like anything bought with disposable income, has unpredictable trends—so you have to know, on an almost instinctive level, how much money you can count on coming in during an average month. Overestimate that, and you're on the fast track to bankruptcy.

Long term survivors of this crazy business—like Margaret and her husband—they likely had it down to a science.

Until a new trend threw everything out.

"What do you want me to do?" I asked Margaret. I had a few

ideas, but I needed to know up front how she expected me to help her.

"I need to know how much risk we're at with these sales. Where is the money coming from? Are the rumors right? Is this some kind of scam?"

"Why would you call me?" I asked. Partly to buy time while I processed her request. But partly out of genuine curiosity.

She gave me an odd look, and laughed. "Why you? Who else would I call? You're the one who took down one of the biggest art fraud rings on Interpol's books. A group they'd been after for years. And you did it in less than a month."

"That's a bit of an exaggeration," I said. "Interpol did all the work…"

She was eyeing me curiously. "You really believe that," she said as if to herself. "Barbara, surely you're aware of your reputation. Everyone in town—hell, everyone in the country, and probably everyone that fraud ring has ever stolen from—knows what you and your team did. Compared to that, my problem is small potatoes."

Now I was staring at her. And at a loss for words.

"Surely you knew this?" she said, leaning forward. "You aren't just small-time any more. Believe it."

"So I've been told," I said, trying not to sound as if the knees had just been knocked out from under me.

Apparently Justine had been right when she talked about the niche my firm was carving out. Which didn't mean I had to take everything she said seriously.

But after this, I couldn't ignore it entirely. Unfortunately.

It was hard for me to realize that a case we'd solved almost despite ourselves would bring any kind of acclaim. We'd all been so caught up in the urgency of finding a missing woman that we'd put it together one piece after another until I was actually calling Interpol about setting a trap to catch an international fraud ring.

A trap that had actually worked.

Then I'd gone straight from that to focusing on getting my show ready.

I hadn't thought about what either success would mean to my business, to my career. To my life. I was going to have to think about it now.

The whole thing made my head hurt.

I put it aside for thinking about later, and focused on the problem in front of me. Was I going to take this case? In addition to Justine's?

Both cases were complex, with the potential to spiral out of control. Each might be more work than I could comfortably handle. On my own, that is.

Which was my old way of thinking. I had access to a team now. A very capable team.

Margaret was watching me carefully, eyes assessing. No way she'd beg. But there was an edge of desperation to the way she sat— a little too tense, a little too close to the edge of her chair.

This wasn't easy for her. Not being in this situation. And not asking for help, either.

What could I say? I owed her, big time. For believing in me, in my art—when I'd given up. And I liked her. She had integrity.

And she cared about art, and about artists.

Knowing Margaret, she probably wasn't lying to me about anything, either. Which would be a nice change. And a welcome contrast to what Justine was probably going to put me through.

"Yes, I'll take the job," I said. "I'll bring over a contract in the morning."

Margaret sagged a little. Hopefully in relief. And nodded. "I'll see you at nine?"

"Make it ten," I said.

LATER, back at the office, my cell summoned me with the ring tone I'd assigned to Nick.

Nicholas Markham and I have been involved for the last year or so. I guess you could say he's my boyfriend—except that sounds entirely too juvenile for the relationship Nick and I have. I didn't have a better term, though.

Live-in would work, except I'd been avoiding even discussing moving in together ever since he brought it up a few weeks ago. My excuse was that I had to focus on my one-woman show. Which was now done with.

And I still hadn't talked to Nick about our future. So what did that say?

But Nick gets me. He really does. And how rare is that? He even gets my job, and the ridiculous hours I work. Mostly because he works ridiculous hours too.

He's with the RCMP, and his current assignment is with the Integrated Homicide Investigation Task Force for Metro Vancouver. Which means when he's on a case, I often don't see him for days. Sometimes not even a phone call. Since I'm not much better at being available for him, I find his crazy schedule comforting.

Or at least I did.

But it's why he wants to move in together. He says at least that way he'd see me most days. He's got a point. Seeing more of Nick would not be a hardship.

Living together? I'm not sure I'm ready for that. Which is why I keep avoiding the issue.

Which didn't mean I was avoiding Nick. I grabbed my phone. "Nick. Where are you?"

"Not with you."

I could hear the grin in his voice. It made me smile. "No kidding."

"So how was the first day back?"

"Long."

"Your office is still standing then? All that angsting was for nothing?"

"That's debatable," I said. "Marie took on a new client, and the two of them decided to transform my office. All my furniture is gone. Except maybe for a file cabinet. Which I can't even find. If it weren't for the name on the door, I'd have thought I was in the wrong office."

There was a silence on the other end, followed by a choking sound.

"That's okay, you can laugh," I said. "You'll probably break something if you keep trying not to."

At my words, Nick did laugh, that rich warm laugh that was probably the first thing I fell in love with. Well, that and his broad shoulders. And his smile. Yeah, I was a goner.

But that didn't mean he got to laugh at my situation forever.

"Okay, that's enough," I said when he was laughing so hard he was practically gasping for air. "It's not that funny."

"I'm picturing Marie, and what she'd probably choose for your office," he gasped out, and was off again. He's met Marie a few times, and I think he's as amused by her as I am infuriated.

Trouble is, he wasn't far wrong. Except in his mental picture of Marie.

"That was the old Marie," I said. "The new one is blond and elegant and talks about brands and the importance of first impressions."

There was a little silence at the other end of the phone. "She what?"

"You heard me."

Another pause. "Nope, can't picture it."

I laughed. "You'll have to come by and see for yourself. Then we'll go for dinner."

"Yeah, about that."

Here we go. "Let me guess. Another case."

"Uh huh."

"You going to be tied up for a while?"

"It looks like it. You?"

"I have a couple of new cases. And yes, probably."

Especially if Justine's case got ugly. Or Margaret's did. Or both of them. But I wasn't going to even consider that. No point buying trouble.

He laughed. "Figures."

There was a little silence between us, despite the laughter.

"And I suppose you can't tell me anything about your case," I said, trying for a light tone.

"Not at the moment." His voice sounded cautious. Not a good sign.

"Well, one of my cases is about design fraud."

"You sound thrilled."

"Yeah, not so much," I said. "But maybe it'll be an easy one, and I can wrap it up fast. The other case…"

I stopped. Margaret's case, the one I was worried could be about money laundering and gangs? Best not to say anything at all until I knew more about it, because it just might intersect with Nick's previous job on the Integrated Gang Task Force.

I didn't want to put him in a position where he felt obligated to bring his former buddies into it.

I was pretty sure it was a minor issue we were dealing with, anyway. Hardly even worth talking about. But I needed to know what Margaret was dealing with here before I involved the police.

"You can't talk about your case, either," Nick said.

He sounded… resigned? Whatever it was, I didn't like the sound of it. "Well, not yet, anyway."

"Me too."

Yup. Definitely resigned. That wasn't good. Not good for him, not good for our relationship.

"Look, Barbara, have you given any more thought to living together?"

And there it was.

"Well, I…" I began, trying to think of the words to head off this conversation. I still wasn't ready to consider living together. There were too many things changing in my life already.

But I didn't want to lose what we had together. And I knew I couldn't stall him forever.

"Wait, Barbara. Don't say anything, not now. This isn't the time. But with our jobs, we mostly can't talk about our work. And with our schedules, we just aren't seeing each other enough to build something more. It's just going to get worse. I'm afraid it'll tear us apart, no matter how much we try. And I don't want that."

"I don't either," I said softly.

"Okay. Okay," he said. "Then we'll talk. We'll go out for Indian food and we'll talk. Soon. I promise."

"Soon," I agreed.

Knowing I'd just about run out of stalling time. And not at all sure what my answer was going to be.

CHAPTER FIVE

The next morning I woke early and went for a very long run. It was cool, but not yet cold, though the heat of summer was gone. Soon the days would be getting shorter. Something else I'd rather not think about.

As I ran along Kits Beach, I could feel the kinks and knots in my muscles from the day before start to fall away. It felt good. Even the memory of walking in and seeing all those colorful desks created a half smile. It was kind of funny, in retrospect.

As I ran in the cool air, the rising sun painted interesting shadows on the path in front of me. I ran on, pacing myself. I wasn't ready to turn back, not yet.

I had some thinking to do.

The sky turned bluer, with no clouds in sight. It was going to be a gorgeous day.

Those changes to my office? I'd figure something out. It was my office, after all. I could change it back if I wanted to—just ship everything back to Justine. I grinned at the thought of her expression when she got it.

I'd never liked Justine much, but she'd made some good points, talked about things I'd never paid attention to, or even thought about. Maybe it was time I did.

And Justine herself—the woman I'd met yesterday had changed, was much more genuine than the young woman I remembered. I could even see this new Justine becoming a friend. Of sorts.

If it wasn't an act.

I'd been burned by clients' lies in the past. I was reserving judgement on Justine. But I was going to help her. Whoever was targeting her was going to regret doing so.

And it was possible Marie and Justine had a point, much as I hated to admit it. It had been really fun working with a team on the Lang case. Maybe I did need an office setup that would allow us to work like that on a more regular basis.

It meant I could keep doing art shows.

Or not.

Not a decision I needed to make now. But it would be nice to have options. It wasn't that I was opposed to change, exactly, more that…

The shrill tones of my cellphone—I had to change that—broke into my thoughts. I stopped running. Stood looking out across the beach at a smooth blue ocean, trying to moderate my breathing while scrambling to dig my phone out of a too tight pocket before whoever it was gave up.

"Barbara O'Grady," I said.

"Barbara?" It was Marie's voice, sounding broken. What was she doing calling me at this hour? "Barbara, she's dead."

Oh no. "Who is dead, Marie?"

"Justine. It's Justine. And she said she was being threatened, and she hired us to help her and…"

And now she was dead.

It made no sense. "Marie, where are you?"

"The office. And they want to talk to you."

"Who does?" But I had a sinking feeling I knew.

Marie confirmed it. "The police," she said. "They're here. And they want to talk to you."

"I'm coming in," I said. Then glanced around me, realized I was at Jericho Beach and called a cab.

I'd been running longer than I'd realized. I didn't have time to run home again.

————

JUST OVER HALF AN HOUR LATER, Marie met me at the office door, her face devastated. "They're in here," she said.

I followed her into the office that still didn't look like mine, half expecting to see my old buddy Jerry Haworth, who is a detective for the Vancouver Police Department. I don't know if I was disappointed or relieved not to recognize either of the men who waited for me behind the partition that now set off my "office" from the rest of the space.

At least they'd managed to sit in those chairs without falling off of them. Whatever had Justine been thinking...

And my thoughts fell off the familiar pathway and collided with the new reality of why the detectives were sitting in my office. Justine.

"Ms. O'Grady?" said one of the officers. Both of them standing as soon as they saw me.

Who else would I be? I nodded.

"I'm Detective Constable Singh and this is Detective Constable Aaron," the one nearer to me said. He was tall, with wavy dark hair and a very neutral expression. The man beside him, also dark haired and dark eyed, was a good foot shorter, much heavier set, and wore a serious expression. "We'd like to ask you a few questions."

I made my way around the eggplant colored desk and sat down carefully on what was now supposed to be my desk chair. "Yes?"

"It's about Justine Grayson." Detective Singh said. He seemed to be the designated speaker. Detective Aaron just watched me, eyes alert to catch the slightest reaction.

"And?"

"I understand she's a client?"

"Yes, she is."

"And you met with her yesterday?"

"Yes."

"Where?"

"Here, and then at the wine bar in the Grand Pacific hotel."

Detective Aaron made a note.

"And how long was she here?" Detective Singh asked.

"Barely an hour. Then we took our meeting to the Harbor Bar."

"Just the two of you?"

"Yes."

"Why?"

"At her request. Though I chose the location."

I watched Detective Singh's quick sideways glance as Detective Aaron made another note.

"And how long were you there?"

"How long? From around two in the afternoon until just after four, I suppose."

"That's a rather long meeting, isn't it?"

It was an odd question. He was fishing. But for what? "Not necessarily. It depends on the client," I said.

His face stayed neutral, but something in his body language said he didn't believe me. He was going to have to work on that if he wanted to keep rising in his field. Unless he just wanted me to think he didn't believe me.

That's the trouble with trying to investigate a P. I. We know all the tricks. At least we do if we're any good.

"Hmmm." Everything neutral again. Which told me nothing. "And where did you go after that?"

"I had another meeting."

"With whom?"

"Margaret Courtland, of the Courtland Gallery," I said.

Margaret has an impeccable reputation in this city. She's also known as a plain speaker, who respects the truth and doesn't pull her punches.

"I see," he said, after a moment. "I assume she would confirm your meeting?"

"She would." I waited to see where he was going with this.

"And Ms. Grayson?" he asked. "What did she do?"

Did that mean I'd taken myself off the suspect list? Probably. He'd gone back to focusing on the timing of my meeting with Justine.

"She was intending to make a few more calls, then take a cab back to her office." I looked from one expressionless face to the other. "I gather she didn't do that?"

"I can't say, ma'am," said Singh. "So you left her there?"

This was sounding worse with every question they asked. Where had Justine died? "Yes, I did."

"And where did you last see her ma'am?"

I hate being called ma'am. "Sitting in the window seat at in the Harbor Bar, watching a seaplane that had just taken off."

I don't know why that image had etched itself in my brain. Except maybe that Justine looked very alone, suddenly. That and the fear I'd heard in her voice when she talked about the threat she was under.

That fear had a new meaning, today.

"What exactly did she hire you to do for her?" It was Aaron this time, as Singh sat back slightly.

Why the handoff? "She was being threatened."

Normally I wouldn't have told them anything, but it no longer mattered to Justine. And it might help them catch her killer.

Both detectives sat forward. "Her life was being threatened?" Singh asked.

"No. Her reputation."

———

THE DETECTIVES LEFT LESS than fifteen minutes later, faces still inscrutable. But their hopes of a quick arrest were gone, if I was any judge. The notion of me as their prime suspect—if that was what they'd been looking for—hadn't stood up under questioning.

Mostly because the timing was wrong, I suspected.

And their interest in the case Justine had hired me for had withered and died right in front of me. The fact that I'd been hired to protect Justine's professional reputation was the real kicker. It was hardly the stuff of murderous fantasies.

Especially when the inciting incident was nearly fifteen years before.

And it left me with a problem. Justine was dead. And she'd probably been killed within an hour of when I'd last seen her, based on the questions the two detectives had asked. And the ones they'd pointedly not asked.

I didn't think they had a viable suspect. Not once they discounted me.

Murder is police business. But Justine was a client. And someone who might even—given enough time—have become a friend.

I don't take kindly to people threatening my friends. Even potential friends. Much less murdering them.

Still, I had no business investigating a murder. Unless…

"Marie," I called.

"Yes?" Her voice on the other side of the partition sounded shaky.

"Can you come here a moment?" I said. "And bring Justine's file, will you?"

There was a sort of hiccuping gasp on the other side of the screen, then I heard a file cabinet bang open. Well, at least we still had paper files. Somewhere.

Seconds later she marched around the partition, dumped the file on my desk and plopped into the chair recently vacated by Detective Singh.

I looked up in surprise. Sorrow met my gaze. Marie's defiant movements were countered by her red-rimmed eyes.

"It will be okay," I found myself saying. Wondering where the words were coming from. "You'll see."

A broken sob was my answer.

"Marie?" Where was the tough-as-nails former bike courier I'd hired? She'd only known Justine a week.

"She was so nice to me," Marie said. "And I was learning so much from her."

Marie had taken Justine as a mentor? Justine? It made no sense to me. Two more different people would be hard to imagine.

Then I looked again at the new, nearly elegant Marie who sat in front of me, and recognized the truth. She'd done exactly that. "I'm so sorry," I said.

"Sorry isn't good enough," she spat out.

So the old Marie wasn't entirely transformed. I found that strangely reassuring, given how irritating I'd often found her.

"Justine is dead," my now perfectly groomed assistant said. "So what are you going to do about it?" Giving me the stink-eye.

Her expression was in such contrast with her grooming that I nearly laughed. Though there was nothing funny about our situation.

"I'm going to make sure whoever killed her pays," I said. "That's why I need her file."

"Oh. Well that's all right, then," Marie said, pushing the file across the desk and closer to me. "What are you going to do?"

"Depends on…ah, here it is," I said. "You did do a contract for her."

"Of course," Marie said.

I was quickly flipping pages, until I found what I'd half-expected. "She signed it, I see. And you signed it, too."

She flushed. She knew full well I'd never authorized her to take on new clients, much less sign contracts that obligated my investigative firm to work with them. We'd had words about this before.

And for once, I was relieved to see she hadn't learned her lesson. "Good."

"It was a simple case, and she needed our help and we really needed what she could offer us…" Marie stopped mid-justification and stared at me. "Good? You approve?"

"No, I don't approve. Signing contracts is above your pay grade. Don't do it again."

Marie was still staring at me. "But you're not mad," she said. "You're relieved. Why?"

"Because in this one case, having a signed contract means we still have an obligation to our client," and I held up a hand to hold off Marie's inevitable questions as I scanned through the rest of the document. She hadn't changed any of the standard clauses. Good again. Except… "What's this clause here?"

She leaned forward. "Which one?"

I pointed to it.

"Oh." She sat back, a grin on her face. "Justine insisted on that one. She added it after she saw this place." A quick sweep of her hand took in the office. "Well, the way it used to be, anyway."

I groaned. Successful completion of the case would result in a really nice paycheck. Plus an expansion and complete re-branding of what Justine had referred to yesterday as my "little business"—to be done either by herself or her senior designer. And I had to implement it and live with it for six months before making any changes, or no paycheck.

And it was a substantial paycheck.

"Why ever did you agree to put this clause in?"

And got the answer I should have expected.

"Because I agreed with her," Marie said. "She took me through what she had in mind, and it made sense. She was really brilliant, you know."

I gave her a skeptical look.

"No, really," Marie said. "And I didn't just let her put the clause in. I made her prove that her ideas were right for our firm."

Our firm? Last I checked, Marie was still a temporary assistant with less than a month to run on her contract.

But that wasn't the part of her statement that stopped me short. "She proved it to you? How?"

"Why do you think I look like this now?" Marie said.

"What?" I'd known it must have something to do with Justine, but I'd thought Marie had copied Justine's style out of admiration. "You changed everything about yourself as an experiment?"

"Not everything," Marie said. "And yes. I liked a lot of her ideas about how this office needed to grow and change. But I wasn't going to let her destroy what you'd built here without proving that she really could do what she said."

I was still reeling from that one, when she added, "And she did prove it to me."

"How?"

"She bet me that within a week, I'd see a huge difference in how clients treated me. And that I'd be able to convince them to sign with us way easier. I was to think of it like a role for me to play."

I was still stunned by the idea. "And you let her?"

Marie nodded. "Sure. If you think about it, it's a kind of performance art. And none of these changes,"—and she waved a casual hand towards her new attire—"are permanent. Some of the things she was proposing for our firm would be a lot harder to change back."

"What changes was she—wait a minute. She bet you could sign more cases as part of your performance art?" Somehow I found the concept of performance art easier to accept than Marie having an entire personality transplant in just over a week.

Marie grinned at me. "I wondered when that would sink in. Yup. I signed a couple of small cases last week. Cory's already done the work, and the checks are in your in basket."

She nodded at a sort-of rectangular container made of a swirly white acrylic sitting on the corner of my desk. And sadness overtook her again. "That's one of Justine's designs."

Belatedly I realized the container held envelopes and pink message slips. That was an in basket? "Cory's already done the work…" I repeated. I think I was in shock.

"Don't worry. They were background checks, easy stuff. Nothing illegal."

Somehow that didn't reassure me. Nothing she'd said so far suggested that Marie's flexible concept of legality had changed any.

I put my head down on my eggplant colored desk and groaned.

"Barbara?" Marie said worriedly. "Aren't you going to yell at me?"

Yelling at Marie was the last thing I had in mind. I glanced at the day Justine's contract had been signed. Two days after I'd left her in charge while I focused on my upcoming one-woman show.

Which meant Marie had been working with Justine for over a week. Maybe she'd told her what she hadn't had time to tell me.

"No. I need you to bring me up to speed on the case," I said.

CHAPTER SIX

Turned out Marie didn't know enough to be much help. But she refused to be sent home.

"If you're going after the maniac that killed Justine, I want to help," she said. "You can't leave me out of this."

Judging by the set of her jaw, there was no point in arguing with her, so I gave Marie my notes on the contract I was intending to sign with Margaret, and asked her to draw it up. She scowled at me.

Apparently doing her job wasn't the kind of help she had in mind.

Why me?

But I explained anyway. "If you can take care of this, I'm free to figure out our next steps in finding Justine's killer."

She looked fierce then, and headed for her desk without another word. Leaving me sitting behind the eggplant monstrosity I now called a desk, staring blankly at a white wall.

While the investigator side of me was still a little stunned by everything that had happened so far this morning, the artist noted that whatever shade of white the walls had been painted picked up and reflected back the warmth of the sun, making the office brighter than I'd ever seen it. And in Vancouver that's important—we get so many gray days that even a little bit of extra light in winter makes the difference between a good day and a bad one.

It's why I spend every December wishing for a nice long vacation to Hawaii.

I don't know why I've resisted white walls for so long—I guess I crave color, and any shade of white just felt too bland. Plus all that 'designer white' nonsense just annoyed me—and the shades chosen by east coast designers were hopeless in West Coast light.

I hadn't thought it through. Now I was wondering how a similar shade would work in my apartment, and particularly in my painting studio. The one that used to be my second bedroom.

Of course, I was also avoiding my shock over Justine's death, and my utter lack of any direction on her case. Figuring out our next steps was easier to say than it was to do.

And sitting here thinking about decorating—decorating!—was not going to get me anywhere.

I grabbed the phone and dialed.

"Detective Haworth."

"Jerry, it's Barbara," I said. "You got a moment?"

"Sure, O'Grady," he said. "But only one."

I didn't have the heart for our usual banter. "Someone was murdered downtown yesterday. Justine Grayson? She's a friend of mine."

Or she could have been, anyway. "I need to know how she died. And where."

The pause at his end was a little too long. "Justine Grayson? That isn't one of my cases. I'll have to look into it. I'll get back to you as soon as I can."

His tone was entirely professional, but we've been friends for too long, going all the way back to grade school. I could hear the hesitation, barely there, in his voice. What wasn't he saying?

But I also knew Jerry too well—asking him what he was holding back wouldn't help. He'd call me back when he had all the info, and not before.

"Thanks, Jerry," I said, and disconnected.

Now what?

I wasn't going to put the case aside until he got back to me. I needed to do something for Justine, and now. Some of her employees might know something. Dragging her file towards me, I skimmed through it, looking for the name I knew I'd seen there. And found it.

David Bittner. Justine's longtime associate and senior designer. He must know something.

Normally I'd call, set up an appointment for the following week. But not on this case. With her sudden death, Justine's office would be in chaos. The last thing I wanted was to add to their grief. But as callous as it sounds, chaos often gets people to open up. And Justine's employees would want to see her murder solved.

Unless one of them was the murderer.

It was a nasty thought, but an inevitable one. I needed to pay a visit to her office.

I'd just stood up and grabbed my purse—which now hung over the back of my chair, since this desk didn't have a drawer for stashing it in—when the phone rang.

"O'Grady Investigations," I said. "Barbara O…"

"Barbara, you have to help me," Justine's voice said. "I think I'm about to be arrested for murder."

I SANK BONELESSLY BACK into my chair. "Justine? Is that you?"

"I've no time for stupid questions, Barbara," she said tartly. "I've just told you they're going to arrest me for murder. I'm in my office. Now, are you coming or not?"

It was Justine all right. The woman who was supposed to be dead.

"But…," I began, and barely restrained myself from asking her why she wasn't dead.

Hadn't the police told me she was? I re-ran the interview in my mind.

No, they hadn't. It was Marie who'd told me. The police hadn't ever said whose death they were investigating. Just that they had some questions about Justine.

In my shock I'd never clarified why they were asking. And the very specific questions they'd asked took on a whole new significance if Justine wasn't dead, but was instead their main suspect.

"Accused of murdering who?" I asked instead.

"David Bittner," she said. "Someone shot him. Yesterday afternoon."

I guess I wasn't going to be interviewing him, then. Gallows humor, but it helped me get my balance a little after my second shock of the day.

And the realization that Justine was alive when I'd barely accepted the news of her death.

"I'm so sorry," I said.

"So am I," she said, her voice cracking. It was the only sign she'd given of the terrible strain she must be feeling.

"Where are you?" I asked her.

"My office."

"Are the police there?"

"No. They left a couple of hours ago."

Just in time to come and ask me questions.

We had a little time then. I didn't waste it asking why she was the main suspect. "I'll be right there. Don't talk to anyone except your lawyer."

"My lawyer..." she repeated.

"You did call her. Or him. Right?"

"No. I'm innocent. I don't need him..."

"Justine," I broke in. "You've had a shock. You're not thinking straight. Call your lawyer. Now. And tell him I'll meet both of you in your office in," I glanced at the clock, calculated the traffic. "Twenty minutes. All right?"

"Yes, fine. I'm not a child, Barbara."

Shades of the old Justine. Maybe we weren't destined to be friends.

"Call him now, Justine."

I quickly updated a stunned Marie, asked her to reschedule my meeting with Margaret, then took the stairs down two at a time.

CHAPTER SEVEN

Judging by the reception station, Justine's office on the twenty-third floor was as streamlined as she was trying to make mine. But where my office was all bold hits of competing colors, hers was elegant in shades of white and cream and soft gold. With here and there a splash of burnt orange, which turned the effect of the whole design from understated to daring. The air smelled faintly of lemongrass.

She really did know her stuff.

So how had I ended up with an office full of Marie-style color, while Marie herself looked like she belonged in this very stylish office?

Me? I looked like I should be working at the Gap, right down to my navy denims and tailored black jacket. I was wearing some rather nice suede ankle booties, though.

Justine, for once, didn't seem to notice. She came forward to greet me, hands outstretched, before I even had the chance to tell the distraught looking receptionist my name.

"Barbara. You came," she said, taking both my hands and squeezing them. Which was a relief. I'd been afraid she was about to hug me.

I don't hug easily. Except with people I know well.

"Thank you," she said. "So much." Her lip quivered. "I…"

Then her voice changed, became softer as her gaze went beyond me to her receptionist. "Jessica, you look awful," she said. "You need to go home and recover from the shock."

"I'm so sorry, Justine," the young—make that very young—woman replied. "It's—David…" And she put both hands over her immaculately made up face and sobbed.

Justine dropped my hands and stepped behind the desk to put her arms around the sobbing woman.

"I know you were friends," she said. "It's so hard to lose him like this, so suddenly and in such an awful way."

"Y…yes," the receptionist choked out.

"Go home," Justine said again.

"I can't just leave," she said. "Who would answer the phones? What if…"

"I'm closing the office," Justine said, her voice suddenly decisive. "We all need to grieve. Transfer the phones to our service, then go and bathe your eyes."

Jessica wiped at her eyes, sniffing. Justine handed her a tissue from a box on the side of the reception desk and Jessica dabbed at her face. Her makeup was still perfect. Waterproof mascara has come a long way.

"You can leave whenever you're ready," Justine said. "But call a cab, on the office account."

Jessica started to protest and Justine held up a hand to stop her. "I'll tell everyone else to do the same. We've all had a horrible shock."

I was impressed by Justine's care for her employee in the middle of her own trauma. And by how well Jessica responded—the young employee's professionalism as she gathered her composure and turned to deal with the task she'd been given.

Marie—the new Marie—had displayed a little of that professionalism today.

"Now, let's go see if you can help me stay out of jail," Justine said, turning to me.

She had a sense of humor? I hadn't seen that before. And taking care of her employee seemed to have snapped her out of her earlier panic.

"And help me find the real killer," she added, turning to lead the way down a long hallway leading towards the back.

———

"JUSTINE, it's up to the police to find the killer," I said as soon as she ushered me into her expansive office.

With large windows and a commanding view of the harbor and the mountains, her office continued the understated elegance of the color theme I'd seen earlier. In more normal circumstances I'd have stood and stared for a bit.

These were not normal circumstances.

Justine strode across the expanse of thick, creamy carpet and pulled out the streamlined white leather chair behind her desk. She motioned me to take a seat in one of the matching chairs facing her.

"Yes, it is for the police to do," she said. "And I'm sure they'll do a good job. Except that at the moment they seem to be focused on me as the main suspect. And since I didn't kill David,"—and her voice broke, just a little, on the words.

It felt mean, but I had to ask. "You didn't kill David Bittner?"

"No, I didn't! How can you even ask me that?"

Very easily. Most of my clients lie, at least some of the time. I needed to be sure I wasn't helping a murderer. I hadn't seen Justine in a long time, after all.

I was inclined to like her now—but that didn't mean she wasn't a killer. And shock is even better than chaos at getting to the truth.

"Because if I'm going to help you, I need to know," I said. "Well?"

"I see. Then no. I did not kill him," she said clearly. "And any time the police spend investigating me is time they're wasting in finding the real killer."

She was absolutely right. What stunned me was the contrast between the near-hysterical woman who'd called me—and met me in the reception area—and this calm, rational executive. Who seemed determined not to show whatever it was she was feeling.

How much of this was a facade, assumed to get through a difficult time?

Or was the real Justine cold-blooded enough to pull off a murder? I didn't know.

And I was no closer to deciding when the receptionist, polished facade firmly back in place, ushered in Justine's lawyer.

Brian Stewart. I hadn't expected that. Brian's wife had been a client a couple of years ago, and they'd both been grateful for my help in unraveling what had turned into a pretty traumatic situation for both of them.

"Justine, what can I do for you so urgently?" he asked as he came in.

She walked to greet him and they shook hands warmly. "David's been killed," she said bleakly.

"Justine, I'm so sorry," he said, genuine feeling in his voice. "He was very talented, and a good man. What happened?"

"The police think I did it," she said.

"What? They're calling it a homicide?"

She nodded and gestured to where I sat. "And Barbara told me to call you."

"Barbara…?" He repeated, and his eyes followed her gesture.

He'd been so focused on her that he hadn't noticed me sitting there. When he did, a smile broke across his patrician features. Brian is a handsome man, and with silvering dark hair and clear blue eyes, he's becoming even more so as he ages.

For a sharp lawyer, he's also a very kind man, and that shows on his face. He's one of my favorite ex-clients.

"It's good to see you again," he said to me. And to Justine, "Barbara is one of the very few investigators I trust."

That was nice to hear. Especially since I didn't think he'd be too happy to hear what I had to tell him. But he got there ahead of me.

Turning back to Justine, he took one of her hands in one of his. "Justine, I'm not the lawyer you want if this is a homicide case. My specialty is corporate law, though I dabble a little in wills and trusts. If you really think you're a serious suspect, you need a criminal lawyer."

Go, Brian! She took it well from him, too. Better than if I'd tried to tell her the same thing. Just nodded, and gestured him to the chair beside mine.

"I don't really think I need a lawyer," she said. "But when the police left and I called her, Barbara insisted I call my lawyer. That's you."

"How long were the police here with you?" Brian asked.

"Nearly an hour."

"Just you?"

"Yes."

"Then you need a criminal lawyer," he said. "I can recommend James Marchant, in my firm. He's young, sharp and hungry. You'll be in good hands."

"Brian, I didn't do it," Justine said, just a hint of the desperation I'd heard earlier in her voice.

"Even better," Brian said. "Marchant will take good care of you. I'll make sure of it."

Justine glanced from him to me, then sat back in her chair as if trying to put distance between her and us. "I don't have any choice, do I?"

"No, you don't," I said. "Not if you want this over with, and David's killer found."

"I agree," Brian said. "Justine, you're too good a businesswoman to leave yourself unprotected in a situation like this. If you get distracted, or worse, arrested, your business will suffer. And making sure that doesn't happen has to be your first priority. Especially now."

I gave him a measuring look. Why now? Was something going on with Justine's business?

If so, it made the timing of the threat she'd hired me to investigate even more interesting.

Why do clients always seem to think they only have to tell me part of the story? They'd never accept only part of an answer from me. First chance I got, I was getting the whole story out of Justine.

She'd been right that she needed help, but from here on, it would be on my terms, not hers. With the kind of pressure she was under, she didn't have time to slowly dole out the facts any more.

Apparently Justine had already figured that out. She glared at both of us. "Fine, I'll hire your James Marchant to deal with the police for me," she said.

"And to make sure your rights are protected every time you talk with them," Brian said.

"Yes, yes, that too," she said. Then dropped her bombshell. "But I'm also hiring Barbara to find out what really happened to David. And who killed him."

Oh no.

"Justine, you can't hire me to catch David's killer," I said.

"You said you'd help me," she said.

"Help you, yes. That doesn't include catching a killer."

"I'm not hiring you to catch him," she said, ignoring my protests. "I told you, the police can do that. I just want you to find out who did it. And then make sure the police know who it was."

I didn't know whether to be complimented or horrified that she had such a high opinion of my skills.

On the other hand, finding David Bittner's killer might well be a logical extension of the problem she'd already hired me for. And I'd never have a better chance to get the answers I needed from her. All the answers.

That quickly, I made up my mind.

"Before I take this on, you need to know that in order to help you, I'll need all the details about what's really going on," I said bluntly. "And you can't hold anything back, no matter how personal or painful it seems. Do you agree?"

I made a production of taking out my small notebook and pen, giving her time to think about it. And making a point. I could just record everything, but sometimes taking notes is more effective.

She just nodded, her jaw set. But her face had gone even paler than it had already been.

"Fine. Since we already have a signed contract, then give me another dollar to hire me for this as well."

She gave me a funny look, but reached for her purse.

Brian held up a hand. "Better yet, my firm will hire you for this investigation," he said.

That made sense. If she was going to share details, they needed to be confidential—and as a contractor for his firm, I was covered under their lawyer/client privilege, and couldn't be called on to testify against Justine.

"Good idea," Justine said. "Can we extend that to include the work I already had Barbara doing for me?"

We both nodded.

Justine smiled. "Good. Bill me," she said to Brian. "And don't question Barbara's hours or expenses. I'm happy to pay whatever it takes on this one."

Whoa. I'd known she was successful, but her firm—Grayson Design—must be doing *really* well.

Brian looked a little taken aback, but his only comment was to me. "Make sure that Marchant knows first about anything that you plan to share with the police," he said.

I didn't contradict him, but Justine was still my client. I'd do whatever was in her best interests. Which didn't mean she'd like it much.

"Then it's question time," I said to her. "And you might not want your lawyer here for this part," I added, glancing at Brian.

Who stood up immediately.

"I'll leave you to it, then," he said. And to Justine, "And you can expect a call from Marchant within the hour."

"No, I'd like you to stay, please," Justine said to him. She turned to me. "Brian knows most of my confidential business, anyway. And I think he needs to hear this."

CHAPTER EIGHT

Outside the office, I could see a tiny seaplane circling against a cloudless sky, ready to make a descent somewhere along the harbor. Inside, a lone bee was buzzing against the window. As I watched Justine's expression, starkly lit in the sunlight pouring through the windows, I wondered idly how that bee had made it inside the sealed tower. Mostly, though, I wondered if Justine was really ready for this.

But she'd made her decision. It was time for me to do my job.

I sat back in my chair, and started off slowly. "Tell me about David Bittner."

In the chair beside me Brian Stewart sat forward a little, as though to interrupt, then settled back. I darted a quick glance at him, but his face gave nothing away.

"David was my first hire," she said, her face falling a mask of grief. "We worked together for more than a decade. He's—he was—a very talented designer, my right hand. And a good man." She slanted a grateful look at Brian, presumably for his earlier remark.

"David is… was a really good human being—caring, considerate, generous. And he could tell a bawdy joke with the best of them.

David, of all people…" Justine's voice broke and she put her hand to her mouth for a moment.

"He didn't deserve this," she said fiercely.

"What aren't you saying?" I asked her.

She glared at me, darted a glance at her lawyer. "It should have been me," she said, her voice clear and strong but her eyes moist.

"Because of the threats?" I said.

Out of the corner of my eye I could see Brian Stewart straighten. His face didn't change, but the furrows in his forehead deepened just a little. He hadn't known about the threats.

"Yes. Or at least I think so," she said.

"You think you were the target? That David died by mistake? Or that he was killed as a message to you?"

Her suffering and guilt were hard to watch, but I needed the truth if I was going to help her. And often the truths we tell ourselves are colored by our own fears and beliefs. I needed to challenge her perceptions if I was going to uncover David Bittner's killer.

"I…" She stopped, looked from me to Brian, who had stayed silent, and back again. "I thought he was killed because I hadn't responded to the threat."

"You thought?" I repeated. "Have you changed your mind?"

"No. Well, not exactly. But when you ask about it like that—for one thing, David couldn't have been mistaken for me."

Now we were getting somewhere. "Okay, let's start with that," I told her. "How did David die? And what were you doing at the time?"

Justine nodded. I guess the questions were making sense to her. "After you left the wine bar, I ordered another martini, and made some calls," she said. "I was there nearly an hour, I think."

"That would bring it to five-ish?"

She nodded. "Maybe closer to five-thirty."

We should be able to check the security footage. "Then what?"

"I grabbed a cab out front, and went back to the office. There were some documents that needed signing." Her eyes flicked to Brian in a tiny, betraying movement.

This was important. "What documents, Justine? And don't forget, you promised me the truth."

This time her eyes stayed focused on my face. I could almost feel the effort she was making not to look towards her lawyer. Had she always been this easy to read?

"I—Grayson Design has an exclusive merchandising offer on the table. For a line of furniture I've been developing."

Was that where my new furniture had come from? That might explain why she was so passionate about how well it would work in my office. "And?"

She sighed. "And it's a hugely lucrative deal. One that will create headlines as well as cause a big stir in the industry. But it's built on the strength of my personal brand, and my company's brand. Anything that goes wrong with either my reputation or the company's could end up with the deal being canceled. And there are a few firms in the industry who'd like nothing better than to ruin my name. And they'd stop at nothing to kill this deal, if they knew it existed."

"So your arrest for murder…"

"Or my head designer being killed because of my past," she finished. "Yes. Either could potentially kill this deal. Both together is practically a guarantee. And the longer it drags on, the worse the impact will be."

"So the industry gossip mills would have a heyday," I said, nodding.

I didn't know much about the design industry, but I knew a lot about corporate culture from my early days when I'd paid my bills as a temp employee. "Which is why you want to hire me to uncover the real killer."

"Exactly."

"So tell me about the threat. And I mean everything about it."

Before she could respond Brian leaned forward. "What threat

are we talking about here? And if it's serious enough to possibly impact the deal, why don't I know about it?"

I looked at Justine.

Who grimaced. "I've been receiving threats for the last few…" she began. Then she hesitated, and visibly braced herself. "The last six or seven months, actually. Pretty low-key threats at first, which is why I didn't say anything. And the negotiations were at a delicate stage."

Brian's face was impassive. "Go on."

"They've been escalating," she said. "The threats."

"Which is why you called in Barbara, I gather."

"Yes."

"She signed with my firm a week ago," I said. Hoping my poker face was firmly in place as I said it. "If I may…?"

Brian nodded, sat back a little, seemingly willing to let me run the interview. But his gaze stayed fixed on his client. Who looked as professionally polished as ever, but her eyes were desperate.

"What time did you get back the the office?" I asked her. "And who was still here?"

"It must have been close to six, because no-one was here," she said.

"Is that usual?"

"No, quite often David and a few other designers are working late. It's also a good time for impromptu strategy sessions, when one of us feels the need for brainstorming on a project. But lately, that's happening less often."

"Why?"

She winced a little. "I guess I've been less available to them. Between the deal and the threats, I've been a little preoccupied. Usually David would pick up the slack."

"Usually?" I repeated.

She frowned. "That hadn't been happening either, for the last several months at least. I guess I was too caught up in my own worries to really pay attention. Everyone was still doing good work, and the team's spirit seemed fine. Or at least, I think it did."

"What was going on with David, then?" I asked.

She shook her head. "I don't know. I don't even know if anything was going on with him. Usually, he'd have told me if there was something…"

"He didn't express any worries? Concerns?"

"No. Nothing," she said.

"How would this deal you were working on have affected him? And your team?"

"We would have grown. Substantially. And they would all have done well out of it, financially. Especially David and the other designers."

"Did they know that?" I asked her.

"No. This was all very hush-hush. I can't afford to have word of it leaking out."

Which was pretty standard, especially if this was a multi-million dollar deal. "So you didn't tell David about the deal? Or the threats?"

"No. I couldn't," she said.

But they all would have picked up that there was something wrong, no matter how careful she'd been. That was the nature of offices, especially ones with creative teams that relied on each other. I'd need to do some digging into the dynamics of her team, and how much they might have figured out about the upcoming deal.

"Which of his colleagues would David have talked to if he did have personal worries?"

Her eyes teared up. "That would be me," she said. "Just like he was the one I talked to. Usually."

Usually again. It sounded like something had changed in Bittner's life. "Did he have money issues?" I asked her.

"David was well paid."

That didn't mean he didn't have money issues. "What about addictions?"

She smiled fondly, then seemed to recollect the circumstances.

"He said—used to say—he was addicted to books. He has... had quite the collection."

"Nothing else?"

"No. Not that I ever knew of."

And that was an interesting choice of wording. Was she holding something back? Or had she sub-consciously noticed a change in his behavior. "Was he married? Single?"

"Single. Very much so."

"So no relationship problems?"

"Oh, there were always those. But nothing significant, I don't think."

Or just nothing he'd told her about? "So how did David die? And where?"

"He... in the hotel," she said. "He'd registered under an assumed name. And he was shot."

"Which hotel?" I asked. With a sinking feeling that I already knew.

"The Grand Pacific," she said.

Great. Because the Harbor Bar where I'd met her the previous day was part of the Grand Pacific Hotel, an internationally known five star establishment with stunning views overlooking the Vancouver harbor. And from that wine bar she could have walked across a wide open space and taken the escalator down to the main floor, or she could have taken an elevator up to any of the hotel rooms.

Justine had been right there—alone—in the same hotel where her employee had been shot. And probably around the same time, to judge by all the questions we'd both been asked.

No wonder the police had been so interested in my meeting with Justine at the wine bar, and who had left first. But I couldn't verify when she'd left the building. Or if she'd left at all.

"The taxi driver would be able to confirm when you left to go back to the office," I said.

"Yes, they can. But I think the timing must be too close. When I left, I mean, and when he... he died."

I'd have to find out exactly what time that was. I made a note. "What taxi company did you use?"

"Yellow Cab. We have an account."

Had David also used that account? I'd have to find that out, too. "Where was he found?"

"I think in one of the hotel rooms—given the questions they'd asked. They think he was waiting for someone. They wanted to know if it was me. And if we'd been having an affair."

She drew in a shaky breath. "We weren't. David was my best friend. But he wasn't into permanent relationships. I'm not sure he believed in them, at least not for himself. He used to say that… that why did he need someone when he had me."

It sounded like he'd been in love with her.

She correctly interpreted my look. "No, not like that. You have to understand, David was gay. And he separated relationships into physical and spiritual. Physical was always with other men. But he always said he cared most about the spiritual."

It still sounded like David had loved her—and had gone to some lengths to make sure that wasn't awkward for her.

"Do you have any idea who he might have been seeing?"

"No. He'd sometimes discuss his various relationships, but with few details, and never names. David was out, had been for a long time, but I had the impression that a few of his lovers might not have been. Especially the married ones."

She grimaced. "That way there was no danger of a permanent relationship. I told him he deserved better than that, but he never listened. And now it's too late."

Justine pressed her hand against her mouth and stared down at the desk for a moment while she regained her composure.

That could explain why David had been in a hotel room at the Grand Pacific. And the timing of it. The hotel was easy walking distance from the business district. And at that time of day explanations like "I had to work late," or "I went for a few drinks with a client," were more believable.

"Had he been talking about problems with a recent relationship?" I asked when she looked up again.

"No. But I may just not have given him the time to tell me," she said bitterly. "This deal, and all."

She was going to blame herself for that for a long time. But there was one burden of guilt that she might not have to bear.

"If David was waiting for a lover," I said. "His death might have nothing to do with the threats someone made against you."

She shook her head. "I'm not so sure."

"Why not?"

"I don't think I can explain it."

"Try," I said.

"Justine, this is important," Brian said. "We're going to need all the details."

I nearly jumped at the unexpected sound of his voice. I'd been so focused on Justine, trying to read her every reaction, and he'd been sitting so quietly for so long that I'd—not forgotten exactly, but discounted, his presence.

Justine gave a choked laugh. "Fine. But it isn't pretty."

———

PUSHING her hair back behind her ears in what seemed to be an unconscious gesture, Justine turned to me. The unthinking change of hairstyle took away some of her polish, making her look younger and more vulnerable.

"Do you remember when I won the Argyll award?" she asked me.

I nodded. "Yes, but not well." Interior design had never been my focus—even back then, I paid far more attention to anything related to painting. "Why?"

"Because there were two of us nominated from our program. Me and Ethan Walker."

"Ethan Walker?" I vaguely remembered that name. But why? Then it came to me. "Didn't he…"

"Commit suicide? Yes, six months later. And the suicide note was a long, vitriolic accusation of failure and hopelessness. And he blamed me for stealing that award from him, and ending his career before it even started."

"I never heard that."

"It was hushed up. He was apparently bi-polar, and had stopped taking his medication in order to compete at what he described as "his best" in the competition. By the time he died, he'd slid from his creative high into a low period. He was severely depressed. And he refused to seek help."

"So how could anyone blame you for his death?"

Justine drew in a shaky breath, glanced from me to Brian, who hadn't said a word through all of this, then fixed her gaze on me. "Because I was responsible. It's why those threats are so vicious."

"What?"

"You remember how frantic our last year of university was? How we were all trying to be the best, and to figure out how to establish ourselves, to start our careers off with a bang?"

I nodded. It had been a recession, too, and no-one was hiring. No-one was interested in new talent. That was when I'd joined Andrea's agency as a temp. My keyboarding speeds were adequate at best, but I'd been really good with spreadsheets.

"It was a tough time," I said.

"Yes. It was." She turned towards Brian. "And the Argyll award— that was an international spotlight, ready to shine on someone and kickstart their career. When I heard I'd been short-listed, I was determined that someone would be me. No matter what."

She linked her hands together on the desk in front of her. Suddenly prominent knuckles told me how much strain she was under.

"I'm not proud of this, but when I found out Ethan was also in the running, I determined to do what I could to make sure it was me that won, and not him."

"How? Weren't all the entries submitted ahead of time?"

She nodded. "Yes. But there was an interview component. And I knew just what to say to knock him off his game."

She swallowed hard. "I was ruthless. Oh, I didn't do anything big, just little snipes in the week before the interview. Just enough to undermine his confidence."

She paused to clear her throat. "I'd like to think I wouldn't have done it, if I'd known how fragile he was. But the truth is, I can never know that for sure. When I found out he'd committed suicide, I hated myself for that. And I vowed then I'd never undercut anyone again. In fact, that I'd support other artists, any way I could."

From the things I'd read about her over the years, she'd done exactly that. I hadn't always believed the news articles, because they didn't match the Justine I remembered, who had always struck me as more than a little petty. I believed those stories now.

"It was all so stupid," she said. "And such a waste. In the end, Ethan wasn't even my main competition. That was a fellow from Toronto, who ended up winning the Argyll the following year. I killed Ethan Walker for nothing."

————

I COULD HEAR THE SOFT, expensive tick of the crystal clock on Justine's desk as the silence stretched. Bright beams of sunshine through the windows cast shadows across the three of us as if we were playing a macabre game of statues. Brian's face hadn't changed, but his muscles seemed locked. Justine looked frozen, as if her words had triggered an evil spell.

How had she lived with herself all these years, believing that?

"Who else might believe as you do? That you killed Ethan Walker?" I asked. My words jarred us all out of that frozen instant.

"I... I don't know," said Justine. "I never asked. My guilt was so obvious to me that I just assumed that all his friends saw it too."

"And who were they? His friends?"

"I don't know that either. I didn't know him at all, really, except for a few classes together. And how he spoke of his art in class—well, how we all did, I suppose—exposed every insecurity we had. Made it easy to play on them." She seemed to fold in on herself as she spoke.

I needed to know a lot more about Ethan Walker. Because despite what Justine thought, she was not the logical target for someone to blame in Walker's death. Not if she'd told us the truth, that is.

Because I remembered those classes all too well. Better than Justine did, based on what she'd just said.

"And what of your insecurities? Did anyone play on those?" I asked her.

"Well, sure," she said, as if it was no big deal. "You remember what some of those classes were like. Andrea Channing thought she was a big deal back then, and she took pleasure in cutting me down every chance she got. Her friend Tracy whatever-her-name-was wasn't far behind."

That's what I'd expected to hear. But Justine seemed to be hearing her own words for the first time, judging by her shocked look.

"And did Ethan Walker ever criticize your work?"

She started to nod, then caught herself and stared at me.

"Sometimes he could be the harshest, most wounding critic in the class," she said softly, half to herself. "And sometimes the kindest. I'd forgotten that. But I didn't know he was bi-polar."

It didn't take her long to process that memory, either. I watched as her posture straightened into its usual confidence.

I made another note. Maybe she wasn't the only one who'd forgotten about the other side of Ethan Walker.

It could be the threats and David's death were unrelated, after all.

Or maybe Justine still hadn't been told the real reason she was being threatened.

"What you've told me about Walker might make a very personal motive for your stalker," I said. "Someone whose only way of dealing with grief is to find someone else to blame. No matter how blameless you really are."

"But I'm not…" Justine said, leaning forward as if to protest.

Too many years of blaming herself for something she hadn't really done would be hard to let go of.

I gave her a moment, and she just shook her head a little and didn't say anything more.

"No, you're not responsible," I said. "And it's a stretch, but I can see a scenario where someone who couldn't accept Walker's loss might still have been angry with you. Might have made these threats against you. We'll be looking into that. And why you were being threatened now, after all these years."

I paused for her reaction. She nodded, but didn't say anything. Neither did Brian Stewart.

"What I don't see is any link between the threats and David's death. Have you any ideas?"

Justine shrugged her thin shoulders, looking uncharacteristically helpless.

Brian seemed to have been asking himself the same questions

"If David's death had nothing to do with the person who has been making threats against you," he said in a quietly compelling voice that made both Justine and I turn towards him. "Then who would gain from his death?"

Justine looked startled, though whether by his question or his tone I wasn't sure.

I was simply curious. I knew Brian didn't spend much time in the courtroom, but he knew how to ask the good questions, the ones that made a client rethink everything. And timing was a big part of that.

His was excellent.

"I can't imagine anyone would," she said after a long moment. "How could they? David dead? That is nothing but loss for anyone he knew."

Brian was right, though. Someone had gained something from

David Bittner's death, even if that benefit was in expressing a moment of rage.

Bittner had been shot in a hotel room, under an assumed name. Which meant someone had arranged to meet him there. A lover?

One bringing a loaded gun to a hotel tryst? If that's what had happened, that was no flash of anger or jealousy. That was planned.

If I was going to try to identify Bittner's killer, I'd need to learn a great deal more about his life. Which Justine either didn't know about or wasn't willing to admit, even to herself.

Given everything I'd heard this morning, it was going to take everyone working as a team to keep Justine out of jail.

Including this Marchant fellow.

I didn't know much about him—but I knew his reputation. Criminal lawyers, the good ones, are high profile hotshots. At least to those of us in the industry—whichever side we're on. And Marchant was the newest, and hottest of the breed.

Just how much of a pain would he be to work with?

CHAPTER NINE

As I drove back to the office, mostly oblivious to the oranges and yellows of turning leaves against a bright blue sky—my artist's eye never quite ignores such things—I realized I needed to focus on my strategy for Justine's case. And putting the right people to work on it.

James Marchant—and whatever problems he might bring—could wait until Brian had briefed him. And he'd talked to his new client.

I just hoped Marchant had strong nerves. Justine wasn't going to be anyone's dream client.

Opening the office door, I was relieved to see Marie, still slightly red-eyed but looking almost her normal self—well, her new normal, the professional version.

She leaped up from her screaming pink desk the moment she saw me. "So it's true, then?" she asked, clutching my arm. "Justine is alive?"

"She is. And she needs our help now. I'll fill you in, but I need coffee first." And I headed towards the back to put on a fresh pot.

"I just made some," she said.

I held back a shudder. Marie doesn't drink coffee—I've never understood why, since she downs Red Bull in quantities that make me wince—and her coffee making abilities reflect that disdain.

I'd have to put on a new pot.

"Just taste it," Marie said, trailing along behind me. Apparently she'd taken up mind reading as well. "It's not bad. You'll see."

I didn't say anything. Whatever I said would result in loud words and hurt feelings, and I wasn't going there.

"Really," Marie insisted, somehow darting around me. Next thing I knew she was pressing a full cup into my hand. Well, at least it was hot. That was an improvement.

I took a cautious sniff. It smelled okay. In fact, it smelled really good, dark and rich.

"It's good. Really," Marie said. "Justine showed me how, after she convinced me that a good cup of coffee can keep clients happy. Which reminds me. We need to update our coffee technology. This"—and she waved a hand at the drip-through coffee pot, which was my lifeline—"is so dated."

She had no idea what she was talking about. Away from the office, I downed cappuccino with the best of them. But at the office? No.

The coffee pot stayed. End of discussion.

I took a cautious sip of the coffee, mostly so I wouldn't have to answer her. To my amazement, it wasn't bad. In fact, it was good. Really good.

Maybe there were more advantages to this new Marie than I'd realized.

Coffee in hand, I sat down at my desk. Marie plopped herself into the chair opposite me and sat forward. "Well? What's going on?"

I briefed her as succinctly as possible.

When I was done, she was wide-eyed. For all of twenty seconds. Then I could almost see the wheels turning.

"That's a lot of stuff to find out," she said.

Leaving me wondering exactly which stuff she'd focused on. Probably the drama of it all.

"The way I see it," Marie said. "We have a thirteen year-old suicide and a recent murder to investigate. Which may or may not be connected. And in both cases we have to learn an awful lot about who the dead guy was, and about his life. With not much time to do it."

She cocked her head to one side. "Plus there's the case at the Courtland Gallery that I prepared the contract for. Which reminds me, you need to get that signed."

I was going to have to learn not to underestimate my assistant.

"This new case is going to take the whole team," she said, surprising me again. "Good thing we have desks for everyone."

And she shot me a sly look.

I rolled my eyes and she grinned.

"Let's start with Cory," I said. "It's just after two now. He should be available by three-thirty." My nephew might be an ace with a computer, but he'd just turned sixteen and was still in high school.

"He has a free period last thing this afternoon," Marie said. "If I text him now, he should be here in half an hour." Pulling out her phone, she started typing.

What was this? As far as I knew, Marie and Cory mostly enjoyed what I called an armed detente, each one waiting for the other to make the slightest error. And now she'd memorized his schedule?

"You'll probably need to call in Badger, too," Marie said, refer-ring to the high-priced computer genius Cory had asked a few favors from in the past. Badger had been so good, I'd ended up hiring her for that case.

I'd expected to use Badger again sometime. Just not this soon. And I wasn't sure this was a case where we needed her level of expertise.

On the other hand, Marie was right that we didn't have a lot of time. And for our client, the stakes were high.

Both Justine's freedom and her reputation were at stake. She needed help. And she was prepared to pay for it.

Maybe we did need Badger now.

"Okay, I left a message for Badger that we need her for a case," Marie said.

Wait, what? "You just texted Badger as well as Cory?"

"Sure. There's no time to waste."

I rolled my eyes, but didn't say anything. I'd come to the same conclusion, after all.

"And Cory will be here in half an hour. Which might give you and me enough time," my incorrigible assistant told me.

I was pretty sure I'd regret it, but I had to ask. "Enough time for what?"

Marie grinned at me, flung her arms wide. "This office isn't working."

I glanced at the jumble of odd colored desks that surrounded us. "No, it isn't. I'm glad you see…"

And that was as far as I got. Marie had already turned and was headed out into the hallway, beckoning me to follow her. Speechless, I did so.

———

MARIE WALKED one door down the hall, inserted a key she pulled from her pocket, and flung the door wide. "Isn't this perfect?" she called over her shoulder as she disappeared inside.

What was she up to now? Too curious to ignore her antics, I followed her inside.

The space was smaller than my current space, but well laid out with two offices—with windows—straight ahead. There was a decent sized meeting room—also with a window—running along the right wall. And a sort of reception area in the open front area, with a large screen against the left wall.

Marie glanced around, then looked at me expectantly.

"What?"

"You don't see it?" She sounded disappointed.

"See what?"

She huffed at me and stomped over to the screen. I grinned at the sight. She might look like a new model assistant, but she was still the same Marie. Then she pulled back the screen to reveal a closed door in the wall, and my grin vanished.

"Tell me that door doesn't lead into our offices."

"Can't."

She was enjoying this way too much. "Where does it open?"

"You know that storage closet that's mostly useless?"

It figured. Great security we had. "So why are you so pleased about it?"

"Because it's perfect. We need more space, and this space is vacant. And already connected to our existing offices."

"What?"

"Think about it. You need a private office. We need space for all of us. And a proper reception area. For when you hire an actual receptionist. And a real meeting room."

Obviously she'd been talking to Justine.

And that private office…

"No, Marie," I said. It was too much change, too fast. And I wasn't sure it was a direction that made sense. Or if I had the cash flow for any of it. "Maybe the firm will need to expand. Someday. But not now."

"But this space is perfect. And it's available now." Her jaw was thrust forward and she'd fallen into a fighting stance. With her new attire, it looked so incongruous that it took everything I had to keep from laughing.

But I didn't want to hurt her feelings. "There'll be other opportunities. There always are."

"Don't you want to grow?"

No.

"I want to be sure my firm"— a not so subtle reminder of whose name was on the door—"survives any growth we might need. A lot of small firms try to grow too fast, and go under."

I'd seen it too often. Doing investigations for people isn't a predictable business. Grow too fast, take on too much overhead and you don't survive the next economic downturn.

"It'll cost you more later, when we have to move," she said.

"That's a risk I'm prepared to take." I glanced around me. "And this is an awkward space for most firms. The landlord may have difficulty renting it any time soon. Especially if they notice the door leading into our space."

She was silent. Apparently I was right. But she also looked thoughtful.

Uh oh. I knew that look. Now what was she up to?

———

I GOT myself settled behind my unrepentantly eggplant desk, and used the time before Cory got there to review the contract Marie had drawn up for Margaret. When he arrived, I briefed him on our new case, and asked him to do some digging into David Bittner's life.

"What do you need to know?" he asked.

"Someone killed him. We need to know why. I'm interested in anything in his life that strikes you as being out of the ordinary."

"Anything that doesn't fit, then?" he asked.

"Exactly."

With a nod, he set up on the burnt orange topped desk—I shuddered—and was quickly buried in some internet search or other.

Half an hour later, I looked up to see him standing by my desk, laptop in hand. His eyes were sparkling. "You have to see this."

"Show me," I said, and moved my own laptop so we could both see his.

"I was digging into David Bittner's life, like you said," Cory said.

"And?"

"And I think he had at least three identities."

"What? You're kidding me."

"Nope. He mostly lived as David Bittner, but I found two other online identities, and both of them have credit cards and everything. And that's just what I came up with on a quick search."

It was probably two more identities than I'd have found. I'm competent, but no expert. If he had more time, and Badger working with him, they'd probably find even more.

This was Justine's trusted second-in-command and best friend. If Bittner had this much of a double life that he kept from her, what were her enemies hiding?

I'd known this case would be complicated, but I hadn't expected quite so much so soon.

"Keep digging," I told Cory.

He nodded and sauntered back to his desk. All nine steps away. I looked across the room at Marie.

"Have you heard from Badger yet?" I asked Marie.

"No. She'll probably drop by in the next hour, though. She usually does."

Badger wasn't doing enough work for us to merit a "usually." I'd have to think about what that meant. Later.

"Good," I said. "I'll call a quick team meeting after she gets here, say around five. Can you order pizza for us all, Marie? And Cory…"

"I'll show Badger what I've found by then, see what she says," he broke in to say. "She's wizard on this stuff. I've still got a lot to learn."

"Good enough," I said and went back to thinking about Justine's case.

CHAPTER TEN

It was nearly four when I looked up to find Marie standing beside my desk. I hadn't even heard her approach. "How long have you been there?"

"Not long. But I need to talk to you before the meeting. In private."

I glanced at the screen in front of me. I just had a few minutes work to finish this off. "Can it wait?"

"No. This is urgent," she said.

Now what? I nodded and stood up.

Marie dragged me to the four stall women's bathroom at the other end of our hall, and checked each stall individually to be sure they were empty—her finger to her lips in a request for silence the whole time—before locking the main bathroom door.

"Marie, you can't do that."

"If someone needs to come in, they'll knock," she said.

This was odd, even for her. "So what's so urgent? And so secret?"

Marie ran a hand through her sleek blond hair. I watched, amazed, as it fell neatly back into place. That was a seriously good cut. On Marie?

The over-enthusiastic, and let's face it, somewhat paranoid assistant that I'd reluctantly hired seemed to be morphing into someone I didn't recognize.

And then she did something like this. Now this was the old Marie. And I was almost glad to see her. What was I thinking?

"I didn't want Cory to hear me. In case he took it wrong," she said.

Now she was worried about the boy she saw as her rival's feelings? We didn't have time for this. "Marie, we're supposed to be working as a team. We don't keep information from each other."

She gave me a withering look.

Okay, maybe I'd earned that. I had a habit of holding back key information until I thought we were at a point in the case where the others needed to know. And I was trying to break myself of it.

Yeah, right. Maybe it was a trust thing.

But the longer I worked with Marie and Cory, the more I did feel I could trust them with the sensitive details of a client's problems. Badger too, if in a different way.

"Just spill it," I said.

"Fine, then." Marie's belligerent expression did not in any way match her attire.

I hid a grin. She'd been around me too much, clearly—she was beginning to pick up some of my expressions. "Well?"

"David Bittner? I think he was selling out Justine."

"What?" And why couldn't Cory hear this? "Selling her out to whom? And why?"

"I don't know who. But because he needed money. What else?"

"How do you know this?"

"Ummm, something a friend of a friend told me." She wouldn't meet my eyes. "He's a gambler."

"Your friend is?"

"My friend's friend. Not mine," she hurried to say. "And no, not him. Bittner's the gambler. He's in debt up to his eyeballs, from what I hear."

How had Marie learned all this? Did I even want to know? "Cory didn't dig up anything…" I began.

Then I put it together. "This friend's friend—he might be in collections?"

"Something like that."

"And for a company that is rather less than legal?"

"Yeah. Like that."

"And maybe they were putting pressure on Bittner for being behind on his payments?"

"That's the way I heard it."

"And you didn't want Cory to know this, why?"

"You know he likes a challenge. Plus he hates stuff he can't find online. You don't want him going searching for any of this."

She was right about that. My sister would string me up by my toenails if I let Cory get anywhere near loan sharking. Never mind the other implications of what Marie had told me.

High gambling debts could have pushed Bittner into borrowing money at ridiculous rates from a low level loan shark. But Marie's reaction told me it could mean something worse.

And if they were really high gambling debts? The source of those loans could be drug money, Hell's Angels, a Chinese tong or even the Russian mob, which is gaining a bigger foothold on this coast than anyone would like to admit. No wonder Marie was being secretive.

"If Bittner was selling out Justine, we need a place to start," I said. "And specific details. Any chance I could talk to this friend of a friend?"

"None." Marie looked determined. And worried.

"Would me asking questions put you in danger?"

"Probably."

That avenue was out, then. "Can you tell me anything about them? Or their connections?"

"No. I really can't."

Fair enough. "Okay, I'll find another way to get the information."

I needed to talk to Nick. Since his last gig had been the Gang Task Force, he still knew a lot of the players. In fact, there was a lot of overlap between the two. Inter-gang turf wars and the resulting violence had resulted in more than half of the murders in Metro Vancouver last year.

Marie was watching me closely, still with that worried look. "Your boyfriend?" she said when I didn't say anything.

Marie was starting to know me better than I'd realized. Which should make me more nervous than it did. I wasn't ready to think about why that might be.

"If Bittner's problems were gang-related, Nick will know most of the players," I said. "It might give us a start. But I need to get a better sense of what he was into, first."

"Put Badger on it," she said. "Nothing surprises her. And she's good. Really good. They won't see her coming. And she won't leave tracks."

Marie was right, but her words surprised me. I hadn't realized she'd come to value Badger. Who was just as hard to work with as Marie was, but in a different way. They were as different as chalk and cheese—with no point of understanding. Or so I'd thought.

It seemed like the dynamics between Marie, Cory and Badger had changed while I'd been out of the office. How had that happened in such a short time?

Since I'd finished my show, everything around me seemed to be changing faster than I could keep up with. I didn't like it much. Sitting on some island somewhere was starting to sound good.

Except that I'd be bored stiff in about a day and a half. Maybe less.

Probably this whole change thing was a blip. It would pass.

So why did the idea of Marie and Badger working well together make me nervous?

———

BADGER ARRIVED JUST AFTER FOUR, and set up her laptop on the acid green desk without a word to anyone. Marie didn't even look up.

Knowing her, she'd probably texted Badger right after our conversation, and filled her in.

Seconds later, Cory wandered over to Badger's desk with his own laptop and began explaining what he'd found. Badger nodded and said something I couldn't hear. Her fingers flew over the keyboard.

Cory watched for a moment, a broad grin on his increasingly mature features, and went back to his own desk with that intense look that I'd come to know meant he was on a mission. My nephew was growing up fast. It looked good on him.

I just hoped that nothing I got him involved in would make him grow up too fast.

CHAPTER ELEVEN

At five the pizza arrived, and we clustered around the folding table that Marie had somehow shoehorned into an empty space near the window. We had to sit on those stupid metal folding chairs, too, because there wasn't space for anything actually comfortable. I looked around the table, then at the office behind us.

I wasn't prepared to admit that the colored desktops had any merit, but having seen Justine's office, I had a new appreciation for what she and Marie had been trying to accomplish here. If I squinted a little and imagined the space was at least half again as big—I could almost envision a very functional office for all of us. With even some room for us to grow.

Grow? Where had that come from?

Six months ago, it had been just me, and I'd been perfectly happy that way. Now? I glanced around me. I'd enjoyed working with this team on the Lang case. And I needed them on this one. But to expand my business this much…

I felt the beginnings of a migraine, just behind my right eye. Justine needed us focused on solving Bittner's murder, not redecorating.

I glanced around the table. "This is a big case. Our first focus needs to be Bittner's death, since Justine may well be arrested on suspicion of killing him. Cory, how did you and Badger make out with Bittner's various identities?"

"We're finding more of them, but it's going to take us awhile," he said.

"He did good work finding them so fast," Badger added. Cory beamed, then tried to hide how pleased he was.

"Yes, he did. Marie, how are you coming on finding out who Ethan Walker's college friends were?"

"Way slower than Cory, here." She feigned a punch at him. He scowled at her.

I ignored the interaction. "Has anyone found anything that ties Justine's stalker to Bittner's death?"

"Nothing so far," Badger said.

Cory shook his head.

"Well, I might have something on that part," Marie said, and stood up.

Once she had our attention, she stomped the three feet to the window, then back again. She walked like she was wearing the Doc Martens she used to wear, not the four-inch heels that were actually on her feet. The disconnect between her new style and her body language was moving fast from amusing to disturbing.

I was going to have to talk to her about that. It wasn't a happy thought.

Then I caught the sideways glance Badger was giving her. Or maybe someone else would do it for me.

"Well?" Cory said impatiently. "Quit stomping and tell us, already."

Make that several someones.

"I am not stomping," Marie said, glaring at him.

He glared back. "What do you call it?"

She made an inarticulate noise, then faced the whiteboard, writing on it with quick strokes. I guess taking the high road was easier than trying to find another word for stomping. One that didn't sound so pissed off. I hid my grin.

Cory wasn't done with Marie yet, though. "Spacious?" he asked, squinting at the whiteboard. "That's your connection? Spacious?"

She let out a ladylike sigh, and kept writing.

Marie? Ladylike?

I wasn't the only one who choked on that one. Cory and Badger exchanged glances.

"It isn't spacious," Marie said patiently, turning to face us when she'd finished her phrase. "It's quite clearly spatial. Spatial relationships."

She was right. It was.

But it still didn't make any sense. At least not in our world. Maybe in Justine's world. But not in the investigative one, where we were trying to save our client's company. Not to mention keep her out of jail.

No-one said anything for a moment.

Then Marie grinned at all of us. "Your faces!" she said gleefully. "If you could see your faces."

Cory looked sheepish.

"Marie, Justine doesn't have time for us to be playing games," I said. "Can you get to the point?"

She sobered instantly. "Right. Sorry. Well, Justine's famous, right? An internationally known designer, and all that. And apparently internationally known designers are like academics. They publish."

"They do?"

She nodded. "Interviews. Predictions for upcoming trends. Opinion pieces. Stuff like that. Even essays. So I've been going through everything Justine's published over the last two years. And there's a lot of it. She's very quotable, you know," she said directly to me, her expression earnest.

I'd take her word for it.

My poker face must need some work, because Marie grinned.

She'd been needling me. And it had worked. I'd have to watch that one.

"Anyway, I was looking for anything controversial," Marie said.

"You know, lots of comments, angry replies, arguments. There was a surprising amount of discussion about some of her ideas, but the one that really set people off was…" And with a flourish she pointed to the words she'd written.

"Spatial relationships?" Cory repeated skeptically. "What's that when it's home?"

He'd picked that phrase up from his mother. I recognized it as one of my sister Susanna's favorites. Which would embarrass Cory to no end if I pointed that out.

I figure I earned big-time aunt points for keeping it to myself.

"Something to do with the best way to have all the elements of a design relate to each other within a given space. Like a kitchen," Marie said. "It's pretty standard stuff, but it seems Justine's been pioneering a new way of thinking about it, and people got pretty het up over that."

Okay. It sounded too much like some academic politics to me, where everything has already been discussed, so people argue about the interpretation of a single word. For years.

"How does this relate to Bittner's death?" I asked.

"I did a search of his publications, too," Marie said. "There weren't so many of them, but he and Justine co-authored a few papers. Mostly about," and I could hear the drumroll in her voice, "the changing paradigm of spatial relationships. Those papers are the ones that brought out Justine's troll."

"Justine's troll?" I asked as Cory and Badger exchanged knowing glances.

"An online commenter who spews hate all over someone else," Marie said.

"I know what a troll is," I said. "What did you learn about Justine's? Was there only one?"

"There seemed to be," Marie said. "But he was prolific. And vicious."

"And how does this relate to Bittner's death?" I asked.

"The last time I could find the troll showing up was on an

article Bittner and Justine co-wrote," Marie said. "And he—Bittner —and the troll really got into it in the comments."

"Have you been able to find out who the troll is?" I asked

"Nope. Just the handle," she said.

"Which is?"

Marie made a face. "*Designexpert1.*"

"Oh, that's original."

"Dead stupid name," Cory said.

And I'm pretty sure Badger rolled her eyes.

"Maybe," Marie said. "But stupid name or not, it got ugly, fast. Well, see for yourself. I'll send you the link."

There was silence for a moment as the three of us skimmed the article and the comments. Marie was right. It did get ugly. And threatening.

"These are some pretty specific threats. Any idea who this guy is?" I asked after I'd finished.

She shook her head. "No, but I can…" she started to say.

"Don't even try to look for him," Badger interrupted her. "I've got this."

"Yeah, you don't want whoever this is coming after you," Cory said.

Marie's jaw thrust out. "Let him try."

I hid another grin.

"Let Badger run with it from here," I said.

————

I HADN'T BEEN HOME LONG when Nick called. It took everything I had not to ask him about gangs. But until I heard back from Badger, it would have to wait.

For one thing, I didn't want to put him in the middle of a conflict of interest, just because I hadn't yet known who I was dealing with. For another, no point having him worried about me when this might be a huge overstatement on Marie's part.

Nick dealt with sharks. Whoever Bittner was involved with could be bait fish in Nick's world.

"It's good to hear your voice," I said.

"Tough day?" Nick asked.

I kept forgetting how well Nick could read me. "Something like that. One of my cases has intersected with the murder of a local designer, David Bittner," I said, knowing he'd already have heard the details of Bittner's death.

"This is your design fraud case?"

"Yes, but the murder doesn't seem to have anything to do with the alleged fraud. Except for the fact that my client may be a suspect."

"Ouch."

"Exactly. But it's nothing…"

"You can talk about," he finished for me. "Yeah, that's my day too. In fact, I'm calling because it looks like we're going to have to take a rain check on that dinner I was planning."

I could hear the frustration simmering in his voice. And I got it. I missed him too.

But postponing dinner meant we'd have to postpone "the talk" about moving in together. I felt guilty about the little spasm of relief I felt.

But only for a moment.

"Our day will come," I said grandly, and got the laugh I was aiming for. Which made me feel better, too.

We're good together, Nick and I. But we've never spent a ton of time together—both of us too busy. I didn't want to jinx a good thing.

Neither of us had much to say after that, so we cut the call short. I went for a run afterwards, trying to get rid of that flat feeling. I hate that feeling.

CHAPTER TWELVE

Justine and I met with her hotshot new lawyer in Justine's office the following morning. James Marchant was a tall, thin man with dark hair, an impeccably cut suit and deep frown lines in his forehead. In another decade, those lines might make him look distinguished. Now, he just looked angry.

Justine seemed pleased with him, though. She looked more relaxed than I'd seen her look since her associate's death. We sat at the big table in her boardroom, just the three of us, with the sprawling view of downtown at our elbows.

No sooner was I seated than Marchant turned those sharp eyes on me.

"I understand that my client has already retained you to investigate this unfortunate matter," he said.

Which one? The blackmail? Or the murder?

"That's right," I said. "And your firm has already formalized it, so that the results of our investigation remain privileged."

"I see."

Sure he did. And he wasn't happy about it.

"And what is your proposed plan for the investigation?" he asked.

"That will depend, at least partly, on your strategy for defending your client against whatever charges they come up with," I shot back.

"You mean you don't have a plan yet," he said.

Justine was looking agitated. I didn't blame her. Your defense attorney wasn't supposed to feud with your investigator.

I drew in a deep breath. Someone had to take the high road here, for Justine's sake. It might as well be me. I did, after all, have a strategy. One that was well underway.

And I did need to know what his plans might be.

Getting Justine clear of this mess would take both of us, working together. Now that was a scary thought. Especially when he was glaring at me like that.

Marchant reminded me of—me, I realized with a sense of shock. Which was immediately followed by a very uncharacteristic desire to giggle. Mostly at the thought of his reaction if I told him what I was thinking.

But it was true. The glare, the sarcasm, the questions?

His reaction was exactly the one I would have if I had to work closely with someone I didn't know or trust. Like him.

"My initial focus will be two-fold," I said calmly, noting as I spoke that Justine's frown had vanished. "My team will be looking into the history of Ethan Walker's unfortunate death, as well as searching for anyone who might blame our client for it. We'll also be looking into David Bittner, and any enemies he may have had."

"That sounds," and he paused, as if choosing just the right word, "reasonable."

"Thank you," I said. Ignoring both his skeptical expression and the mock surprise in his voice. "It's a start."

He nodded, but didn't offer anything further.

Forcing me to ask. "And your strategy?"

"I think it's too early to share that," he said. "Once you've gathered your facts, we'll see where we are."

I reminded myself I was a professional and kept my tone even. "I'll look forward to it."

It was an effort not to grit my teeth as I said it. Some people make me hate being a professional. It looked like James Marchant was going to be one of them.

I checked my watch. "And now I'm afraid I have another appointment. Justine, I'll be in touch."

And got myself out of there before he said something else to annoy me. Marchant was probably an excellent trial lawyer—with that attitude, he'd infuriate the opposing counsel.

Angry enough to make errors? Judging by the way I felt now, probably so. Good.

Now, all I had to do was find the real murderer, and make his job really simple.

Piece of cake.

———

IT WAS a good thing I'd walked to the meeting with Marchant—the twenty minute walk across the Granville Street bridge to the Courtland Gallery gave me a much needed chance to decompress afterwards.

It was another crisp fall day, the skies that clear, cloudless blue that made my fingers itch for a paintbrush. I caught glimpses of the mountains here and there—the view corridors downtown that allow views of the ocean and the mountains haven't been preserved nearly as well as I think they should have been. But on a day like this, Vancouver is a glorious city to live in.

Even the snarl of traffic downtown didn't detract from it—not when I was on foot, instead of stuck in long lineups of frustrated drivers.

And my meeting with Margaret, which I'd postponed from the previous day, took no time at all. I gave her the contract, she signed and gave me a cheque. I promised to report back in a few days. Done.

And Margaret didn't even hint about me doing another show. Or ask how my painting was coming. Which wasn't like her.

What should have been a relief from a pressure I didn't need right now—wasn't. Now I was going to have to worry about Margaret, too.

Still, I should have been ready to head straight back to the office, as I'd planned to. Back to the investigation into whoever had killed David Bittner. But I was hungry. And I was already on Granville Street. Beans, my favorite neighborhood coffee shop, was only two blocks away.

Uh huh

I know myself too well. Yes, the thought of the "Everything but the Kitchen Sink" muffins and the good coffee had me drooling. And I think better when I'm not starving. But I was also avoiding my office.

And I needed to think about why. Right after I had that muffin and coffee.

When the barista called my name, I grabbed the enormous muffin and my extra-large cappuccino and headed for a small booth in the corner with a good view of the street. I find the bustle and color of the busy street helps me think. Plus no-one could sneak up on me from any direction in that particular spot.

Yes, I care about not having my back to the room. Call me paranoid.

I just think I'm careful. Except for sometimes, when I'm convinced protecting your back is part of a universal human fear, left over from our earliest days when we were as much the hunted as the hunters. And that some of us are still more tuned into our primitive side than others.

I'm not sure what that says about me, though.

Sipping my coffee, I reviewed my notes on Margaret's case, and thought out who to assign to it. Normally I'd have worked out my game plan before I had her sign the contract, though with my standard contract terms it isn't strictly necessary. This time, the urgency of Justine's case had taken over.

Still, what Margaret really needed was information. Which was probably a pretty straight-forward search for someone who knew their way around the darker side of the webs, including the Dark Web.

Someone like Badger. In fact, it might fit in nicely with the search Badger was already doing on Bittner's gambling. She could probably uncover the answers Margaret needed in a couple of hours. Perfect.

I texted Badger the details. I was really going to have to consider hiring her full-time. If I could afford her.

One down, one to go. I ate some of my muffin, drank my cappuccino, and ran through the notes I'd taken in my recent meeting with Marchant, and with the one Justine the previous day. Then I stared out the window for a bit, not really seeing anything as I digested what I'd just read.

And my intuition leaped into overdrive.

I re-read my notes on what Justine had said. Then I turned to a blank page, and began to put together a timeline of David Bittner's last night, flipping between Justine's comments and the work my team had done the previous day.

There wasn't a lot to go on.

It was time to talk to my team.

CHAPTER THIRTEEN

By the time I'd run up the seven flights to my office, I was ready for anything. Well, almost anything. I hadn't expected to be met at the door by Cory, practically bouncing with poorly suppressed excitement.

"What are you doing here? You're supposed to be in school."

"Teacher's conference," he said with a grin.

"And your mother knows you're here?"

He gave me a sheepish look. "She said I'd probably get in less trouble here than anywhere else."

Wow. That was the first sign of softening I'd seen in my sister Susanna's attitude towards her son working part-time for me. To be fair, he tends to be a risk-taker, and working for me has given him more opportunities than either Susanna or I had anticipated.

But this case was not going to be one of them. I'd make sure of that.

"Aunt B. You need to see this," he said, his voice breaking higher on the last word.

"In a minute. I need coffee first."

"It's on your desk," Marie said. Her voice sounded odd, too.

I glanced across the crowded room, and sure enough, there was a mug of coffee sitting there. Still steaming.

How had they known when I was coming? Oh.

I gave Cory a firm look. "Tell me you're not tracking the GPS on my phone."

"I'm not," he said.

"Then how did you know..." I broke off as I registered that Marie was avoiding looking at me. She didn't have the skills to set up a trace on my phone. But my nephew did.

I glared at him. "Plausible deniability? Really?" I said.

He grinned at me. Obviously thinking he was off the hook if I was making a joke. He was so wrong.

"So you set it up so Marie could track my phone," I said.

He nodded. "We were worried about you. After the last few cases..."

I rolled my eyes. He had a point. Not a good one, but it was a point.

"Turn it off," I told him. "And don't do it again. Not unless you're both prepared to have me track your phones. Got it?"

Cory looked apprehensive. Marie looked horrified. Both of them nodded.

Cory I could understand—at sixteen, he's at that stage where he spends a lot of time making sure his mother doesn't know what he's up to. And some things I would have to tell her—it's in the sister code.

But what was Marie hiding?

Still, as long as she showed up for work on time—and didn't track my phone—it was none of my business.

"Good. Now, what's got you so revved up?" I asked. I sat down and reached for my coffee.

"Badger will be here in a few minutes," Marie said. "We need a meeting."

Which was exactly what I'd been thinking. But there was something in Marie's voice.

Now what?

———

TWENTY MINUTES later we were all crowded around the fold-up meeting table. I opened my laptop. "Okay, what have you got?"

It surprised me a bit when Badger was the first to speak. Usually she sat back and listened first.

"Bittner had a gambling problem," she said. "And he was borrowing money from some very nasty types. His death may have nothing to do with Justine or her business at all."

So Marie's intel had been good. I smiled at my assistant, and she flushed a little.

"Can you be more specific about who Bittner was borrowing the money from?" I asked Badger. "Are we talking money lenders? Gangs?"

"I'm still digging," Badger said. "I've found the first thread of the money trail, but it's still low level. I need to see where it goes."

"Fair enough. Keep me posted."

I still intended to talk to Nick. His perspective on my cases—with identifying details safely removed, of course—is always useful. I'd wait for Badger's update, though. For all the same reasons.

"Bittner's death might not have had anything to do with his gambling, though," Cory said, surprising us all. Badger gave him a look I couldn't read. My nephew turned red and wouldn't meet her eyes.

What was that about? I made a mental note to find out.

"What have you found?" I asked him.

"The hotel security cameras show a man leaving the suite Bittner had rented. Really quickly."

"What time?"

"Just after five."

"That falls right in the middle of the timeframe for the murder," I said.

He nodded.

So why had the police been looking at Justine? "Show me," I said.

All four of us crowded around his laptop, and Cory pressed a key to start the surveillance recording he already had cued up.

We were looking at an angle that showed David Bittner's hotel room door, 1517. The recording was in black and white, and the focus wasn't as sharp as I'd have expected from a high-end hotel.

Seconds later the door to 1517 opened, and a figure—male, and wearing a suit—emerged.

As the recording ran, Cory provided the commentary. "You see how he's got one side turned away from the cameras in the hallway. And here, he takes the stairs down, and somehow evades the rest of the cameras. Almost like he knew they were there."

He paused the recording, and turned to me. "Do you recognize him?"

I had a sinking feeling that I did. Despite his attempts to minimize how much the camera caught, it looked like Michael Gainer. Who was a prominent—and very married—lawyer who rumor had it was up for a judgeship.

Gainer's kept his occasional affairs —with partners of both sexes—fairly private, but they were the stuff of quiet rumors in certain circles. Was Bittner one of those affairs?

Or was there another reason for them to be meeting privately in Bittner's hotel room that night?

And yeah, Gainer would have scoped out the cameras. Especially if the hotel was a regular meeting site for him.

"I think so," I said. "I think it's a local lawyer."

Who might or might not be Bittner's lover. Justine couldn't tell me much about Bittner's personal relationships. Or had she just chosen not to?

"Think?" Marie said. "You can't be positive?"

"No. Run it again, will you Cory?"

He did so, once at regular speed, and once in slow motion. We all four squinted at the screen, looking for any detail that might help identify a killer.

"Well?" Marie asked as Cory paused the recording after the slow motion run through. They all turned to look at me. "Is it him?"

"Yes, I think so." I still couldn't see any details, but I'd seen Gainer pacing in a courtroom often enough. The guy had a distinctive walk, even on a bad recording.

"So who is this guy?" Cory asked.

"Michael Gainer," I said.

"The one who's up for a judgeship?" Marie asked.

Now how did she know that? "That's the one," I said.

"I thought he was married," she said.

"He is. " And happily, from everything I'd heard. On the surface, anyway. Maybe it was an open marriage.

"And we don't know why they met privately. Making assumptions without proof is the mark of an amateur."

"But…" Cory started to say.

I held up a hand. "Not open for discussion. It might, or might not, be Gainer. And they might, or might not, be lovers. What this recording gives us is more things to investigate. And more ways to find Bittner's killer."

I paused, to make sure they heard me. "And we don't gossip. Ever. Especially not about rumors. Got it?"

I was answering Cory, but I wanted my point clear to all of them.

Cory mumbled something. Marie nodded. Good. It was those two I was worried about.

Badger just smiled. As far as I could tell, she never willingly told anyone anything.

"Anyone spot a gun?" I asked. As far as I knew, the murder weapon hadn't been found yet.

"It's the same problem. It could under his jacket on the side we can't see," Badger said.

"But he's angry. Or maybe upset. See how tight his shoulder muscles are, and the controlled way he's moving," Marie said.

"Run it again, please Cory," I said.

He did so, and we all watched intently.

"You're both right," I said. "Good work. So we have two possible motives for Bittner's death that have nothing to do with Justine's case," I said, glancing from Badger to Marie to Cory.

"Ummm," Cory said. Not meeting my eyes.

Oh, this wasn't good. "What haven't you told me?" I asked sharply.

"Well, after Gainer leaves…"

"Go on."

He flushed a little, darted a look at Badger. "You'll need to see this for yourself," he said.

He winced a little, then pressed a key. It was a view from the same camera that had caught Gainer leaving Bittner's room. I glanced at the time stamp. Twenty minutes later. Well within the time frame we'd been given for the murder.

There was a movement at the end of the corridor. A medium height figure, dressed in black, with a hoodie pulled up. Must have come up the stairs. The elevators were in the other direction.

As the figure came closer, it resolved into a woman. Who looked very familiar. In fact, she looked a lot like Justine.

I cursed under my breath. Watched as the woman rapped on Bittner's door, waited a moment, then someone inside the room opened the door—it was impossible to see who—and she went in.

No wonder the police were looking hard at Justine.

If it was her. Those weren't the clothes she'd been wearing in the bar, and she hadn't had a change of clothes with her. And she never looked directly at the camera.

But her height, her coloring, even the way she moved—those were all Justine.

And if it was her, why hadn't she mentioned this little visit to anyone? She must have known she'd be caught on camera.

Sometimes I hate clients.

I glanced around the table. Cory looked nervous, Marie looked defensive and Badger wore her trademark blank expression. This case was turning complicated, and potentially nasty for all of us. Nobody wants their client to be guilty of anything, much less murder.

It would take some handling if this fledgling team of mine was going to get through this without tearing each other apart. Or worse.

"So what time did Justine leave?" I asked Cory.

"Ummm…" he said, and fiddled with the keyboard.

Ummm? "What exactly does that mean?" I said.

He knew that tone. It was written all over his face. "I don't know when she left. The recording skips."

"Skips?" I said.

"It's missing, like, close to two hours. The tape jumps from five-thirty to quarter after seven. See?" he said, backing up the recording to where the woman in the hoodie appeared, then playing it in normal time.

We all watched as she knocked, then vanished into Bittner's room. Then we watched a minute or so of nothing at all happening.

"Was there no-one else staying on that floor?" I said half-seriously as we continued to watch nothing happening.

"All the rooms around 1517 were booked. Want me to find out who'd already checked in?" Cory asked.

"That would help. Thanks. Was the missing time deleted?"

"I don't think so," Cory said. "But I'll need Badger's help to be sure." He glanced at her, and she gave him a smile. His expression relaxed the tiniest bit. It wasn't much, but it told me a lot.

"It looks to me like someone's disabled the recording for that period." He sounded more confident now.

"Could that have been done remotely?" I asked him.

Cory looked to Badger, who said, "Yes. But these systems are designed not to be hacked. Someone knows their stuff."

Why was I not surprised. My gut said that nothing about this case was going to be easy.

"Okay, I'll talk to Justine," I said. "If she's the one in the recording, we need to know what was going on."

"And if Bittner was alive when she arrived. And when she left," Marie said.

I looked up in surprise. She was right—and those were the key questions.

"Run that sequence again, will you Cory?" I said.

He did so. Several times, in fact.

It was the right room number, and the figure who opened the door was the right height and build for David Bittner. But you couldn't see enough to be positive it was him.

Any more than I could be positive the woman was Justine.

"Cory, can you send a clip of just that sequence to me?"

"Easy," he said, his fingers flying. "And done."

I'd meant later, but now was good too.

"Thanks," I told him.

And to Marie, "That's good spotting you did on that sequence."

She looked pleased, but shrugged. "I'd already watched it a dozen times, before the meeting. You don't notice all the details at first," she said.

All true. "But you kept watching until you saw them all. That's good detective work."

"Yeah, thanks. But I'm getting nowhere on whoever is threatening Justine," she said.

"Keep working on it—it was a long time ago. And whoever is threatening her will be pretty motivated to stay anonymous," I said. "That's good work, all of you. Anything else?" Glancing around our small circle. Nothing.

"So to sum up, so far we have four possible reasons for why David Bittner was killed." I numbered them off on my fingers. "Gambling debts. A lover's quarrel. A troll, who may or may not be related to Justine's stalker. Or a fight with Justine herself—or whoever it was the camera caught going into his hotel room."

Nods all around.

Okay, then. "I'll talk to Justine. You three, focus on the other angles. Including Bittner's various identities. For now, finding Bittner's killer has the priority over identifying Justine's stalker. And at least now we have three possible scenarios, not just the one."

We all knew which scenario I was referring to—the one the police favored.

The one where our client was the killer.

———

I GLANCED AROUND THE TABLE. Cory looked nervous, Marie looked defensive and Badger wore her trademark blank expression. This case was turning complicated, and potentially nasty for all of us. Nobody wants their client to be guilty of anything, much less murder.

It would take some handling if this fledgling team of mine was going to get through this without tearing each other apart. Or worse.

"So what time did Justine leave?" I asked Cory.

"Ummm…" he said, and fiddled with the keyboard.

Ummm? "What exactly does that mean?" I said.

He knew that tone. It was written all over his face. "I don't know when she left. The recording skips."

"Skips?" I said.

"It's missing, like, close to two hours. The tape jumps from five-thirty to quarter after seven. See?" he said, backing up the recording to where the woman in the hoodie appeared, then playing it in normal time.

We all watched as she knocked, then vanished into Bittner's room. Then we watched a minute or so of nothing at all happening.

"Was there no-one else staying on that floor?" I said half-seriously as we continued to watch nothing happening.

"All the rooms around 1517 were booked. Want me to find out who'd already checked in?" Cory asked.

"That would help. Thanks. Was the missing time deleted?"

"I don't think so," Cory said. "But I'll need Badger's help to be sure." He glanced at her, and she gave him a smile. His expression relaxed the tiniest bit. It wasn't much, but it told me a lot.

"It looks to me like someone's disabled the recording for that period." He sounded more confident now.

"Could that have been done remotely?" I asked him.

Cory looked to Badger, who said, "Yes. But these systems are designed not to be hacked. Someone knows their stuff."

Why was I not surprised. My gut said that nothing about this case was going to be easy.

"Okay, I'll talk to Justine," I said. "If she's the one in the recording, we need to know what was going on."

"And if Bittner was alive when she arrived. And when she left," Marie said.

I looked up in surprise. She was right—and those were the key questions.

"Run that sequence again, will you Cory?" I said.

He did so. Several times, in fact.

It was the right room number, and the figure who opened the door was the right height and build for David Bittner. But you couldn't see enough to be positive it was him.

Any more than I could be positive the woman was Justine.

"Cory, can you send a clip of just that sequence to me?"

"Easy," he said, his fingers flying. "And done."

I'd meant later, but now was good too.

"Thanks," I told him.

And to Marie, "That's good spotting you did on that sequence."

She looked pleased, but shrugged. "I'd already watched it a dozen times, before the meeting. You don't notice all the details at first," she said.

All true. "But you kept watching until you saw them all. That's good detective work."

"Yeah, thanks. But I'm getting nowhere on whoever is threatening Justine," she said.

"Keep working on it—it was a long time ago. And whoever is threatening her will be pretty motivated to stay anonymous," I said. "That's good work, all of you. Anything else?" Glancing around our small circle. Nothing.

"So to sum up, so far we have four possible reasons for why David Bittner was killed." I numbered them off on my fingers. "Gambling debts. A lover's quarrel. A troll, who may or may not be related to Justine's stalker. Or a fight with Justine herself—or whoever it was the camera caught going into his hotel room."

Nods all around.

Okay, then. "I'll talk to Justine. You three, focus on the other angles. Including Bittner's various identities. For now, finding Bittner's killer has the priority over identifying Justine's stalker. And at least now we have three possible scenarios, not just the one."

We all knew which scenario I was referring to—the one the police favored.

The one where our client was the killer.

———

NO ONE HAD MUCH MORE to say, so the meeting broke up. Marie and Cory moved our meeting table back out of the way and everyone was soon back at their own desks and focused on their computers.

Except me. I was still fuming about the recording, and the likelihood that Justine had left a few pertinent details out of my briefing.

After setting me up to find a murderer for her.

I needed her to explain that recording. I checked my watch. Knowing Justine, she'd likely still be in the office. Good.

I was going to enjoy this conversation, even if she probably wouldn't.

I glanced through my notes again. Thought through the timeline.

The hotel surveillance footage showed a man who was probably Michael Gainer leaving Bittner's room at 5:05. And a woman who was probably Justine arriving at Bittner's room at 5:25. Someone who was probably Bittner had met her at the door.

Which meant Gainer probably wasn't the killer.

Leaving Justine as the primary suspect.

Or Justine's stalker. Or whoever David had owed money to. Because of the missing time on the video recording, the timeline could work for any of them.

If Justine could explain her presence in David Bittner's room, we were starting to make real progress in figuring out what had happened to Bittner.

With a little luck, we might even solve this thing in time for Justine's big furniture deal to go through.

Not that I cared about her furniture deal. But Justine did. And she was the client.

I should care what the client wanted, right?

Looking around the colorful chaos that now passed for my office, I wasn't so sure about that. I wished I had my old, familiar office back. It was hard to concentrate when I was so aware of what each of the others was doing.

But all three of them really did need room to work in. Which they hadn't had before.

Maybe Marie was right—maybe I did need to take on additional space. If only so I could have my own office again.But first I had to go talk to my client about her apparent starring role in that recording.

Out of habit I checked my phone before I left, and found a text from Nick. That wasn't like him. What was up?

One click and I was staring at an ad for a two bedroom apartment for rent.

Subtle, Nick. Rolling my eyes, I sent him a cross-eyed emoji in return.

I was smiling as I left the office.

CHAPTER FOURTEEN

I'd stopped smiling by the time I got to Justine's office. The front office was deserted, but she was still there. Which didn't surprise me, given everything she had on her plate.

As I walked into her office, I saw her in silhouette against a deep blue sky, slumped in her chair. She had colored pens in every shade imaginable spread across her desk, and a half finished sketch on her desk, but she was just staring into space.

Justine looked very alone, and weighted down with worries. I felt some of my anger dissipate.

She heard me then, and startled, as if she'd forgotten she'd buzzed me up. Then she frowned. "I don't understand why you came here? Why didn't you just phone?"

"Why didn't you tell me you saw David Bittner the night he was killed?" I said, closing the door behind me with a solid thunk.

Her face froze and she gaped at me.

"No answer? How about the truth?" I said.

"I don't know what you mean."

"Justine. I saw the hotel security recording. You can't deny it's you."

Though she might try. The recording wasn't clear enough to

stand up in court, and she had to know that. Although with the right digital enhancement, that might not hold true for long.

"What recording?"

"Oh, come on, Justine," I said, dragging the chair opposite her forward and sitting down so that we were almost nose to nose. "You're smarter than that. You have to know that the hotel has cameras on every floor. Surely you knew you'd be recorded?"

"No, I know. I mean… yes of course I know they have recordings. But how did you find out about them?"

I noted that she still hadn't denied it was her in the recording. But she hadn't said it was, either. "The police have them. Surely they've already questioned you?"

"Of course they did. But they wouldn't share the recordings with you."

Still no denial. But she wasn't acting like a guilty woman. More like she had something—other than murder—to hide. What was this?

"No, they didn't," I said slowly. "But you hired me to find out who killed your associate. You didn't think I'd look at the recordings?"

"I didn't think you'd have access to them," she mumbled. "Hoped you wouldn't have, really."

She gave me an angry look. "I wanted you to look at things the police haven't considered. Not just focus on me," she said, jabbing a thumb towards her chest in a very un-Justine-like move. "The police are already doing a fine job of that."

I held up my hands in the classic time-out symbol. Justine stared at me for a moment, then started to laugh.

She sounded on the verge of hysterics. But at least she'd stopped glaring at me.

"Timeout? What for?" she said, on another hiccuping laugh.

"We need to start this conversation over. Justine, I'm on your side. My team has already identified two, possibly three other parties that might have had reason to kill David Bittner."

Reasons I hoped I wouldn't have to share with her. At least not while she was so stressed.

That got through to her.

"You have? People who wanted David dead? Not just my stalker?" She sounded—shocked? And just a bit hopeful.

She really hadn't expected me to find anyone else with a motive for killing David Bittner. Just how well did she know the man she called her best friend?

"Yes, people who might have reason to want him dead. One of whom might be your stalker. But if you saw Bittner the night he was killed, then that changes some of the variables in our investigations."

Especially given the time when she seen him. If it was really Justine on the recording. And I still wasn't sure of that, though I wasn't going to tell her that. Not yet.

I leaned forward, and was relieved to note she didn't lean away from me, even a little. "You need to be honest with me, completely honest, if you want me to find out who killed your friend."

The play on her emotions was deliberate on my part—I needed to get past her instinctive reaction, which seemed to be to tell people as little as possible about what really mattered to her.

But this was a murder investigation. Her secrets would put her behind bars for life, if she wasn't very careful.

Justine dropped her head in her hands, her perfectly cut hair sliding forward to form a frame around her. "I'll do it," came the choked words. "I'll tell you what you need to know."

"Everything?"

"Everything."

"Good," I said, and pulled out my notepad. I didn't realize until much later that with her choice of words, Justine had given herself another out.

———

"LET'S start with the big question," I said. "Was David Bittner alive when you got to his suite?"

She gave me an irritated look. "Of course he was," she said. "Who do you think opened the door?"

I wasn't buying it. "I don't know. That's why I'm asking."

"Of course it was David. Who else would it have been?" But she started fiddling with some of the colored pens on her desk, picking them up and putting them down in random paths of color.

"And was David alive when you left?" I asked, watching her.

"Yes. Yes, of course he was. You don't think I killed him, do you?"

Despite her indignant tone, she didn't look at me. And her hands were taking apart the patterns she'd just laid, and reassembling them into something resembling a mandala.

"It wasn't you, Justine, was it? On the video."

Now she looked up. "What do you mean? Of course it was me…"

"But you think you know who it was. Who are you protecting, Justine?"

"What? No. You're imagining things." She glared at me, but it wasn't her best effort. And her hands never stopped moving.

"Who looks that much like you, and is worth facing a murder charge for?" I threw at her.

She tried another glare, which failed miserably. Glares are my stock in trade—I know a real one when I see it.

Justine sighed, and gathered up the pens, plopping them into a narrow drawer on the left side of her desk. Then she rested her hands quietly on the table in front of her. "Anything we say is covered by client confidentiality now, right?"

"Yes."

She nodded slowly. "All right. Then I'm glad I hired you, Barbara. You always were too sharp for your own good. But I never expected you to get to this point so fast."

"It wasn't you, was it?"

"No."

"So who was it?"

One of her hands quivered a little on the desk, as if wanting to reach for those colored pens again, but she quickly stilled it.

"Do you have a copy of the footage from the hotel?" she asked instead of answering.

"Of course," I said, and set up my laptop between us. Silently, we watched the recording play out.

"Again," she said when it ended.

We ended up watching the recording half a dozen times before Justine was ready to say anything.

I was willing to be patient—I could see how hard this was for her, and I needed whatever information she had too badly to push her.

And whoever it was that had gone into David Bittner's hotel room on the night of his murder, I needed to talk to her.

"What time was this taken?" she asked at last.

"Twenty-five after five."

She nodded. "I was still making calls and working on my second martini then. Practically next door. Why did she…?"

"Who is it?" I asked, my patience at an end.

"I can't be certain, the quality isn't good…"

"Justine. You're the one who's up for murder."

She sighed. "My niece. I can't be sure, but I think it's my niece."

"Why do you think it's her?"

"Because as a result of some odd genetic quirk, from a distance she looks exactly like me, right down to the way she moves."

No wonder Justine had hired me to identify Bittner's real killer as soon as the police told her they about the recording. "Your niece's name?"

"Chelsea. Chelsea Martin."

"And how old is she?"

"Twenty-six. My much older half-sister's daughter."

"I'll need to talk to her. Where would I find Chelsea?"

Her hands wound around each other on the desk in front of her and gripped tightly. "I have no idea. I haven't seen or heard from her in five years. More."

That had to be hard. "Okay, when did you last hear from her?"

"Five Christmases ago. She and I... We had a falling out."

"Where was she working then?"

"She was freelancing as a graphic designer."

Interesting. "Was she any good?"

"Yes. And she could have become even better."

"Any idea who her major clients were?"

"No. She didn't want to trade on my reputation, and insisted that I know nothing about her business. I don't even know if she was using her own name as her business name."

"And you didn't try to find out how she was doing after your falling out?"

Justine's gaze flickered away from mine. She seemed to lose herself in the gold-tipped view of city and ocean spread in front of her for a moment.

"It was hard," she said. "But I'd promised. So no, I never checked."

I couldn't have done that. If I'd been at odds with Cory or his sister, I'd have kept tabs on them at the very least.

And probably interfered at the first opportunity. But that was me. And I'd never have promised not to keep out of their business in the first place.

I was impressed that Justine had honored her promise. But at what cost?

She couldn't find her niece. I could. "Where was Chelsea living then?"

"Here. In Vancouver. In a small loft off of Commercial, I think."

"Can you get me the address?"

"Just a sec." She pulled a sleek keyboard towards her, pressed a few buttons, glanced at the screen, nodded and clicked again.

"This is the most recent one, but it's from six years ago. I didn't even know that she was still in town. There. You should have it now."

I did. "Thanks. I'll find her."

"Barbara, when you do find her—be gentle with her, won't you? She's fragile, for all she thinks she's tough."

She wasn't the only one. Justine had deep shadows under her eyes, and her cheeks seemed hollower than last time I'd seen her.

How much of that was for David? And how much for Chelsea? "I'll keep that in mind."

"Thank you."

I glanced down at the notes I'd just taken, and the ones from the team meeting earlier. "Did Chelsea know David?"

"They'd met once or twice, I think, at parties I'd thrown."

"And can you think of any reason Chelsea would be meeting David in a hotel room downtown?"

"If it is her on the recording, you mean," Justine said.

"Yes, if it is her. Well?"

"Not from what I know of either of them, but the obvious reason would be that they didn't want to be seen meeting in public."

I'd wondered if she'd go there. "Any thoughts on why that might be? If it is her, I mean," I added.

She started to frown. "No. If they had any kind of connection five years ago, I never knew about it. And I can't think of anything the two of them would need to be secretive about—business or personal."

Okay, that was pretty clear.

I thought about what Marie had told me about David Bittner's gambling problems. Problems I was pretty sure Justine hadn't known about, from everything she'd told me. "Did Chelsea have problems with gambling?"

"How could you know that?" Justine said. She hadn't expected the question, and the words seemed to have slipped past her filters.

"Just a good guess," I said. And a logical transition based on what we'd learned about Bittner. It was too soon to share that with my client, though.

I hadn't reckoned on Justine's intuition.

"Not David?" she said on a gasp. "He has—had—," and she swallowed hard, "gambling problems?"

"It's pretty early in the investigation to say," I hedged, "but it seems possible. You didn't know?"

"No. I had no idea. David? I can't believe it." She drew in a slow breath, visibly calmed herself. I was impressed. "Maybe you'll find your sources are wrong."

"Maybe." My words felt hollow.

But Justine wasn't thinking about David now. "Chelsea was supposed to be getting help. Five years ago. Surely she doesn't still have problems."

But there was no belief in her voice.

"That's why you haven't seen her in five years, isn't it?" I said. "She asked you for money once too often, and you laid down the law about her getting help before you'd bail her out again?"

Too many of my investigations had started based on exactly that set of facts.

Justine nodded. The sun was low in the sky now, and a trick of the light made her face look like a golden mask in the slanting light. Tragedy. "She has so much promise. She's a gifted artist, you know. Or she was."

It sounded as if Chelsea was like her aunt in more than appearance.

Justine was staring at her hands. "But my second husband—he was a gambler. You can't change them, no matter how much you're willing to do," she said softly, as if to herself.

Then she looked at me. "When you talk to Chelsea—if she needs help, if she'd accept any help—please let me know."

"I will," I said. And I left.

Any further questions I had for Justine could wait until I'd talked to Chelsea.

CHAPTER FIFTEEN

I went looking for Justine's niece. Who no longer lived in the apartment above the busy grocer on Commercial Drive, the one with bins of fresh Chinese and Italian vegetables out front. I love the local neighborhood shops, the ones whose products—and prices—reflect the local population's shopping habits. And often the history of the area.

The young couple who did live in Chelsea's former apartment had never heard of her, and had only lived in the apartment for six months themselves.

"We'll likely have to move soon, too," the young woman told me. "There's rumors this building is going to be sold and new condos put up. I'm not sure where we'll go."

She sounded sad. With a sky-high real estate market and a vacancy rate that was so close to zero as to be irrelevant, her story didn't surprise me. But it made me sad, too.

Vancouver used to have room for everyone—and I suppose Metro Vancouver still did. With access to Skytrain, some of the outlying communities aren't as far away as they used to be. But a lot of the more diverse and interesting neighborhoods seemed to be pricing themselves out of the very diversity that made them interesting in the first place.

Still, there are other areas that are becoming even more interesting, just in different ways. European friends of mine say we're on our way to being a world-class city, with all the challenges that brings. And the city is growing as fast as it's changing.

But change is hard when it hits up against personal memories. Especially when favorite haunts start disappearing.

My old favorite Italian coffee shop was still there, though, and still making the incredible cappuccinos that first made me a coffee fanatic back in my university days. I soaked up the familiar atmosphere, all battered tiled floors and marble pillars, along with an atmosphere that wouldn't be out of place in Rome or Naples, while I did a quick search on my phone, looking for Chelsea Martin.

Nothing. Then I searched for a website, or some indication of her business. Not finding either, I sent a quick text to Cory, asking him to look into it when he could.

By the time I'd finished my coffee, I had a text back. He'd found an old, no longer active website that she'd used under that name, but nothing newer. He'd keep digging.

I wondered if Chelsea's freelance business had failed. Maybe she'd given up on freelancing and was working for someone else? Which should make her easy to trace.

It seemed odd that she'd have given up her website if she'd stayed in the same business, though. Unless she was either using a new name, or had changed businesses entirely.

Looking at the familiar walls around me, the familiar faces behind the counter, even after all these years, I had a sudden inspiration. Neighborhoods might be changing, but it took more than a little change for the people who were comfortable living in them to leave. Often they changed along with their neighborhoods.

I texted Justine, asking how long her niece had lived around Commercial Drive. She texted back. At least six or seven years.

Okay then. I did a search on Gambler's Anonymous. There was

a meeting in a church basement about ten minutes from Commercial that very evening.

I made a note, cleared my table and left, feeling surprisingly satisfied with my little exploration into my past.

————

I'D JUST GOT into my car when I got a text message from Nick. I clicked on it to see a photo and a listing for a three bedroom townhouse for sale in Kits. What?

Out of curiosity I scrolled down, and nearly choked on the price.

Before I could figure out a response, his next text popped up, "Just looking. It never hurts to know what's out there."

Um. "Nice, but pricey," I sent back.

He texted an image of a bouquet of flowers.

Okay then. I just hoped this wasn't going to get too intense.

Keep it light, Barbara, I told myself as I searched through emojis. And sent back a virtual donut. With sprinkles.

Hey, it beat thinking about the damage addictions can cause.

With a grin, I started the car.

————

THE MEETING ROOM in the basement of the well-worn church on Twelfth was windowless, with white walls that could use a paint job and long overhead fixtures that hummed softly. The air was slightly stale, and smelled of bad coffee and desperation. This was an open meeting of Gamblers Anonymous, so friends and family were welcome, making it easy for me to blend in.

With its plastic stacking chairs and too bright lights, the place reminded me of similar meetings when I was a teen and my mother had dragged my sister and me to Al-Anon. Those meetings were supposed to help us cope with my father's drinking problems, but I guess Mom decided that they were making things worse. After a few meetings we stopped going, and went back to pretending everything was fine. Which mostly it was.

Mostly.

I chose a seat towards the back—in what would have been the shadows had the place not been so brightly lit. It was hard to feel anonymous in a place with no shadowy corners. Which struck me as odd for a program named Gamblers Anonymous.

I hid behind the pamphlet they'd passed out at the door while I kept watch for Chelsea. If she didn't show up, I planned to slip back out that door.

A quick scan of the material told me that GA was non-profit, funded by donations from members, similar to Alcoholics Anonymous. In fact, it was clear, even from the little I remembered from Al-Anon, that GA followed the same principles and the same structure as AA.

The pamphlet explained that chronic gambling is an addiction and an illness, not something the chronic gambler can control by willpower. This addiction can and will destroy the life of a chronic gambler—just like alcoholism, in fact—but that by facing the illness and being willing to do the work and make changes in their lives, a chronic gambler can recover.

But never enough to gamble again. Just like an alcoholic. One drink is never enough…

The pamphlet set out the twelve steps of recovery—the same twelve steps I remembered AA using—emphasizing the difference between supporting an addict in their recovery and being co-dependent with their addiction.

It surprised me that I found the words—and the memories they brought back—hard to take. That had been a long time ago.

There was no sign of Chelsea. And a rustle of movement at the front of the room told me the meeting was about to start. Time to get out of here.

Just as I gathered my things ready to stand up, someone ghosted in the back door and sat in a chair at the other end of the row I was in. Someone else trying to hide?

Good luck with that. I glanced over—and recognized the woman's profile.

It was either Justine herself—meaning she'd been lying to me again—or it was her niece, Chelsea. I couldn't tell which, because she was dressed in much the same way as the woman in the recording, and she had the hood of her hoodie up.

Which looked odd indoors. Though it was drafty in the hall, so that was some excuse.

I was pretty sure this must be Chelsea, because I couldn't imagine Justine ever wearing a hoodie. Watching her out of the corner of my eye, I waited for her to turn so I could be sure who I was seeing. She didn't.

Instead, the woman in the hoodie faced resolutely forward, but something in her body language told me her eyes were sweeping the rows of chairs in front of us.

I kept an eye on her without making it obvious as various members came to the front to tell their stories. Who was she looking for?

Or should I be asking who was it she was afraid she'd find here?

Chelsea—because after half an hour of surreptitiously watching her, I was certain it wasn't Justine, which left her niece—had kept her hoodie up and had barely moved.

But she hadn't relaxed at all. There was enough tension in her shoulders to give her a migraine if she wasn't careful.

In between watching her, I scanned the room. There were some interesting dynamics among what I recognized as family groups, but nothing that suggested any link to David Bittner. Not that I'd expected anything, not this early in an investigation.

No, it was Chelsea I was interested in.

Finally the meeting wound to its end. Practically as the last words were said, Chelsea was up and out the door. That was okay. I'd been expecting that move for the last ten minutes or so—her shoulders had grown even tenser, as if they were readying to pull her to her feet—and I was right behind her.

I followed her down Twelfth. She stopped beside a battered

twenty-year-old Civic that was parked under the twisted branches of an old cherry tree. She had her keys in her hand when I stopped on the sidewalk side of the car and said her name.

She jumped, and looked up, stark fear on her face.

"Your aunt Justine sends her best," I said. Though she hadn't actually spoken the words, I can read undertones with the best of them. "I'm Barbara O'Grady. I'm a P. I. And I need to talk to you."

"Not now," she muttered, fumbling to get the keys in the lock.

"Not here," I said, as if agreeing with her. "How about Calabria Café? Coffee's on me."

She had the door unlocked and had started to swing it open, but with my words, she stopped and stared at me. "How do you know I'll come?"

I shrugged. "I don't. But I suspect you need help. And I can help."

"Why should I trust you?"

"Calabria is a public place. And we're both known there. It's a free coffee." I paused. "And it's damn good coffee."

She gave a half nod, slid into her Civic and jackrabbited out of there.

I could only hope she'd be at Calabria's.

CHAPTER SIXTEEN

Commercial Drive at night takes on a convivial persona that's a mix of a warm evening air, laughter and the smell of good food. Half of the crowd seemed to be gathered at Calabria, which was noisier and more crowded than ever. Every table was full.

I paused in the doorway, glanced around. There was no sign of Chelsea, but one of the small marble-topped tables along the far wall had just come free. I grabbed it, staked my claim to both chairs, and waited.

Surely she'd show up—for the coffee, if nothing else. Or maybe out of curiosity.

Paolo was working tonight, and in a brief lull between waves of customers, I caught his eye, and signaled for a coffee. As I did so, I caught sight of Chelsea hovering in the door, her eyes searching the room. I held up a second finger, and waved towards her.

Paolo gave her a big smile and me a nod, then hurried to fill our order before the next onslaught of customers.

Something in the interaction had reassured Chelsea. She put her hood back, sauntered across the room and dropped into the chair opposite mine.

That earned her a couple of glares from the table beside ours, who'd been keeping a covetous eye on that chair for the last ten minutes. I'd expected a battle royal over the chair if she hadn't arrived soon.

Our coffees—cappuccino for me, double espresso for her—arrived at nearly the same time. I gave Paolo a quiet thanks and a twenty.

"Just keep 'em coming," I said with a smile.

He grinned, and tucked the bill into the pocket of his spotless white apron. As he whisked away, Chelsea stared at me. Table service is not the norm at the Calabria Café.

"You really are known here," she said.

"Paolo knows me, anyway. And clearly he knows you, too."

I hadn't needed to tell him Chelsea's order—he already knew it. Though how she could make a habit of drinking double espressos at this time of night, I didn't know.

"Paolo's the one who matters," she said.

She had that right. Which meant she had half a brain. Good to know.

I just smiled, and waited for the questions. Which weren't long in coming.

"So Justine hired you?" she asked, leaning towards me and pitching her voice low enough that it wouldn't carry far over the cheerful din that surrounded us.

"Yep."

"Why?"

I leaned in a little towards her. "To find out who killed David Bittner," I said softly.

At my words her face lost all color. Even her lips were white.

"D...David's dead?" She sounded shattered, and her hands were shaking.

Well, that answered my first question. It would take an extraordinary actor to fake that reaction.

"You didn't know?" I asked. Mostly to give her some time to recover. I already had my answer.

"No. I was looking for him tonight. That's why I went. To the meeting, I mean."

"Really? It looked to me like you were trying to hide."

"I was."

"From whom?"

"No. It's too soon. I can't trust you yet."

But she needed to trust someone. It was clear in every move she made. Chelsea was scared.

No, make that beyond scared.

"But Paolo trusts me," I said, deadpan. And she trusted Paolo. Whom we both knew was an excellent judge of people.

It got me the half-smile I was going for. And she relaxed just a little.

"Yeah," she said, and busied herself dumping sugar into her espresso.

"When did David die?" she asked when she'd finished turning her coffee into syrup. I could see her brace herself for the answer.

"Tuesday night. Not long after you the Grand Pacific, the police think. That was you on the security recording, going into his hotel room, right?"

"Yes," she said, probably not even aware of what she'd said in the shock of what I'd told her.

Then she stared at me. "Wait a minute. You mean I was the last person to see him alive?"

"Did you kill him?"

"What...? How could you...? Of course not!"

"So he was alive when you left?"

"Yes, of course..."

"Then you weren't the last person to see him alive. That would be the killer."

She swallowed hard, and swigged back some of her coffee flavored syrup. "So David was... Someone really killed him?"

I nodded.

"But who?"

"They haven't arrested anyone. But they're looking hard at your aunt Justine."

"My aunt? But she loved David. Why would they think…?"

She stopped dead. "Oh. The recording. They think that's her on the recording."

"The police haven't exactly clarified why they're interested in her, but I think that's a safe guess. Until I found out about you, I thought it was Justine, too."

She just stared at me. "You mean I'm a suspect?"

"Once the police figure out it's you on the recording, I'd imagine so."

Chelsea grabbed her espresso and drained it. Then she glared at me. "What about you? Do you think I did it?"

I considered her question, the attitude behind it, and the fear hiding behind that. Then added in everything I'd learned about her today.

"No. I don't think you did it," I said. "But I do think you're in trouble."

———

CHELSEA PICKED up her empty cup, glanced inside as though surprised to find it empty, and put it down again. As if by magic, Paolo hustled over and placed two fresh cups in front of us.

"You were paying attention," I said to him, while Chelsea grabbed the new cup and started adding sugar.

"No, *bella*," he said with a wink. "It is quiet for a moment, so I bring your coffees. I know how the two of you love your coffee."

It was true. Both of us had finished our first cups in record time. And I had a feeling it was going to take a lot of coffee to get through the rest of this conversation. "Thanks, Paolo."

Chelsea stirred her small cup vigorously, then downed a slug of it. I held back a shudder. It was a bad way to treat good coffee.

But if it got her through this meeting, and got me the information I needed to help Justine, I was all for it.

"You're right," Chelsea said suddenly, looking up from her contemplation of her espresso. "I am in trouble. That's why I was hiding at the meeting."

I said nothing. Just waited.

She nodded a little, as if I'd given her the answer she'd hoped for, and swallowed more espresso.

Sugar was good for shock, I told myself. She probably needed it after hearing about Bittner's death.

"I don't gamble any more," she said, as if she was answering a question I hadn't asked. She leaned forward, her voice low but intense. "I can't. It cost me too much. And trying to rebuild—it's just hard."

She finished her espresso in one gulp, met my gaze. "I can't afford to gamble. Not on anything. Not ever again. It's been nearly three years now, and every day I have to fight the need to take just one more risk."

I gave her the respect her words deserved by listening quietly. She'd said these words before—I could hear it in the cadence of the words.

Probably she'd told her story many times in GA meetings. It didn't diminish the power of her words. Or the impact of them.

"David couldn't afford to gamble anymore, either," she said. "But he couldn't see it. Maybe he hadn't destroyed everything in his life enough yet. He still had his job."

Probably for not much longer, if he really had been selling Justine's secrets as Marie had heard. "Why did you meet him in that hotel room on Tuesday?"

"I was worried about him," she said. "David said he hadn't been gambling, but he'd been twitchy lately. Distracted. I know the signs. And he'd missed the last GA meeting."

"How did you know where he was on the night he was killed?"

"I called him, and he told me."

Why would Bittner tell this young woman where he was? Especially when he was at a hotel under an assumed name. It seemed odd to me. So I probed further.

"Why the meeting at his hotel room, though?" I said. "Why didn't he just arrange to meet you the next day?"

"I wanted him to go to a meeting with me that night. He wouldn't."

"So he told you to come to the hotel instead?"

"Yes."

I was missing something here. Obviously it was a bad time for David Bittner. He'd sent Gainer away not long before Chelsea arrived. Maybe even because she was coming.

Then why had he agreed to see her? Unless... "What time did you call him?"

"Maybe ten after five."

I flipped through my notes. Gainer had left less than five minutes before Chelsea called Bittner. Maybe Bittner had needed company.

"And how did he sound on the phone?"

"He sounded upset," Chelsea said. "And a bit desperate. It's why I insisted on seeing him."

And there it was again. "You insisted?"

Instead of answering, she reached for her espresso.

"Why would David agree to a meeting just because you insisted?" I asked.

"Because I'm his sponsor," she said.

———

I STARED at Chelsea blankly for a moment, trying to take it in.

"You were David's GA sponsor?" The person he could call anytime he felt the urge to gamble, the one person he could rely on —day or night—to talk him out of gambling.

The person he might share his deepest secrets with.

Chelsea nodded. "Yes. I've been dealing with gambling addiction—my own and other's—for a long time now. And David really did want to quit gambling. So he'd listen to me when I told him he was getting too close to giving in to the need to gamble. Mostly, anyway."

"Getting too close?"

"Gambling addictions come from different roots," she said after a moment. "But for a lot of us, gambling becomes our escape, the one safe place where the rest of the world goes away. So any kind of emotional stress can send us right back to that feeling of safety—even when we know it's destroying our lives."

I'd never heard that about gambling before. But I'd heard it about drinking. I guess there was a reason the structure and rules of GA were so close to the AA ones.

"So you got there about fifteen minutes later?" I said.

"That sounds right. I grabbed Skytrain on Commercial, so it didn't take me long."

It all fit. "Any problems getting up to his room?"

"No. No-one even looked at me sideways."

Vancouver's a pretty casual place, but that hotel is not. "Even with the hoodie up?"

"Oh, I didn't put it up 'til I got to his floor."

"When you came out of the stairwell."

"Yes."

"You took the stairs all the way up?"

"No, I got off on eight, and took the stairs from there." After glancing at me, she seemed to decide that needed explaining. "David asked me to try not to be seen."

That was convenient for her. Or maybe for him. "Why would he do that?"

"He didn't say."

"But you did it anyway." I didn't wait for her to answer—if she had an answer—just moved on to the answer I really needed. "What time did you leave?"

"Probably about quarter to six. I wasn't there much more than twenty minutes. David really didn't want company. I think he was just humoring me."

"And how was David doing?"

"Not too good. He was upset."

"And what did you talk about in those twenty minutes?"

"David told me he'd just had a hard conversation with a lover—now an ex-lover—which was why he was upset. And that the relationship hadn't been going well for a while. No details."

So David Bittner had been one of Gainer's lovers. Unless he'd lied to Chelsea for some reason. "Did David normally share personal information with you?"

"Yes. He was discreet about names and details, but he'd usually talk pretty openly about stuff that was stressing him out."

"Did he talk about having debts?"

"Not that night. I already knew a lot of it."

"Gambling debts were an ongoing issue for him. And he knew that you knew it," I said.

"Yes."

"But he wouldn't go with you to the GA meeting?"

She flinched a little. "No."

"Why not? Did he have plans for later?"

"I don't know. He just said he needed a quiet evening. And that he'd be fine."

"Did you believe him?"

"No. I didn't. I thought he'd go looking for a high stakes poker game before I'd even left the hotel."

Chelsea's eyes filled with tears. She blinked them back. "But I'd done everything I could. The rest was up to him. And he wasn't ready yet. Not really."

She rubbed a finger around the edge of her tiny espresso cup. "David couldn't quite let go of that last chance. The one perfect game that would fix all his money problems, and let him walk away clean."

"It's every gambler's dream. Only it doesn't exist," she said. "If you win, you just keep going until you lose again. And he'd run out of time."

"How?"

"He'd borrowed too much money. And every time he needed

more money, he found a way to get more. Each time the cost was higher."

"And the consequences worse," I said. I knew this story. And how it ended.

"Yes."

The look on Chelsea's face told me she knew it too. And had been way too close to the ugliness it could lead to. "You?" I asked her.

She shook her head. "No, thank God. Not me."

But someone she cared about. She didn't need to say it. "I'm sorry."

"Thanks. It's one of the reasons I go to so many meetings. Some are for me, to make sure I stay out of the action. And some are to see if I can help other people. The ones who get in too deep, and can't see it."

"Like David," I said.

"Yes. Like David." And this time her silence was a mourning, and an acceptance that this time, the help she could give hadn't been enough.

"Did he talk to you about what kind of trouble he was in?"

"No. He'd never give details, or talk about his loans. I just recognized the patterns. I'd seen them before."

"So you have no idea who he'd borrowed money from?"

"No," she said softly. "But they might think that I knew."

"Because you were his sponsor?" I asked.

"Yes. It's why I didn't want to be noticed at the meeting."

"Do many people know that you were his sponsor?"

"No. At GA we mostly keep it a private thing. But when David got desperate—well, he'd say anything to convince someone to lend him more money."

"You think he was desperate enough to name his sponsor, and put you at risk?" I asked her.

"I think David was self-destructive, too much so to care who he took down with him." Chelsea's face was white and her eyes bruised looking. It looked like she hadn't been sleeping well.

"It's a pretty common phase," she said. "And an ugly one. And it usually comes right before the gambler finally accepts they have to quit gambling once and for all."

"So you think he what? Tried to use you as some kind of guarantee?" I asked.

"Maybe. He was desperate enough."

I sat back while I took that in. "If that's true…"

"David was that kind of desperate. I just don't know what he might've done about it."

"Whom he might have talked to, you mean," I said.

She nodded. "I've seen it before. And even the suspicion that I might know things I shouldn't can be poisonous."

"Then you need to get away from here for a bit." And I needed to talk to Nick. And maybe Jerry too. He'd been assigned to the Integrated Gang Task Force for a time as well. Just not at the same time as Nick.

She glanced around. "I'm as safe here as I am anywhere in this city," she said.

"I meant you need to get out of town. At least until David's murder is solved."

Chelsea gave me a twisted grin. "Chance would be a fine thing. I'm broke. And they'd find me, anyway."

"What if you had the chance?" I said, thinking of the pain in Justine's face when she talked about the niece she hadn't seen in five years.

The niece who apparently had freed herself from the addiction that had separated them. "Could you leave town immediately?"

"Where would I go?"

"Just answer the question."

"Yes. Given the chance, I could leave town tomorrow. Tonight, even."

"Then come with me," I said, and led the way out of the café.

It was faster than answering her inevitable questions.

CHAPTER SEVENTEEN

Justine's lawyer—not Brian, the irritating one—had arranged a meeting for me with Michael Gainer. The man I now suspected had been Bittner's lover. The one who'd argued bitterly with Bittner on the night of his murder.

Gainer was in the midst of a criminal trial, so his time was limited. He'd suggested we meet in his office before court.

I needed to talk to the man, not the lawyer. Which wouldn't happen if we met in his office. But an early morning walk on the beach might just do the trick.

It's a Vancouver thing.

Logistically, it should work. I happened to know Gainer lived near Spanish Banks, a peaceful stretch of shoreline with a long sweep of sand and and a panoramic view of the city.

The beach would be mostly deserted at that hour. And there was tons of free parking. I suggested meeting in the far lot on Spanish Banks.

To my surprise, he'd agreed.

I showed up at the parking lot we'd agreed on at seven a.m. with two coffees in hand, and sugar and creamers tucked in my pocket. A gleaming silver Jag suggested he was already there.

As I pulled my battered Civic a couple of slots over from him—wouldn't want to risk marring that impeccable finish—his door swung open. A tall, impeccably groomed and ruggedly handsome man stepped out.

In jeans, he'd have looked at home in any outdoor setting. His beautifully cut suit transformed his look to a power look, without losing that approachable feel. I'd bet the juries loved him.

Michael Gainer was in his early fifties, I'd guess, but he wore it well. He had the weathered face of a man who loved to sail, and the squint lines to prove it.

"Ms. O'Grady, I presume?" he said, striding towards me.

"Yes. Mr. Gainer?"

He nodded, held out a hand. "Michael is fine. We're not in a courtroom now. You come highly recommended, Ms. O'Grady."

I stifled a laugh. How Marchant had managed to recommend me without choking? "Barbara, please," I said.

"Barbara, then. And just so you know, that recommendation is the only reason I agreed to this unorthodox meeting."

But his gaze had moved past me, to sweep the ocean beyond, assessing the wind, the water and the currents with the familiarity of the experienced sailor I knew him to be. And the look of a lover.

This was a man who loved the ocean, in all its moods. He wouldn't have passed up a chance to start his day here.

I wondered how he and David Bittner had ended up together. From what Badger had texted me, Bittner didn't sail—in fact, his preferred habitat was indoors. Restaurants, parties, large gatherings—anywhere he could find the energy of a crowd.

But then, all of Gainer's relationships, except the one with his wife, were clandestine ones. His relationship with Bittner would have been spent away from both their usual worlds, where none of their differences mattered, only what they shared.

Maybe it was a relationship that was only possible because it had to be kept secret?

"Shall we walk?" I asked, waving a hand towards the path that ran along the shoreline, only feet from the waves. "If you have time, that is? I have a number of questions I'd like to ask you."

And I suspected that he knew as well as I did that the questions were likely to be uncomfortable ones. It would be easier for both of us if we were in motion, and not staring directly at each other.

Usually, I'd want to watch every nuance of someone's expression when I question them. But this man would be too good at hiding his thoughts—it went with the job.

If I could talk directly to the Michael Gainer—and not to his professional role—the nuances of his voice should tell me what I needed to know.

"Your questions are about David Bittner's murder, I gather?"

"Yes."

"And you're representing his employer, Justine Grayson?"

"Yes."

"Very well," he said, and walked to the path. "I can only give you fifteen minutes, though," he added as I fell into step with him.

It was more than I'd expected. "Thank you. I'll try not to waste your time."

"Let me make it simple for you. David was a good man, and his loss is a harsh one for everyone who knew him. He valued Justine greatly, and he'd be horrified to hear she was even suspected of killing him. This is the only thing I can do for him now."

He paused, and we walked without speaking for a moment, the waves on our left making a shushing noise that was echoed by the salt-flavored wind in the branches of the sprawling oak tree on our right.

I waited, letting him choose his moment, choose his words. Everything I knew about Gainer said that he made a point of preserving his privacy.

This was for David, he'd said, so he'd force himself to talk. But a moment in the quiet of this place might make it easier for him.

After a few more moments, he said, "I'm assuming you know about my relationship with David Bittner. So you know my secrets."

Well, I knew one of them, anyway. And his relationships weren't so secret in some circles. But I wasn't about to argue with him.

"I've heard a rumor or two. But I'd appreciate it if you could confirm the nature of your relationship with Bittner."

———

GAINER NODDED, kept walking.

"I'm good at keeping people's secrets," I said. "Anything you tell me will go no further. Unless and until it is the only way to keep my client from a murder conviction."

He glanced sideways at me. "I've heard that about you. And I appreciate your honesty in not sugar-coating the worst case."

"It's the right thing to do," I said, uncomfortable with his recognition. I gave him a quick smile. "Besides, you've seen too many murder cases—you'd never believe me if I sugar-coated anything."

He chuckled, returned his gaze to the waves. "David and I were lovers. But he had some personal issues."

"His gambling."

He startled a little, glanced at me, then back at the ocean. "You know about that?"

"I spoke with his sponsor. Since he's gone, she was pretty open about the challenges he faced. That's not an easy demon to fight."

Michael Gainer seemed to relax a little. "No. In the last few months, he'd grown extremely frustrated. And erratic with it. Sometimes he'd feel he'd won out over his addiction, and he'd be euphoric. Sometimes he'd be so angry with himself for succumbing again that he'd be impossible to be around. Or worse, so depressed I feared for his life."

He sped up his steps, his words coming faster. "Too often, he'd be chasing that one last win that would solve everything. And he'd lose. He'd just end up deeper in debt, and the cycle would start over. Those were the times that worried me the most."

"Why?"

"He wouldn't talk about where the money was coming from,"

Gainer said. "To me that said his sources weren't strictly legal. And I've been part of too many trials not to know the type of people he'd be dealing with, and how lethal that kind of loan can be."

Some of them had probably been his clients. "Any idea who he was dealing with?"

"No. I might have some guesses, but I can't share those."

He probably had some stories, too. "How long were you and David together?"

"A little over three years. He was a good man."

I hadn't realized they'd been together so long. "And was your relationship a good one?"

"Yes, despite some of the tensions we were both under. It was."

"What tensions were those?"

"David's gambling, and the stress it caused him. The pressures of my work."

Were Gainer's other affairs were part of the problem, too? I didn't press him. It was clear from his tone that I wasn't going to get more detail. And I had other ways of finding out.

"Did David ever express concerns about his work, or about Justine?" I asked instead.

"No. He loved what he did, and he loved Justine."

"Tell me about the last time you saw him. How did David seem?"

Gainer's pace sped up a little, and his fingers clenched. "He was tense. Edgy. He got to the room late, where usually he was early. He didn't tell me where he'd been, which was normal. But he was clearly upset, and he wouldn't talk about it. That wasn't like him."

"Do you know what was bothering him?"

"I assume it was to do with his gambling. But I don't know for certain."

That was the lawyer talking. "What time did you get there?"

He gave me an odd look. "Don't you know?"

"Humor me."

"About quarter to five," he said.

"And you left twenty minutes later?"

He scowled. "Yes."

"Why?"

If we hadn't been walking along that beach, I doubt I'd have gotten an answer. But we were. And I did.

"David… wanted to end our dealings together," he said, his voice quiet despite the fact we were the only ones there. "And I couldn't talk sense into him. So I left."

Stormed out, I was guessing. Which explained the body language on the recording. No wonder David had been upset enough to invite his sponsor over.

"Was this sudden? Or had the two of you talked about ending the relationship before?"

"I didn't see it coming."

"So why did he suddenly want to end a three year relationship?"

"He said it wasn't safe to be connected with him anymore. Despite how careful we were. He was convinced he'd end up undermining my career if we kept seeing each other."

"Why?"

"He didn't want to say. Finally I got it out of him that he was being threatened. And he was afraid of what might happen next. That the fallout would splash over onto the people around him. His words."

"You. And Justine," I said.

Justine hadn't mentioned anything. Maybe David hadn't had a chance to talk to her. Or hadn't wanted to, if she didn't know about his gambling problems.

"Yes."

"And you think whoever he'd ended up borrowing money from was threatening him?"

"Yes."

Which was what Chelsea thought too. "And did you accept that the relationship was over?"

"No. Because it wasn't. I intended to talk to him again, when he was calmer. We weren't done."

Until someone killed David. The thought hung unspoken between us. "Did David have any enemies? That you knew of?"

Gainer stopped, stared at me for a moment, then turned and strode back in the direction we'd come from. I hurried to keep up with him.

"David? Hardly," he said.

"What about professional rivalries?"

"If he did, he never talked about them. No, this was about his gambling. And the lengths he'd go to in order to keep gambling."

His voice was bitter, as if I was hearing one piece of an old argument. "Did you know David had a gambling problem when you first became lovers?"

"No. I started to wonder if he had a problem about six months ago. But it was still easy to decide I was wrong, to ignore it."

I wondered how David Bittner had hidden his gambling addiction for so long. "What made you suspect it then?"

"That something was really wrong? I attended a week-long conference in Vegas last March, thought David might like to join me. It turned out to be a bad idea. We managed a few dinners together, but I was tied up most of the time."

There was some undercurrent here I was missing. "And he was gambling?"

"Yes. It was after that that I started to see cracks in his behavior."

"He got in too deep?"

"I think so. If I'd realized he had a gambling problem, I'd never have suggested Vegas. But up until then, it seemed an enjoyable pastime for him. I thought him as successful at the tables as he was in everything he did."

And there it was. As Gainer talked about his lover's gambling addiction, there was a bitterness I hadn't heard earlier. I wondered what damage that bitterness had caused between them.

For David to maintain his facade that his life was under control as he grew more and more desperate must have taken a high toll on him, and on his life. It had clearly damaged his relationship with Gainer.

What else had it impacted?

And Gainer had given me a place to start.

Vegas, last March.

Maybe what began in Vegas hadn't stayed in Vegas.

———

I'D JUST GOT BACK to the car and put the key in the ignition, when I got a text message from Nick. The first emoji was a cup of coffee. He knows me pretty well.

The next text—with photo—was a listing for a two-bedroom and den townhouse for sale. Just off Commercial Drive.

And I did love that neighborhood. The place looked nice, with lots of windows. And 2BR/+Den was a nice compromise.

The price was still choke-worthy, though not as bad as the Kits 3BR.

"Nice location. Good light. Still pricey," I texted back.

Nick was right, this was kinda fun. As long as I didn't think about what finding "the right place" would mean.

Then he sent me a blue ribbon. Which made me smile.

I sent him a pineapple. Because he likes them. And because it would probably make him laugh.

CHAPTER EIGHTEEN

By the time I got into the office, it was nearly eight. I'd hoped to have some time before the others showed up, but Marie was already there.

"Barbara," she said, looking up and beaming at me. "How did you do?"

"Well, I know who our mystery woman was on the recording," I said, pausing by her desk.

"Tell me it wasn't Justine."

"No. It was her niece. Who says David Bittner was alive when she left his hotel room. And I believe her."

"You're sure?"

"Pretty sure. So we need a new suspect. And we need to know who KO'd the recording system that evening. Is Badger coming in today?"

"She said she was."

"Good. And Cory?"

"After school."

"We'll need a meeting then, with all of us. Can you set it up?"

Marie nodded, her fingers flying over her keyboard. "I've sent the invites. You'll be there?"

I nodded.

"Good," she said, then paused. "I hoped you'd be in early," she said in a rush. "I need to talk to you."

Uh oh. "Let me make some coffee first," I said, probably a little desperately.

I was still having trouble switching from my investigative mode to the mindset where I was responsible for managing others. Especially Marie.

Although even that was getting easier. Problem was, I didn't trust easy—especially not when it came to Marie. I never knew what to expect from her any more. Though not all of it was bad.

Just unpredictable.

"Oh, I already put the coffee on," she said. "And there's fresh cream in the fridge."

See what I mean?

I poured my coffee, then pulled up a chair at her desk. "So?"

She fidgeted with her hair, staring at me. The action was at odds with her normally forceful personality. Now she was making me nervous.

"Marie? You had something you wanted to say?"

"It's kind of a confession. I'm supposed to be looking into Justine's college friends, and it isn't going very well."

I relaxed a little. "There's nothing to confess. That's a pretty normal state for most investigations—one dead end after another, until finally it starts to come together. How far did you get?"

"I know she graduated from the Emily Carr College of Art—it's in her CV. Though it's a university now."

"Go on."

"But I can't find any hint of her at the University of BC. I'm beginning to think Justine didn't have any friends at all."

Given the Justine I remembered from those days, it sounded very possible. But much as she'd annoyed me, Justine had been popular. Which meant Marie was right. She was missing something.

"Why are you looking at UBC?"

"Well, that's where you went, right? You said you had classes together."

"We did. But at Emily Carr. I did a couple of semesters there one year," I said. There had been a few instructors I'd really wanted to study with. "They had an exchange program with several universities at the time. That's where I know Justine from. And that's where you need to look for her friends."

"Oh. And her award?"

I swiveled her computer to face me, typed in the relevant website. "Try this."

She swiveled the monitor back and her eyes scanned the screen. Then she grinned at me. "That's great. I knew you'd know. Thanks."

And her fingers began to fly over the keyboard. Apparently I was dismissed.

With an inward smile, I took my coffee and headed for my own desk. I'd gathered a lot of information since yesterday, and I needed some time with my notes to figure out what my next steps were.

———

I WAS JUST THINKING about whether I needed to go to Vegas or not when Badger came in. She gave Marie a nod, and strode straight to my desk.

"I understand you wanted to talk to me," she said, swinging out the chair beside my desk and sliding into it.

She hadn't even talked to Marie. How… oh. "Marie texted you?"

"Yeah."

It figured. "I talked to the woman in the security recording from the hotel, the one in the hoodie who looked like our client. She's Justine's niece, Chelsea Martin. According to Chelsea, Bittner was alive when she left his hotel room."

Badger cocked her head slightly, watching me. "And you believe her."

There was neither question or judgement in her words, just a statement of the facts as she knew them. It was typical of her. And told me a lot about how much information Marie was sending her.

And something about how Marie saw her own role, too. Which seemed to be expanding in directions I'd never anticipated. I'd have to think about that.

A statement I seemed to be making all too often lately, I thought with an inward grin.

"Yes, I believed her," I said. "But if Bittner was alive when Chelsea left, then the segment of recording that's missing from our tape becomes critical."

"Stands to reason. What time did she leave?"

"Chelsea says she stayed maybe twenty minutes. Which puts her leaving around quarter to six."

"Not long after the recording feed went out."

"Exactly. Is there any way of identifying who might have disabled the security recording that night? I'm assuming it needs to be someone associated with hotel security."

"Probably. Unless the whole system was hacked. Which might be a possibility. Let me see what I can find out."

"That would be good. If we know who, it could lead us to the killer."

"Or not," Badger said with something that might have been a slight grin. "Was there anything else?"

"Did you have any luck identifying whoever's been threatening Justine?"

"I'm working on it. I could have something for our meeting later, I think. I've got some stuff on her troll, too. I haven't found any connection between her stalker and the troll, though. Not yet."

Which meant either there wasn't one, or the stalker was really good. But Badger was better.

"Thanks," I said. If it were Cory, I'd be complimenting his work. Badger would just be annoyed if I tried it. "On the money trail that you're following—Chelsea said Bittner's debts were too high, that he'd got in too deep. Is that useful?"

"Might be. I've still got some digging to do there. Anything else?"

She'd summed it up nicely. "No, that's it."

"Then I'll be back for the meeting," she said. And with a nod for Marie, she was gone.

Shaking my head, I went back to my notes. And figuring out my next move.

———

THERE WAS something about the conversation with Gainer that morning that was niggling at me, but I couldn't put my finger on it. Something he'd said? Something he hadn't said?

Whatever it was, it was going to keep bugging me until…

"Barbara?"

Marie's voice broke into my thoughts, just as I'd almost caught the fleeting thought. "What?" I snapped.

"Sorry," she snapped back.

"No, I'm sorry. What is it?"

"This isn't making sense to me. Can you come have a look?"

I stood up. "Sure."

Maybe taking a break would help me figure out whatever I was missing. I moved to stand behind her, looking over her shoulder at her screen. "What am I seeing here?"

"The Argyll Award has attracted a lot of controversy over the years, and there are a few sites that talk about the entrants and the winners every year. This is Justine's year."

"Okay."

Marie clicked on a link. "Someone posted a copy of Justine's college transcript here. She didn't graduate."

"What?"

"She didn't graduate. See here," she pointed. "These last three courses are marked incomplete. Without them being completed, she wouldn't have earned a college degree."

I stared at the screen. "Sometimes an incomplete could be

finished if the professor agreed and the work was done later. An amended transcript would be issued."

"According to the poster," she clicked again, brought up the content, "Justine never finished these courses. Or her degree."

"But the Argyll award—it's only awarded to recent graduates. If Justine didn't graduate...?"

"How did she win the award? Exactly."

"Fraud?" I said. I was thinking out loud. "Can you access the records from the competition for that year?"

"No," Marie said. "I already tried that. They're still sealed. We'd need Badger if you really wanted to get into them. I just wanted to be sure I wasn't missing something."

"This post is dated the same year Justine graduated. But how did someone get ahold of Justine's transcripts?" I looked more closely at the screen. "How hard did you have to look to find this?" I asked her.

She shrugged. "I think I'm a pretty good researcher. But I'm no hacker. Why?"

Marie had surprised me more than once with the information she'd been able to find. But it wasn't technical skill—before she started working here, she avoided computers on principle. Luckily for all of us, she'd changed her mind when she decided to help me out.

Personally, I thought it was a mix of persistence and that odd quirk to Marie's personality—one of many—that had her starting from a different angle than most. A quirk that I was beginning to rely on.

Still, the fact that Marie had found Justine's transcript—with its missing course credits—so quickly meant it wasn't buried very deeply. Which, strategically, made no sense.

"If Justine's stalker hates her as much as she thinks," I said. "Then this is a more subtle strike than I'd have expected."

"His threats doesn't seem exactly subtle," she said with a snort.

No, they didn't. "Maybe no-one was supposed to have found

this yet," I said, working it out in my head. "What if this transcript isn't real?"

"You mean Justine's stalker might have faked it?" Marie said. "But why?"

"Well, he is threatening to undermine her reputation," I said. "What if these were posted recently? Something the stalker planted here for a later reveal."

"In a blaze of publicity." Marie nodded. "Okay. Or maybe they are real, and this is the threat her stalker is holding over her head."

"It isn't much of a threat once it's public, is it?" I said.

Marie shrugged. She didn't look happy.

"It looks like it's time for me to have another conversation with our client," I said. "But could you talk to Cory, see if he can dig into the site and find out when this thing was actually posted."

"Yeah. I just hope it's a fraud, and all the stalker's doing," she said. "I just don't see how this fits with the Justine I know. She's such a brilliant designer."

And I hoped Marie's new idol didn't have clay feet.

"We don't have all the facts yet," I said. "But either way, this isn't who Justine is now. All of us grow into who we become. The early version usually has a flaw or seven."

She smiled at that.

I glanced at my watch. "With any luck, I have time to see Justine before the meeting. I'll be back in a few hours."

"Aren't you going to call first?"

"I think this should be a surprise visit. Don't you?"

CHAPTER NINETEEN

When I got off the elevator on Justine's floor, the atmosphere seemed subdued despite the autumn sun pouring in through the big windows. The receptionist I'd met the other day greeted me warmly enough, but didn't bother to ring through to Justine.

"She's in her office. Why don't you go on in," she said.

As I made my way down the open hallway, I glanced at the workstations I passed. Cloud shadows played on the walls as the sun moved behind white clouds, but there was no excited conversation here. Not even the murmur of voices. The stillness felt unnatural. People had their heads down, seemingly focused on whatever was in front of them, but their hands weren't moving.

Something was very wrong.

Opening Justine's door, I saw the same thing. She had white orchids blooming on her desk, and a lovely bouquet of white and yellow chrysanthemums on the round meeting table. Sun poured in through the windows. But Justine herself was sitting with tensed shoulders, staring fixedly at her computer screen.

"Justine? Is something wrong?"

She startled, and looked blankly at me. "Barbara? Why are you here?"

"I had some questions. Do you have a moment?"

"I suppose so. Come in." And she waved a hand towards her chair. But she didn't get up.

Everything about her seemed entirely out of character. Even her bright lipstick had worn off, and not been repaired.

"What's wrong, Justine?" I asked as I sat down opposite her.

"I'm afraid we're going to be shut down."

"What? How is that possible? And by whom?"

"You'd have to ask Brian," she said flatly.

"Brian Stewart? Your lawyer?"

She nodded, but barely.

What could have gone wrong? I took a wild guess. "Are you being sued?"

"That's what I'm told."

"By whom? And why?"

She just stared blankly at me.

I know shock when I see it. "Was Brian here?" I asked quietly.

"No, he called. An hour…" her eyes went to the clock. "A few hours ago."

"Have you talked to anyone else?"

"No."

That was bad. "Look, sitting here like this isn't doing you any good. Is there someone you can talk to?"

"David…" It was a despairing whisper.

"Okay," I stood up. "I'll talk to Brian. But first, I'm taking you home. Is Chelsea still there?"

She nodded.

I'd taken Chelsea to her aunt last night. I figured no-one would look for her there right away, and it would give us time to figure out where she'd be safe.

Right now, it meant Justine wouldn't be alone tonight. Which was a very good thing.

"And I think you should send your staff home too. It doesn't look like they're getting much done," I told her.

Justine just looked at me.

I wondered how bad the rumors in the office were, and where they'd started. But that was a concern for later.

"Justine, call your receptionist. Tell her you're closing the office for the rest of the day, sending everyone home," I said. Then I paused, waiting.

No reaction from my client.

This wasn't good. On so many levels. "Now, Justine," I said, putting just enough force behind the words to get her moving.

She made the call, then I convinced her to get her purse and her jacket. As I followed her out, I wondered what was behind this latest disaster.

And how I was going to get her out of this mess.

———

HALF AN HOUR after I'd left Justine with her niece—after a quick explanation to Chelsea and a promise to look in later—I was being shown into Brian Stewart's sprawling fortieth floor corner office, with its view of downtown Vancouver, the ocean and mountains in the background. On a sunny fall day, it was breath-taking. With a view like this, how did the man ever get any work done?

Brian came forward to greet me with his hand outstretched and a broad smile. As he waved me to the artisanal glass and steel meeting table that took up the right side of his office, I noted he was sat with his back to the view. Leaving me to try to follow the conversation instead of getting lost in watching the play of puffy clouds against that flawless blue sky.

It was obviously a strategy he habitually used to his advantage. Smart man.

James Marchant was already there, seated on the same side I was. So what did that say about Brian's relationship with the other man? It could be a generous gesture, sharing that amazing view. Or it could be a subtle one-upmanship. In reverse.

Or maybe I just think too much. I looked from one lawyer to the other.

Nah. The games might be subtle, but they were there. I hid a grin.

I sank into the ergonomic leather chair. Wow. Maybe I'd just stay here.

"Barbara. I'm glad you called," Brian said as he took his own seat. "How is Justine?"

"She's in a state of shock," I said. "Your news seems to have been one disaster too many. I'm worried about her. That's why I'm here."

His forehead creased. "In shock? But she handled the call in her usual delightful style. She was professional, as she always is, and asked all the pertinent questions. But Justine is never one to hold back on her opinions. And they're usually pithily expressed."

"And that was the case with this call?" I asked.

He nodded. "Very much so."

"Then it must have been one shock too many," I said. "It all seems to have hit her after your call."

"That's truly unfortunate," Brian said, his frown deepening. "She isn't alone, is she?"

"No. I left her with a family member." I wasn't about to mention Chelsea. Not yet.

"Good."

Marchant leaned forward. "I trust this is a temporary situation? She is still far from being in the clear with the police."

I hadn't had a chance to tell him about the security recording, and this wasn't the time. I'd wait until I had more information about those missing hours.

"I expect it will be temporary," I said. "Justine has always been resilient. And I doubt she'd be where she is now professionally without a very thick skin."

Brian was nodding. I turned to face him. "But I do need to know more about the current problem. It may tie in directly to her case."

Did it? I wasn't so sure. But Justine couldn't help herself in the state she was in. "Is she being sued?"

"She didn't tell you?" Brian asked.

"Not clearly," I said.

"I wouldn't go so far as to say she was being sued," Brian said. "It's more of a threatened suit at this point."

"From whom?" I asked.

Marchant sat forward a little as if he was about to object to my question, then settled back on a look from Brian. Who was the senior partner, after all.

"The company she's been working with on her new furniture line," he said. "And at this point, since you're officially working for us now, I think you need details. But because of the confidentiality of the deal, we can't afford any more leaks."

Marchant frowned at that, but didn't say anything.

"There will be no leaks from my end," I said.

Brian Stewart nodded. "Good. Then Justine is negotiating with Hughes Furniture International on a major design contract with international distribution."

Even I had heard of Hughes. "She's going to have her own line with them?"

"Yes. The deal is for two separate lines under her name, with the possibility of a third."

No wonder Justine was paranoid. This was huge.

"Let me guess," I said. "Hughes is reacting to a rumor that Justine has done or plans to do something that would be in contravention of that deal."

"How did you know?" Brian asked. "Or is it a good guess?"

"It's a good guess," I said. "But based on how the person I'm calling her stalker has operated in the past, it's a logical progression of his behavior."

Marchant sat forward again, his face intent.

"This is the person who is threatening her, that she talked about in our last meeting?" Brian asked.

"Yes. He's been gradually escalating." I was now pretty sure those transcripts had been faked.

"Do you suspect he's also the killer, then?" Marchant asked me.

"It's one possibility, but at the moment, no, I don't. I think the stalker is out to destroy Justine's credibility and her career. This would be a predictable next step for him. Or her."

"So who, other than my client, do you think might have killed Bittner?" Marchant asked.

"Bittner's personal history suggests several suspects," I said. "We're still in the process of identifying and narrowing them down."

Before Marchant could ask anything else, I turned back to Brian. "I'm going to need to know everything you know about the rumor that has Justine's would-be partners threatening to sue. It may help us identify the stalker. Is that information you can share with me?"

He thought about it for several seconds. "Yes. I think we have to do so, now. It's a rumor, but there are a couple of details that no-one else should have known. We need to shut this down. Now."

"I'll need to know how Justine's would-be partners became aware of that rumor. It must have been targeted in some way," I said.

"Is she right?" Marchant asked Brian. "Did whoever spread the rumor target it specifically to her partners in this deal?"

"I don't have that information," Brian said. "I'll see what I can find out."

"Because if they were targeted," Marchant said. "Then there's a leak somewhere. Either in their shop. Or Justine's. Or ours."

Brian stared at the other lawyer. "You're right. And that would be a major problem. No wonder Justine was so shocked, if that occurred to her."

"And it would have," I said.

Thinking about Marie's comment that Bittner had sold Justine out, I hoped this wasn't what she'd meant—that Bittner had been involved in this. Such a betrayal would hit Justine even harder than his death had done.

"Yes," Brian said. "It would."

There was a small silence that no-one seemed to want to break.

Finally Brian spoke. "I don't know how quickly I can get an answer on how Hughes heard about the rumor. But I will get every detail. I'll get back to you as quickly as I can."

He paused again, his face determined. "And if there is the slightest hint the leak came from this firm, I'll get to the bottom of it. That I can promise you."

"If you can get me the details of the rumor itself, I may have someone who can track how and where the rumor—or rumors— spread online," I said. "And the sooner we can identify and deal with him or her, the better it will be for Justine."

Brian pressed a button on his phone, and asked his executive assistant to send the latest email on Justine's file to the three of us. What seemed like moments later, I felt my phone vibrate.

"I have it," I said, and raised an eyebrow at him.

He nodded permission, and I signed into my email and skimmed the email. "That should give us what we need," I said, looking up.

"Good," he said. "Now, what are we going to do about Justine and this case of hers?"

CHAPTER TWENTY

Two hours later I was back at my office, to find Marie had set everything up for a meeting, including providing a tray of mini-cupcakes. I wasn't going to argue—I snagged a red velvet one. But she and I needed to have a serious talk about office finances.

I was discovering that Marie's instincts were often excellent, but she had serious gaps in her grasp of cash flow. Especially for a small business. For Marie, money was either not available at all, or didn't matter.

From what I could tell, that mindset stemmed from the deprivation of her childhood. Her aunt had raised her in poverty—monetarily, and of the spirit. If it hadn't been for her sister, I don't think Marie would have survived it.

But that childhood pain was making Marie's art brilliant. Judging by the few pieces she'd let me see, anyway.

And her new lavish approach to money, ironically, might never be a problem for her. Not with the money she'd just inherited from the sale of her late mother's paintings. Although they say lottery winners who don't understand how to make money work for them often end up broke after a year or two. So her feast or famine mentality could still be a problem for her in the future.

Here and now, it was my firm she was likely to sink.

Or maybe not.

Until the last year or so, I'd been scraping by on so little money, I'd got in the habit of squeezing every dollar until it screamed. Now I had some rethinking to do, too—not on the basics, but on my priorities.

When a business starts to grow, you can squeeze it so tightly it dies almost as easily as you can drown it in debt. I'd spent so long avoiding the latter, that maybe I was in danger of the former?

I'd rather not do either.

Grinning at my own pontificating, I grabbed another cupcake and went to pour myself a coffee. By the time I was ready, Cory and Badger had both shown up, and the three of them were already seated at the meeting table. It was a good thing I'd already had two cupcakes—the tray was now empty.

"Cory, do you have that list of what other rooms were booked on the fifteenth floor of the Grand Pacific the night of the murder?" I asked as I pulled out one of the folding chairs.

"Sure do," he said, and bent over his laptop. "I've sent it—you should see the email now."

"Got it. Thanks." I looked round the table. "Who wants to start?"

"I do," Cory said. "I did some digging into Bittner's various identities. He had one—the one he used to book the hotel room on the night he was killed—that he used mainly for hotels and dining out. Stuff like that."

Used when he was trying to keep a relationship a secret? I thought about what Gainer had told me. "How long ago did he create this identity?"

Cory glanced down at his screen. "Just over three years."

That fit. "He'd been seeing Gainer for three years."

"So he created that one to keep some of his lovers' secrets," Marie said.

"Looks like it," Cory said. "Unfortunately Bittner was using his other identities—and I found another one—to keep his own secrets."

"He had five identities?" I asked. How did the man keep them all straight?

Cory nodded.

"What was he hiding behind the other three?"

"A ton of debt," Cory said. "The guy was in big trouble. He'd maxed out his credit, and then some, as four different people. As David Bittner, he was in financial trouble. And three of the other identities are worse."

Wow. When Justine said her head designer was in trouble, she hadn't known the half of it. But why hadn't she?

From everything she'd told me, Justine knew what desperation looked like. And Bittner had been desperate.

So how had Justine missed exactly how much trouble David Bittner was in?

She'd talked about how close they were. And she'd seen out of control gambling before with her second husband. And with Chelsea. Yet she hadn't noticed it in the man she called her best friend?

And Bittner was a big part of her business success, too.

Justine had told me she hadn't been paying as much attention to her day-to-day business lately, because of the deal she was working on. But this was a pretty big problem to miss. Especially in someone she saw every day, and said she was so close to.

"Where did Bittner borrow the money from?"

"Taking all four names together—and not counting the identity he used with Gainer—he had loans and lines of credit at eight different banks. And twenty-two credit cards, all maxed out," Cory said.

"As David Bittner, he was still making the minimum payment on most of his debt, but his credit scores were bad. And his condo had three mortgages on it," he added.

Wow. "So we're talking hundreds of thousands in debt?" I asked.

"Including the mortgages, more like three-quarters of a million, a lot of it with high interest rates. And that's just the stuff I could find," Cory said.

"I had a look too," Badger said. "And Bittner had a couple of big loans off the books."

"How big? And with whom?"

"So far it looks like another half million or so. Maybe more. And I'm having trouble tracing the source of some of the money. I'll keep digging."

I couldn't wrap my head around being more than a million and a half in debt. I worry way too much about meeting my office rent and my mortgage payment each month.

And if Badger couldn't find the source of Bittner's loans, the origin of that money had to be really shady. And owing that much money to some kind of criminal organization? Did the idiot have a death wish?

No. He had an addiction. One he hadn't yet been able to over-come. And now it was too late. David Bittner's life was gone, along with his chance to make different choices.

And someone needed to pay for that.

Preferably someone not my client.

———

"THAT'S REALLY GOOD WORK," I said, looking around the table at the three of them. "And I have some related information. First off, I found the woman in the hoodie from the recording. She's our client's niece, Chelsea Martin."

And I filled them in on my conversations with Chelsea, and what she'd told me about David Bittner. As I did so, I watched the three faces around the table.

Cory looked even more horrified than when he'd told me what he'd found, Marie looked sad, and Badger—I couldn't read Badger. As usual.

"So Bittner was actually in Gamblers Anonymous," Marie said. "It wasn't doing him much good."

"It might have, eventually," Badger said unexpectedly. "Sounds like he was struggling to get clear, but he'd dug himself in too deeply."

"That's how Chelsea saw it," I said. "As if he'd just needed more time."

"Which he won't get now," Marie said.

"No. He won't." I let the silence sit between us for a long moment. It felt almost like a mourning for David Bittner. And a pause we all needed.

I've sometimes found that in solving cases, I learn so much about the victim that I end up sad for their loss even after a case is closed.

When it was just me working a case, I just ignored the feeling, maybe had an extra glass of wine or two at Guido's bistro—a place that felt almost like home to me, but came with built-in company.

But now, working with these three, I'm seeing the same thing. And somehow it felt important to honor that. Which was an odd feeling.

"I also spoke with Bittner's lover, Michael Gainer this morning," I said after a bit. "Chelsea's story alibis him—Bittner was alive when Gainer left. And he also talked about Bittner's gambling, though he didn't seem to know the details."

"Or maybe he didn't want to know," Cory said. "He's a lawyer—some things he has a duty to report, if he knows about them."

"You're not supposed to know that stuff yet," Marie said.

Cory just grinned at her.

I was pretty sure I didn't want to know where—or why—he'd learned it. I knew Cory's father talked business at the dinner table. I'd thought it probably bored his kids, but might end up being a good education for them. Maybe I'd been wrong.

"I've just come from a meeting with Justine, followed by a meeting with both her lawyers," I said. "She's been threatened with a lawsuit. Someone's been spreading rumors about the very hush-hush deal she's engaged in, and it's serious enough to put her career and her company at risk."

And her sanity. But I held that back, protecting her privacy. Justine was a fighter. She'd bounce back.

I was almost sure of it.

"Just like her stalker promised," Marie noted. "And maybe the transcript thing ties in too."

"You're probably right on both counts. But we can't afford to make any assumptions about who's behind this. We're going to have to follow every lead we have," I said, opening my laptop and forwarding the email Brian Stewart had sent me.

"I've just sent you the relevant email from Hughes Furniture International, the company Justine is negotiating with," I said, my tone serious. "I'm sharing that name—which is highly confidential—with all of you, because we need it to do our work. But if that name, or anything about this case gets out—we'll have killed Justine's career ourselves."

I waited a moment to let that sink in, meeting each of their eyes in turn. Marie turned pale, and nodded. Cory looked determined. Badger looked—like Badger.

"All right, then," I said. "The probability is that the rumor that triggered this email came from Justine's stalker. The lawyers are going to see if they can get us any information on how this was sent to Hughes. That might tell us a lot more about whoever is causing all this trouble for our client."

I paused, measured their intent faces. "But whoever it is, I want to know how they had enough information about Justine's business dealings to spread this rumor. It reeks of insider info to me."

As I'd hoped, Marie spoke up.

"I heard that Bittner was selling Justine out. Maybe he's the one who had this information. And he sold it to the stalker." She paused, glanced at me. "Or whoever."

That's what I'd wondered.

"Because of his debts? Yeah, that works," Cory said. "Can you find out?"

Marie shook her head. "It wasn't first hand, and I can't go back to the source. But Badger's been looking into it. Quietly."

Both she and Cory turned towards Badger.

Who had been watching the two of them with a furrow between her brows. "I have," she said. "And I might have been looking in the wrong direction."

"Which doesn't happen often," Cory said.

Badger gave him a half-smile but the furrow remained. Too bad there was no quick way to clock how fast a person's brain worked. I suspected she'd be setting new records right about now.

"The info I did find wasn't going anywhere. I hate that. These guys," and Badger waved a disdainful hand at the email I'd sent them all. "Weren't even in my focus. They are now."

And she gave us all a tight little smile.

I was glad it wasn't me she was thinking about right then.

"So—I'm guessing you didn't ask Justine about her transcripts then, and whether she really graduated," Marie said to me.

"No. It wasn't the right time." And Justine couldn't have handled another shock. Not then.

"She didn't graduate?" Now it was Cory who sounded shocked. Don't tell me he'd made an idol of her too.

"I found a transcript that shows she didn't finish all of her courses in her last year," Marie said. "But faking something like that seems like the kind of thing her stalker would do."

"I can look," Cory said. "See if I can get hold of her original transcript. No-one with the smarts she has just doesn't finish a degree."

Oh. That's what he was shocked about. His mother would be pleased to hear that Cory valued an education so much. Especially given his current lack of focus on school. If I hadn't made passing all his grades a condition for working with me, I wondered sometimes if he'd even bother attending most of his classes.

"I didn't finish mine," Marie said.

Cory frowned at her. "Doesn't count. You're working on it now."

"I didn't finish either," Badger said.

Oops. Justine might not be one of Cory's idols, but Badger was.

"Why not?" Cory asked.

A shrug. "I had other things to do."

He leaned forward, his face bright, then glanced at me. And sat back again. "Oh," was all he said.

I suspected he'd be asking her more questions later, out of my earshot. I couldn't decide if I'd rather know what was said. Or not. Right now, I had plausible deniability with his mother.

Not that Susanna would care. If Cory decided against going to university, my sister would find a way to blame me. Even if she had to twist the facts until they screamed.

"I might make a different choice now," Badger added.

Bless her.

And Cory looked even more intrigued. Good.

"Don't worry about the transcript," I said. "Justine probably has a copy. Let's focus on Bittner for the moment. What do we know?"

"We know who the woman in the hoodie is, now," Marie said.

"And how much financial trouble Bittner was in," Cory added.

"I did some digging on Justine's troll," Badger said. "*Designexpert1*, whoever that is, doesn't seem to exist outside his attacks on Justine and Bittner."

"But the attacks started with Justine?" I asked.

"Yes. Then spread to Bittner," Badger said. "I'll keep working on it."

"*You* need to do more digging?" Cory said. "Wow. Somebody's put a lot of effort into hiding. And for a one-off? That's weird."

"*Designexpert1* wants to stay anonymous. And he or she is good at covering their tracks." Badger smiled. "I enjoy a challenge."

And I wouldn't want to be him or her right now. "Have you found anything to suggest that *Designexpert1* might be our stalker?"

"Too early to say," Badger said. "I did find out that the missing time on the hotel security recording was an external hack, though. And a good one. They had to bypass a few extra layers the hotel security had installed to prevent hacking."

"So what does that tell us?"

She shrugged. "Hotel security already has a patch in place, but I could still find enough. I didn't recognize the coding, but I know a few people who might. I suspect it was a hired job, and an expensive one."

"Not the stalker, then?" Marie said.

Badger gave her an enigmatic smile.

Probably not. And maybe not the killer, either.

Expensive, hired hackers with an interest in security sounded more like criminal enterprises. The kind who made a business out of unsecured loans, among other things. And they'd want their victim alive.

Dead gamblers don't pay off their debts.

Unless someone was sending a message. And Bittner's death was an example.

I felt sick at the thought.

———

OUR MEETING DIDN'T LAST MUCH LONGER. As it wrapped up, I glanced at my watch. Nearly five. I needed to talk to Nick, and if he wasn't in the field, this was probably a good time to catch him.

But I wasn't about to call him in the fishbowl that was now my office. I was getting a kick out of working with these three, but I was quickly figuring out they were inveterate gossips when it came to each other's lives. And mine.

Well, except maybe Badger. Her I wasn't quite sure about.

I needed someplace quiet. Hmmm.

"Marie, do you still have the key to the office next door?" I said.

She looked excited and started to get up. "You're really thinking about it? I'll come with you."

I held up a cautioning hand. "Not so fast. I just want to take another look. A quiet look."

"Oh." She handed me the key and sat down again. "I guess that makes sense."

Good thing. It was the only explanation she was going to get. I felt a little bad for squelching her like that, but I needed some privacy for a change.

Marie grinned at me. "You don't really need the key, you know. You could just go through the door in our closet."

What? "Isn't it locked?"

"Nope." She looked smug.

So much for security. Note to self—a little sarcasm isn't enough to squelch Marie. Which was probably just as well if she was staying on as part of the team I seemed to be building.

But it was almost guaranteed to get on my nerves.

———

THE OFFICE next door felt really empty. And really boring—just a sea of beige. Don't tell me I was getting used to Justine's odd ideas of decorating.

To make my call, I went into the office Marie had tagged as mine on our earlier tour. Just to see how it felt. And my luck was in.

Nick answered on the second ring.

"Markham," he said, in what I called his official voice. He was in the office, then.

"Hey, Nick. About those texts I keep getting…"

"Sending them to you makes my day better," he said quietly.

Great. Some women get roses—which I've never understood, by the way. Hothouse roses, beautiful though they may be, strike me as too formal, too rigid. Give me big, shaggy chrysanthemums any day.

But my man doesn't send roses—he sends me photos of places he wants to live in with me instead.

No pressure, though.

Yeah, right.

But how could I complain about those photos when he said things like that? So I asked him about loan sharking, instead.

"I thought you were looking into a case of design fraud. How did loan sharking come into it?" Nick asked.

"David Bittner's murder. He's connected to the original case because he's a designer, like my client. But it turns out he was also a gambler, with a seven figure debt problem."

"Let me guess," Nick said. "The ponies? Or high stakes poker?"

"Poker. How did you know?"

"I was on the gang task force for four years, remember?"

"I know. And drugs equals a lot of money. Which then creates other issues. Like money laundering."

Which reminded me—I needed to follow up with Badger about Margaret's problem.

"That's part of it," he said. "But there's also the question of how to make all that money work for them."

"So loan sharking works?"

"Always has, right back through history. That and prostitution. Money that doesn't have to be laundered, since it's going into another illegal business. And the returns are sky high."

I thought about that one. He was right.

"There's a lot of money to be made in things that feed people's addictions. And addictions tend to feed off of each other," I said, thinking about it.

"Yep."

Which just made this case harder. "What can you tell me about the local gangs who are involved in loan sharking?" I asked him.

"They're bad news. All of them. Stay away," he said.

Oh, that was a lot of help.

Especially since he got an urgent call and had to hang up before I got a chance to ask for details.

It wasn't my day.

CHAPTER TWENTY-ONE

I had a brief word with Badger about digging out the information that Margaret needed. She just nodded and made a note. Content that my team had their assignments and were more than capable, I left them to it, and went to check on Justine.

Justine's home was a corner suite on the twenty-third floor in trendy Coal Harbor. Which meant it likely had a seven figure price tag. With more windows than walls, she had panoramic views of Vancouver's best vistas. The apartment looked out over Georgia Straight on one side and had the north shore mountains framed on the other.

If I'd thought her office decor was stark, it was nothing compared to her home. Her apartment was open plan, with the huge kitchen flowing into a spacious living and dining area. Everything was white, keeping the entire focus on the views. Except it had been done by a master designer, and that white—or rather those whites—were subtly rich with variety in shade and texture.

The artist in me stopped for a moment to understand and appreciate what Justine had done. She'd layered white on white, each complementing the next. But she'd subtly clashed a hint of a shade here, a hue there. Then she'd added touches of her signature orange—a pattern on a cushion, a stripe in a rug—with the occasional hit of vibrant pink. The overall effect was vibrant but restful, a combination I would have said was impossible if I hadn't seen it.

Justine was sitting on the long eggshell white sofa that faced out over the water. She looked better than she had earlier, but still exhausted. With her too pale face and white yoga gear, she fit into her home perfectly—a study in whites.

She had a cup of tea steaming on the small table beside her, and several plates on the kitchen counter said she'd eaten. Chelsea was still there, and hovering. But she had the sense to do it out of Justine's sight. I suspected the tea and the empty plates were her doing.

"Thanks for seeing me," I told Justine after Chelsea showed me into the living room. Chelsea then vanished into a room on the right. Tactful of her.

"Thank you for bringing me home," Justine said. "I'll be fine."

The simple fact that she said that told me how un-fine she was feeling right now.

"I know you will. By tomorrow those idiots will regret they ever listened to rumors."

"Have you found anything?"

"We're working on it. But we will."

She nodded.

"Is there anything you've remembered that might help us?"

She shook her head. "Tomorrow, maybe," she said with a faint smile.

I needed to ask her about Bittner's debts, and if there was any way he could have known about the deal she was working on. But I couldn't do that to her, not now.

But I could ask her about Gainer.

"You said David Bittner talked to you about his relationship troubles. Did you know about David's relationship with Michael Gainer?" I asked her.

"Yes, I did," she said. "They'd been together three years or so, after all. I won't gossip about David, though. Even though he's…"

Her breath caught on the word and she buried her face in her hands.

"I know, Justine," I said, placing a hand on her shoulder. "I'm not asking for gossip. And I wouldn't ask now. Except his killer needs to be found."

She straightened, wiping her eyes. "Before we have to tell them about Chelsea, and they arrest her," she said. "I won't have that, Barbara. You have to know that."

"I know." I paused, letting her regroup a bit. "Were David and his lovers exclusive?"

She paused. Shrugged. "Some were, some weren't. Most of them were what David considered exclusive. Which meant he had one main relationship at a time. But he had other... trysts, he called them. He could be old-fashioned."

She wiped her eyes again. "Which I found either an endearing or annoying trait in him. Depending what he chose to be old-fashioned about."

They really had been friends. And had probably known each other much better than I'd realized. She just might have some of the answers I needed.

"Did Gainer consider them exclusive?" I asked. "Using David's definition?"

"I have no idea," she said tartly. "He was married, after all. Hardly in any position to set limits on David's behavior."

"That sounds like a sore spot," I said. "David's?"

She looked sheepish. "Sorry. My ex-husband. It comes out when I least expect it."

"The gambler?"

"No, my first ex-husband. The second one at least didn't cheat on me with other women. Though gambling turned out to be a more demanding mistress than anyone my first husband hooked up with."

Sounds like her marriages had been challenging. And people wonder why I'm still single. "So David never complained about his relationship with Gainer?"

Justine smiled, her eyes sad. "David did nothing but complain about it. Gainer was married, and kept all of his affairs very quiet. Which limited their time together. David hated that. He was more than open about all of his own affairs. Except his relationship with Gainer, of course. But that wasn't his choice."

Yet they'd stayed together for three years. Something must have been working for them. "Had he always complained about it?"

"Oh, sure. But it got worse back in the spring. I'm not sure why —he'd never say. And then I got too busy to ask." She looked sad.

The spring. When David Bittner and Michael Gainer had gone to Vegas.

Gainer had said Bittner's gambling grew worse after that trip. Now Justine said he'd been more unhappy in their relationship after that too.

What, exactly, had happened in Vegas?

And did it have anything to do with Bittner's death? Or Justine's case?

I was about to ask Justine if she knew, but judging by her pallor, it was time for me to go. She'd had a rough day.

"Is there anything I can do for you?" I asked instead.

"Can you follow up with what's his name, my second lawyer, for me?"

What's his name. I loved it. "Marchant?"

"That's it. Can you follow up with Marchant for me? Make sure he's up to date on everything that's going on."

"Yes, I can do that."

"But Barbara? Don't mention Chelsea to him. Not yet."

Interesting. She'd have to tell him eventually that it was her niece in the recording and not her. "Sure. Anything else?"

She gave me a weak grin. "That's plenty. It means I don't have to talk to him tomorrow. Frankly, I can't stand the man. But I might need him."

If she was arrested and her case came to trial, she meant.

Without the recording evidence the police were probably relying on, that looked like a long shot to me.

———

AFTER I'D LEFT Justine's apartment, I walked back along the seawall that borders Coal Harbor to where I'd left my car, taking deep breaths of the rich salt smell of the waves. As I walked I put in a call to James Marchant's office.

To my shock I was put through immediately.

"Ms. O'G... I mean, Barbara," Marchant said. "Have you heard from Justine Grayson?"

"I just left her apartment," I said.

"Good. How's she doing?"

"Pretty well, all things considered," I said.

He muttered something.

"What's that?"

"Nothing. Look, I need some information. Any chance you can come by our offices today?"

I'd planned on a phone call, but I needed to clear my head. I drew in another lungful of sea air. A brisk walk would do it.

And there were a few things I hoped Marchant could tell me, too. It would be an easier ask in person than over the phone. "I can be there in twenty minutes," I said. "If that works?"

"Great." He sounded surprised. And worried? "I'll see you then."

You'd think a trial lawyer would know better than to ask for things he didn't really want.

———

I HAD TWENTY MINUTES. I lengthened my stride.

My phone chirped, and I glanced at the message. Nick. And he'd sent me a photo of yet another place we could live.

Subtle, he isn't. Well, not when he wants something, anyway. Should I be flattered? Or terrified?

Persistent, like water dripping on stone—that's Nick. It's what makes him such a good cop. And such a terrific lover.

I glanced at the photo again, a small cottage with big trees and a quiet garden. I could picture us living there, looking out over that garden as we argued over whose turn it was to make the coffee.

It's just that the image froze my brain.

I needed more coffee.

———

TAKEOUT COFFEE IN HAND, I arrived at James Marchant's office nineteen minutes later. His office was a slightly down-market version of Brian Stewart's. It was smaller, not a corner office, and being two floors lower, the view wasn't quite so sweeping. But it had the same ocean view, the same built-to-impress mahogany furniture, the same feeling of solidity and tradition.

Marchant met me at the door with an outstretched hand and a broad smile.

I immediately wondered what he wanted. Cynical? Me? Nah.

Once we were both seated he got straight down to business. "I'm going to need a meeting with Justine as soon as she's up to it. Do you have any idea when that might be?"

Given how much better she was this afternoon compared to this morning, I suspected she'd be back in the office the next day. Best to give her a day's grace, though. "Probably day after tomorrow," I said.

He looked relieved. Something was definitely up.

"Why?" I asked.

"The police are requesting an interview. They're being polite about it—for now. But I doubt that will last if I can't produce her."

"She's still a serious suspect?" Surely they must know about Bittner's gambling debts by now. And the missing time on the security recordings had to be raising questions for them.

"It seems so." His brief words and calm delivery were at odds with his request to meet with me right away.

"What do they have on her?"

"That's part of the problem. I don't know yet. Which makes it hard to prep Justine for an interview."

"Have they shared the security recording from the hotel with you?"

His eyebrows drew together, the movement reminding me of those dark fuzzy caterpillars that make white tents all over the birch trees in my neighborhood every summer. "And which recording is that?"

"This one," I said, and emailed it to him. "It should open from the email."

It did, and I watched as he ran it. Then ran it again, several times.

Finally he looked up. "Is that Justine?"

I shook my head. "No."

"It's probably the main reason the police are so interested in her. Are you sure it isn't her?"

"Yes. Very sure."

"Do you know who it is?"

"Yes."

"I see." He considered me for a moment, his face expressionless. "Given the resemblance, I would guess whoever it is, she is related to our client. Correct?"

"Yes."

He nodded. "Fine. I won't ask questions. For now."

"Fair enough."

"But we'll need to be able to produce her too, if necessary."

"Noted." Which didn't mean I agreed, just that I'd heard him. I wondered if he'd caught the difference. Probably. He gave me a sharp look.

But it was Justine's life, after all. And her decision.

He probably knew that too.

"There seems to be a time jump in this recording after our mystery woman leaves," Marchant said.

It wasn't quite a question. I'd expected him to spot that, and he hadn't disappointed me. Maybe working with him on this case wouldn't be so bad.

"Yes. I have someone looking into it."

"Was Bittner alive when the mystery woman left, do you know?"

"She says he was."

"She being the woman in the recording?"

Yup. He was a lawyer, all right. "Yes."

"Then you've spoken with her?"

"Yes."

"And you believe her." It wasn't a question.

His instincts were pretty good. Despite all that legal training. Good to know. "Yes."

A nod. "Which makes that missing time segment critical. Have you other suspects in mind?"

"We're pursuing several other avenues," I told him. "Bittner owed a lot more money than was good for him. And quite possibly to some very unsavory people."

"Drugs? Or gambling?"

"Gambling."

"Hmmm."

Exactly. "I also talked to the man Bittner met in the first part of the recording."

"Gainer?" He smiled at my look of surprise. "I recognized him. And I've heard the rumors too."

I nodded. "I talked to him this morning," I said.

"Let me guess. He says he wasn't there."

"No. Gainer is very firm that he's not the killer. But he admits to being there. Which doesn't really matter, because our mystery woman is willing to swear Bittner was alive when she got there. And Gainer had already left by then."

"So why did he leave so early? I gather hotel room meetings were a regular thing with them?"

"It seems so. Gainer says they quarreled and Bittner ended the relationship."

"I'll bet that went over well."

Interesting reaction. Curious, I asked him if he'd seen Gainer in action.

"The man's a bulldog," Marchant said. "Once he gets hold of something, he never lets go. Must make him a real pain to face in a courtroom."

And what did that say about him as a lover? Gainer had said something this morning about not letting things end there with Bittner. But he'd lost that chance when he stormed out, since Bittner was killed shortly afterwards. Unless…

Marchant hadn't noticed my inattention—he was still thinking about Gainer-the-lawyer. "He's like a force—doesn't let up until he's won. Or leave an opponent time to regroup, he just attacks again. And again."

The man Marchant was describing didn't bear much resemblance to the man I'd talked to that morning.

Marchant's Gainer wouldn't let himself be kicked out by a lover, then wait tamely to continue the discussion the next day. He'd get right back in there, arguing for what he wanted.

Would the missing time on that recording have shown Gainer returning to Bittner's hotel room to continue that argument with his lover?

Was it possible he was guilty?

———

DRIVING HOME in rush hour traffic, I got stuck at one red light after another. Which gave me too much time to kick myself for all the questions I should have asked Gainer. And hadn't.

If Michael Gainer had gone back to Bittner's hotel room during the two hours the recording didn't show, he could have killed his lover. Or former lover. Or whatever they were to each other.

Or he could have seen something.

Part of me wanted to confront Gainer immediately. But the more rational side of me knew that asking Gainer about it now would be a waste of time—he was a criminal lawyer. He'd be prepared for that question. And probably anything else I might ask.

No wonder he'd been so relaxed on the beach this morning.

He'd been prepared for far worse. And I'd prided myself on choosing the right setting for that conversation.

I hadn't even thought to ask him if he'd seen or talked to Bittner again that night. Nice one, Barbara.

Now I needed another way to find out if Gainer had gone back to Bittner's hotel room after the cameras had shown him storming out.

Once I knew that, I'd know what my next step was.

CHAPTER TWENTY-TWO

I walked into the office on Saturday morning just after eight, balancing three coffees, a smoothie and a huge box of donuts. If I was going to ask the team to work on a weekend, I figured I'd better reward them. And Lee's Donuts are amazing.

So I'd made a detour on the way downtown and stopped in at Granville Island. I love the bustle of the place early on a Saturday, when most of the shops are still setting up for the day.

Marie was already in, to my surprise, and it looked like she'd been busy. She'd moved the dividers against the far wall, and done something to rearrange the desks, which gave us a larger meeting area. For today it was great, but it wasn't going to work very well during a typical week.

"Don't worry," Marie told me. "Everything moves back the way it was after today. That's the beauty of these desks. They can be set up so many ways."

Uh huh. Sure they could.

But she was trying, I reminded myself.

"It looks like it'll work for today, though. Thanks," I said. And handed her a mango smoothie.

"You got me a smoothie?" She grinned as she took it. "Awesome.

You want me to get a plate for the donuts while you get set up? The other two should be here anytime."

Marie glanced at the door behind her, then lowered her voice. "I think Badger is making a special effort to get here. Mornings aren't her thing."

"I don't think mornings are a thing for any of us," I said, earning myself another grin. Not morning meetings, anyway.

While I waited for the rest of them to arrive, I reviewed my notes from the previous day. I couldn't stop thinking about Gainer —and Marchant's opinion of the guy. Wondering if Gainer had it in him to kill Bittner.

A text from Nick was a welcome distraction. This time, he'd sent a listing of a three bedroom townhouse a couple of blocks off of Commercial. The price was right and the place was well designed, but...

"Too little light," I texted back. "Depressing when it rains." In other words, half the year or more. Then I waited to see what he'd send back.

He sent me a sunflower.

I grinned, and sent him a beach ball. Wishing I could see his face when it arrived.

Nick followed up with another listing, which surprised me. This was a two bedroom cottage with an unfinished attic. And it had a garden. But it was even further east, and the price—while surprisingly good, still made me gulp.

I could see us living there. And it tied my stomach in knots.

"Too pricey. And too small," I sent back. I didn't mention that I'd loved the garden.

I should have known Nick would see right through me. He sent me a shower of garden flowers. But no questions, thank goodness.

I sent back a palm tree. Maybe we could talk about a tropical vacation, not living together.

Just then Badger and Cory arrived—it amused me to see Cory rush in last, his hair all every which way—and grabbed their donuts. Once we'd all settled around the meeting table, I turned to Badger.

"Have you been able to recover the security recordings from outside Bittner's room the night he was killed?" I asked her.

"Turns out that's a problem," Badger said. "They weren't deleted. The camera feed was blocked, so nothing was transmitted to be recorded. Which means there's nothing to recover."

Dammit. I filled them in on what Marchant had told me about Gainer. And the question I hadn't asked.

"So you're looking to find out whether Gainer went back to Bittner's room?" Cory said. "Why not just ask him?"

"He's just going to say he didn't go back," Marie said. "Even if he isn't the killer, if he went back to Bittner's room it would look incriminating. And he's a lawyer. He'd know better than to take that risk."

I drank some coffee to hide my shock at Marie's insight. "What she said. What about the recordings on the rest of the floor? Do they show anything useful?"

"None of the cameras on that floor were recording then," Cory said.

"On the entire floor?" I asked, startled.

"Yup," he said, and Badger nodded.

Someone was determined. "And whoever hacked the system turned the cameras off remotely?"

"Yes," Badger said.

"Isn't that a bit unusual?"

"These guys are good," Badger said. And she sounded impressed, if only a little.

Which told me quite a bit about whoever we were up against. It took a lot to impress Badger. "Anything point to who hacked the cameras?"

"Not yet," she said.

But her jaw was set and there was a flinty look in her eye that I'd seen before. Badger does not give up easily.

"Do you have copies of the recordings for the other floors in that time frame?" Marie asked. "Or were they turned off too?"

Badger looked at her with interest. "Yes, I do, and no, they weren't turned off. Why?"

"Because it might tell us what escape route the killer took," Marie said. She glanced at something she'd jotted on the legal pad in front of her. "The cameras on the main floor, including the lobby, were all working the whole time?"

"Yes," Badger said.

"Can I get copies of those for the same time frame? The missing hours, I mean?" Marie said.

"That's a lot of recordings," Cory said. "You're going to go cross-eyed watching it."

Marie made a face at him, and I smothered a smile. So much for elegance.

"If you tell me what areas you're interested in, I can isolate those feeds for you," Badger said. She glanced at me. "You good with this?"

Nice that someone realized this was going to cost money. But I was too curious about where Marie was going with this inspiration of hers to stop her now. "Sure."

Marie grinned at me, then turned back to Badger. "If Bittner was alive when Justine's niece left him, then the killer had to get to his floor sometime in the next two hours. And then get out again."

"During the time the security cameras were off," Badger said.

"Exactly," Marie said. "And if the killer was smart, he—or she— would have taken one way up, but left a different way after the killing. So can you send the feed from all the cameras that cover exits on the main floor?"

Cory had been peering intently at his computer as she talked. Now he swiveled his computer, and showed all of us the blueprints of the hotel he'd been looking at. "That's three stairwells and six elevators. You'd want to look at the second floor, too, where the escalator down to the main floor is. And the housekeeping and kitchen floor. And the two parking floors, as well, if you want to get everyone."

Marie rolled her eyes. "Fine. Those too."

Badger nodded.

It wasn't an approach I'd have considered. Probably because it would take forever. Wouldn't it? "What are you looking for?" I asked.

"Bittner let the killer in. It had to be someone he knew," Marie said.

Cory looked at her in surprise, then grinned. "You're planning on using facial recognition," he said. "Good one."

Marie returned the grin.

"I didn't think you'd know how it worked," he said.

"I don't. But I figured you or Badger would."

"You got that right," Cory said.

"And if you guys can do that part, I can get photos of everyone we know Bittner interacted with," Marie said. "Then we'll see if anyone interesting went upstairs during that same time."

Her plan was brilliant.

"It won't put the killer on Bittner's floor," I said. "But if we really can pull everyone entering and leaving from all possible exits during that time…"

Then it gave us a wider suspect pool. Depending how good our information was on who was in Bittner's life.

"Working with that missing time frame will really help," Cory said.

"Unless the killer was staying on another floor," Badger said. "Then you'd miss them entirely."

Marie pursed her lips, not about to be squelched so easily. "Sure," she said. "But if the first scan doesn't work, then we look at one from all the floors. You can get the data, right?"

"Badger can," Cory said with confidence.

Badger didn't say anything, just gave Marie an unreadable look. Then she turned to me.

"How urgent is this?" she said.

"The police still want to talk to Justine about Bittner's death. And she won't give up her niece."

Though her lawyer might. Especially since Chelsea wasn't guilty. But I kept that thought to myself.

"So it's up to us to keep our client out of jail," Marie said.

I liked the "our client". Marie was clearly all in—but I wasn't quite sure what Badger's response would be. This wasn't exactly the international high-stakes crime that the last case I'd hired her for had been.

Badger's face was inscrutable. But her tone was decided. "Then let's get on it," she said.

CHAPTER TWENTY-THREE

I got back home at noon, and put on a pot of coffee. The team were busy running the facial recognition software to see if Gainer had left the hotel when he left Bittner's room. And there wasn't a thing I could do until they had some results.

I thought about lunch—I'd ordered pizza for the others, back at the office—but I wasn't hungry. I couldn't stop thinking about Gainer and Bittner. I was missing something, but I couldn't figure out what it was. It felt like an itch between your shoulders that you can't reach. Only this itch was in my brain.

I took my coffee out on the deck, but the view out over Granville Street didn't hold me the way it usually did. The image of the little house on the East Side that Nick had found crossed my mind—it was cute, but I couldn't imagine us living there. And I didn't want to move.

But I couldn't imagine Nick living here, either. What did that say about me?

Sitting here thinking about it wasn't going to help. I called Andrea. That's what best friends are for.

She wasn't in. I didn't leave a message.

Instead I went back inside, wandered into the spare room.

Looked at the canvas I'd barely started right after the show. And hadn't touched since. The painting stared back at me. Waiting. I couldn't get up any interest in that either.

Something else was niggling at me. It wasn't just the case. Or Nick's wanting us to live together. Or that I wasn't painting.

I had an uneasy feeling I'd missed something. But what?

Annoyed with myself, I went back to the kitchen, dumped my half-cup of cooling coffee and poured a fresh one. As I reached for the milk, I saw the covered—and half-full—can of tuna that had been shoved to the back of the fridge.

That's when it hit me. I hadn't seen Cat for at least a week. Which wasn't like him.

And I'd been too busy to notice. Had something happened to the little guy?

Okay, he's more of a big lug than a little guy. But for a cat, he's good people. Even if he is annoying.

And the idea of something happening to him…

———

LEAVING the coffee on the counter, I double-timed it down the stairs to the apartment just over from mine, but two floors down. The one with the huge fir tree right beside the balcony. Mrs. Pinkton's place.

And Cat's home when he wasn't busy mooching off me.

I knocked. And held my breath. For long moments there was nothing.

Maybe Mrs. Pinkton and Cat had moved?

Finally there was a shuffling sound and I could hear the chain being taken off. The door opened a crack, then wider. My neighbor stood there in a ratty bathrobe.

The last time I'd come down to talk to her was more than a year ago, when I'd finally figured out where Cat belonged. That time, he'd come darting out into the hall to investigate the minute the door was opened. This time, there was no sign of him.

Mrs. Pinkton had lost weight since last time I saw her, and she was paler. And she stooped more than she had. She had to be in her late eighties, but a year ago, I'd been impressed by her energy and her indomitable spirit.

Now she just looked tired.

"Mrs. Pinkton? Are you all right?"

"Not really," she said. "I had a fall a while ago. Not a bad one, but my leg isn't as strong as it was. It's harder to get around."

I felt awful. I lived just upstairs, and I'd had no idea. "Can I help? I could pick up groceries for you?"

"Oh, that's sweet of you. But I just get them delivered."

Of course she did. She didn't let much stop her. "Well, if there's anything I could help you with…?" I said, feeling awkward.

I couldn't just ask about Cat, not when there was no sign of him. And she hadn't mentioned him. What if he'd been hit by a car, and hadn't made it?

I should have given Mrs. Pinkton credit for reading people better than that. She looked hard at me. "Actually, there is something you could help with. Why don't you come in and have a cup of tea."

I agreed immediately, with only a twinge of regret at the thought of that cup of strong, rich coffee sitting waiting for me upstairs. But I know better than to ever turn down an offer of tea. No matter how weak that tea is likely to be.

It isn't the tea that's being offered, it's hospitality, and the ritual of guest and host. It's a ritual that makes talking—and asking the hard questions—easier for both parties. My mother taught me that.

Even though I've never understood her love for the actual taste of the stuff.

Mrs. Pinkton's apartment was quiet and smelled just a little stale. None of the windows were open, and the bedroom and bathroom doors were closed. She waved me into the living room, and vanished into the walk-through kitchen that was the duplicate of mine. Presumably to make the tea.

There was no sign of Cat anywhere.

When the tea was ready, I carried it to the oval wooden dining table and put the tray down on the green place mat in the center of the table. Mrs. Pinkton quickly set the cups, saucers and spoons where they belonged, set the creamer and sugar bowl within easy reach, and poured the tea.

A clear golden brown, the tea had been steeped just long enough. And it wasn't bad. For tea.

When both our cups were properly doctored, she set down her teaspoon. "You'll have been wondering why you hadn't seen Buttercup lately," she said.

Buttercup being the name she'd given a tiny scrap of a kitten. He's now a seventeen pound monster cat. I can't even think of him as Buttercup and keep a straight face. Which is why I still call him Cat.

I just nodded. Physical ailments or no, she was still sharp as a tack.

"He'd gotten too much for me," she said, her face sad. "He's too heavy to pick up, and I can't bend down properly any more. So I was keeping him inside. And when someone came to the door, I had to shut him in the bathroom. It was hard on both of us."

So she'd given Cat away?

"Now my children want me to move to somewhere that there's care available. If I need it. Which I don't."

"I can see that." But I could also see that she might need a little assistance now. And how hard it must be for her to admit that.

"It's a nice place. The one I'll be moving to," she said, as if trying to convince herself. "And I can take most of my things. But they don't allow cats. So Buttercup will need a new home."

So Cat was still here? Where?—stuck in the bathroom? That didn't seem fair.

Then it hit me what she was going to ask. She wanted me to take him.

Me? A cat owner? No. Just no.

The occasional feeding was fine, but my life was too crazy to fit another living being into it.

Sure, I'd gotten used to having Cat around. And I missed him when he wasn't there—even if it had taken me a week to notice. But I lived alone. And I liked it that way.

"You know what a wonderful cat he is," she said. She tried to keep her tone brisk and matter-of-fact, but her voice broke just a little. "But I can't keep him."

Here it came. I braced myself.

"You'd be the perfect person to find him a new home. He deserves that. Someone who can take care of him, and give him what he needs."

She wasn't asking me to take him. I was getting off easy.

And how hard could it be to find him a good home, after all? Even if he was a large, demanding and annoying cat.

Then Mrs. P's hard-won composure broke and she dabbed at her eyes.

"Don't worry," I said quickly. "I'll take him. Buttercup can come and live with me."

Wait, what?

CHAPTER TWENTY-FOUR

I opened a new can of tuna for Cat, and made a fresh pot of coffee for myself. To wash away the taste of the tea.

Cat devoured the tuna like he hadn't eaten in days, then looked back at me for more. I gave it to him. "This time only," I told him.

He ate the second helping. But he didn't purr.

He did follow me into the living room. Then he sat by the sliding doors, looking out. He turned to stare at me, then back at the sliding door, then back at me. He didn't understand why I'd carried him up two flights of stairs from Mrs. P's place to mine—and hadn't that been a treat—or why he couldn't go out on the balcony, the way he was used to doing.

Did he know he'd lost his person, that Mrs. Pinkton couldn't look after him any more? How did you explain that to a cat?

And how was I going to explain adopting Cat to Nick?

I could hear it now. "Nick, I just can't see myself living with you. Too much change. So I adopted a cat instead. So if we ever do live together, you get both of us—me and the cat."

Yeah, that would go over well.

Cat was still staring from the windows to me. Waiting. What was I supposed to do now?

I slid the sliding doors open a little—enough for fresh air, not enough for him to get out.

Cat stared at me, and fished a paw through the opening. Was he trying to push the door open?

"Sorry, Cat. Not today," I said, and locked the slider in place.

The phone rang. The team?

I dashed for the kitchen, where I'd left the phone. Glanced at the display. Andrea's number.

Not the call I'd been hoping for. But maybe the person I needed to talk to.

"Barbara?" Andrea said. "Is something wrong?"

"How did you know?" We've been best friends for a long time, but I didn't think we'd got to the mind-reading stage. Or maybe I'd just missed it.

"You called?"

"Oh. Right." I'd forgotten that. I guess I was more distracted than I'd realized. "But I didn't leave a message."

"You didn't need to. What's up?"

"I think I blew it," I told her.

"You told Nick you can't live with him, didn't you?" Andrea said.

"I haven't told him anything yet," I said. "That's the problem. Well, part of the problem."

"I don't know how you could keep a man who's so perfect for you dangling like this," Andrea said. She was annoyed with me, I could hear it in her voice. "So what is the problem?"

This was not going to go well.

"I've taken on a roommate," I said. Deciding I might as well get it all out there. She was going to laugh at me, no matter what I said.

"You won't live with Nick, and you've taken on a roommate? Oh, Barbara. How could you? You're going to lose him, you know that, right?"

"That's what I'm afraid of," I said. "But when I say roommate, I mean…"

But Andrea wasn't listening. "It's like your life was too perfect, and you can't handle it. You have the best relationship I've ever seen you in. Your business is flourishing. You've just finished holding a one-woman show at the Courtland Gallery, which has been your dream for as long as I've known you. And it's all too much for you. You're trying to kill that dream."

Where had this come from? "But…"

"I'll bet you haven't even picked up a paintbrush since your show. Have you?"

I'd picked one up, but I hadn't done any real work with it. But she was wrong about the rest of it. "Andrea…"

"And I don't get why you're treating Nick like this." She was in full rant now. It doesn't happen often, but she can be a terror when she gets going.

"But…"

"And now you've taken on a roommate. Instead of Nick. Which makes no sense. And you won't even have space to paint. You're going to lose everything, Barb."

Way to hit all the pain buttons, Andrea. I did not need this. "About that roommate…"

She wasn't hearing me. "I can't stand watching it. Not again. You finally got everything working after the damage that Jayson did…"

Oh boy. Andrea hasn't mentioned Jayson Ho, my last live-in—from five years ago—since she figured out I was serious about Nick. Time to derail this train. "Andrea!"

There was a tiny silence. She knows that tone in my voice as well as I know the tones in hers. "What?"

"I've adopted Cat. He's my new roommate."

There was a longer silence. I noticed that Cat had followed me, and was sitting with his tail curled around him, staring at me. How much do cats understand, anyway?

"Cat? You've adopted a cat?" Andrea finally said.

She sounded stunned. Here it comes. "Not a cat. Cat. You know, the big orange striped tom…"

Andrea didn't let me finish. "You mean the twenty pound

orange monster that scams you for tuna every time you see him? Who gets in and out of your apartment at will, and you still don't know how? That cat?"

"Yeah."

She started to laugh.

It figured.

"Maybe there's hope for you yet," she managed to choke out through gusts of laughter.

"Thanks a lot."

"But… how did this happen? And when?"

"About half an hour ago," I said. And explained my current dilemma.

"So what does Nick think about this?" she asked.

"I haven't told him yet. That's why I called you," I said.

Which set her off again.

Great. Clearly Andrea wasn't going to be much help. She was enjoying this way too much.

I was just going to have to call Nick and get it over with.

———

NICK ANSWERED on the first ring, which was unusual. Usually we end up trading messages for a while. I'd been counting on that delay—mostly to figure out what to say—so his voice took my by surprise.

"Uh, Nick…? It's Barbara."

There was a small silence on the other end of the phone. Then Nick's warm voice. With a cautious note that I didn't often hear. "I'm guessing you're not calling about the photo of that cottage-style house I sent you. And I'm not going to like what you're going to say, am I?"

How to answer that? "Um, probably not."

"Then we need to have this conversation in person. Where are you?"

"Home."

With Cat still staring at me. Though after my conversation with Andrea, he'd started purring. "But I have stuff…"

Nick wasn't listening. Or didn't want to listen? "I can grab a few hours," he said. "Why don't I come over. We can go for a walk somewhere. Spanish Banks? We'll get more privacy there than anywhere else today."

Spanish Banks was too tied up in this stupid case right now. And for some reason I didn't want to leave Cat on his own. Not now, when he'd just lost Mrs. Pinkton.

But I'd explain when Nick got here. "Okay."

CHAPTER TWENTY-FIVE

I met Nick at the door with a kiss and a cup of coffee. But I was still thinking too hard about exactly what to tell him. And he—I wasn't sure what Nick was expecting. But I don't think we'd been this awkward with each other on our first date, let alone since.

I grabbed my own coffee and silently led the way into the living room, still trying to find the right words.

But Nick hasn't been promoted so often because he misses things.

He spotted Cat sitting by the sliding door, staring out. "Cat looks like he wants out. Want me to open the door wider?"

"No, he has to stay in," I said before he could reach for the door.

Nick stopped and stared at me. "Why?"

Great, now he and Cat were both staring at me.

"Ummm…" I said. Not the words I was looking for.

"This is what's upsetting you today? Has something happened to your neighbor?"

I nodded. Still no words. "She fell."

"So you're looking after Cat until she's better."

"Not exactly." I was still having trouble finding the right words. Which wasn't like me at all.

He grabbed my hand, dragged me to the sofa. "Barbara, sit. Have some coffee. Then just tell me. Whatever it is, it can't be that bad. I'll help you."

I felt worse than ever. "Well, actually… I adopted Cat."

"Good for you."

Whatever I'd expected to hear, it wasn't that. "What?"

"Cat obviously needed a home. He already likes you, and you like him. So you gave him a home. It sounds like a pretty good deal to me."

"You don't mind?"

He gave me a funny look. "Mind what?" he said. Like he really didn't see a problem.

"You want us to live together. And I just can't. Not right now." I'd finally found the words. "I don't know why. And now I've taken on Cat…"

"Given him a home," Nick put in softly.

"…So I can commit to him. But not to you. What does that say about me?" I got the words out, all right. And I felt like an idiot.

He took my mug, put it down, and held my hand in his. "I wouldn't have expected anything else."

"What?" Great. I was back to having no words again.

"Barbara, you have a huge heart. Cat needed a home—so you gave him one." He grinned at me. "Besides, it gives me hope."

"How?"

"You took him in. Once you get used to the idea and see how well that works, I'm hoping you'll take me in too." And he picked up my hand and kissed it.

I was still staring at him when Cat jumped into my lap and started purring. He'd never done that before.

Apparently both the males in my life approved of this new move.

Even if it did send Andrea into hysterics.

———

QUITE A WHILE LATER, after Nick and I had both showered and dressed again, I made sandwiches and put on a fresh pot of coffee—since we'd both skipped lunch. Apparently Nick really did approve of my adopting Cat—he'd proceeded to demonstrate how much.

I really approved of his demonstration.

From the dining room, I could see Cat curled up in the comfy chair in the corner, dozing. He'd never done that before, either.

Had he figured out that this was his home now? How smart were cats, anyway?

"So what did you think of the last picture I sent you?" Nick asked. He'd just polished off the roast beef sandwich I'd made him and was sitting back with a cup of coffee, looking satisfied with his world.

I'd been feeling pretty good about my world, too.

Right up until he asked his question. I'd been hoping the "moving in together" conversation had been put on hold. At least for now.

And I refused to deal with any more drama. "It looked nice," I said.

"Nice isn't very enthusiastic."

"I can be enthusiastic about other things," I said with a sly look.

He grinned. "I know. Why do you think I want to live together so badly?"

"I was hoping it was my sparkling personality."

"Sparkling?"

"Now you sound like Andrea."

That made him laugh. "Look—I want us to move in together. But for now, just for fun, we could just look at a couple places…"

He glanced at me, grinned and added, "Real places, not virtual ones."

He was still leaning back in his chair, coffee cup in hand, but his eyes were fixed on mine.

"You call that fun?"

"You don't?" He got up, cleared our empty plates and poured us both some more coffee. "This doesn't have to be some big deal."

Nick was a keeper.

And maybe this would help me figure out why the idea of moving in together was freaking me out. "Like we'd ever have the time. Given our schedules."

"Point. But we're both free for the next hour or so. And that cottage isn't far from here."

As if on cue, a phone rang. We both grabbed for our phones.

"Mine," I said, glancing at it. Cory. "I'm sorry, I have to take this."

Nick nodded. He understood, bless him.

"Cory?" I said.

"We're still working on facial recognition from the recordings," my nephew said. "But Gainer was still in the hotel after he and Bittner quarreled. It looks like he went straight to the bar. Then he took the elevator back up at just after six."

So Gainer had probably talked to Bittner again. My gut had been right. Even if we still had no way to prove if he'd actually got off on Bittner's floor. "Do you have him leaving?"

"Just a glimpse of him in the lobby. At nine. It looks like he took the stairs down."

That was a lot of stairs. He'd taken the elevator down the first time. "Does the image show anything useful?"

"No."

Of course not. Gainer knew exactly where the cameras were. "Can you send me what you have?"

"Done," Cory said. "And we're still working on other images. Just in case."

"Thanks. Let me know what you find."

"Will do," and he hung up. He'd already be thinking about what he was working on next.

I looked up at Nick.

"Give me another moment here," I said, and clicked through to the recording Cory had sent. It was short, and he'd been avoiding the cameras, but it was definitely Gainer. So now what?

I was frowning at the screen, thinking fast, when Nick cleared his throat. I nearly jumped—I'd shut out everything but the case.

"I suspect this is the other thing that was worrying you," he said.

"Yes."

"And your possible suspect just became a lot more interesting? Hypothetically speaking, of course."

Sounds like Nick had figured out most of it, just from hearing my end of the conversation. Typical. There was a reason I was so attracted to him. And it wasn't his smile. Or his shoulders.

Well, not just those, anyway.

"Something like that," I said.

"Can I help?"

Maybe it would help to talk it out. Hypothetically, of course.

I filled Nick in on the hypothetical lover who was a hypothetical suspect. "But when I updated the team on what I'd learned since my conversation with the lover, I realized what I hadn't asked him. And the problem that posed."

Nick thought for a moment. "What if he came back later to continue the argument?"

"Yes. Hypothetically."

"I gather from your side of the conversation earlier that he did come back?"

"Well, he was still in the hotel. And he went back upstairs in the right timeframe, pushed the button for the right floor. Which is also the period when there was no recording for that floor."

"Which means you don't know whether or not he went back to the victim's room."

"Right."

"Or what might have happened there."

"Yeah."

"So how do you prove it, one way or another, when you can't ask the suspect?" he said.

"Exactly."

"Do you think he did it? Hypothetically."

"No," I said slowly, a little surprised. On a gut level, I sensed something was off about what Gainer was telling me. Or not telling me. But I didn't believe he'd killed David Bittner.

But I've been wrong before.

"I think whatever happened between them that second time might be the key to who did kill him," I said.

"Hypothetically," Nick said with a grin, still watching my face.

I nodded, still thinking hard. "I need to know more about their relationship. And the victim's lover did tell me they went to Vegas in the spring—somehow it sounded like a turning point."

"In their relationship?"

In Bittner's gambling problems. But maybe something in the relationship had been the trigger?

"Maybe," I said, still trying to pinpoint what I'd heard in Gainer's voice when he talked about that trip.

"Let me guess," he said. "You're heading for Vegas."

He sounded resigned. What was that about?

"No," I said, thinking out loud. "Even if Vegas was a turning point, Bittner wasn't killed in Vegas. Whatever lead up to that turning point, whatever happened after it—they all happened here."

"It still sounds like you need to go to Vegas," Nick said.

"Playing devil's advocate now?"

He grinned. "Maybe. But if you're not going right away, how about that cottage showing?"

My face must have given me away.

"I know. You need to get back to the office."

"Yup. We're finally getting some momentum on the investigation. I hope, anyway. I don't want to lose it."

Nick got it. I knew he would. His job was no different.

And then his phone rang. From his face as he answered it, I knew he wasn't going to be looking at the cottage, either.

CHAPTER TWENTY-SIX

Marie, Cory and Badger were all still in the office when I got in. I hadn't expected it.

"You guys know it's a Saturday, right?" I said.

No response. They were all clustered around Cory's desk, staring at the big monitor he'd plugged into his laptop. Monitor? Now where had that come from?

Probably Marie had been abusing the office credit cards again. I could hardly complain, since we clearly needed it. Rolling my eyes, I moved around behind them so I could see the screen too.

They were watching a digital feed from one of the cameras. Make that several cameras. We were looking at a group of people heading down a hallway, getting more and more distant from the camera. The date stamp told me it was the night Bittner had been killed, and that this was camera one on the second floor.

Then there was a tiny jerk on the screen, and we were watching the same group coming towards the camera, and boarding the elevator. Camera two, still on the second floor.

Another tiny jerk, and we were watching a smaller group get off on the seventh floor and walking down the hall. A couple stopped at what was presumably their suite, and went in. Another man did the same further down the hall.

A tiny jerk, and another camera picked the three remaining members of the original group. Two of them disappeared into the stairway. The third used a key to disappear into a room at the far end of the hall.

Another jerk, and a stairway door opened. What appeared to be the same two, a man and a woman, emerged on the sixteenth floor. One floor above Bittner.

Camera two picked up the pair—it was obvious now these were the same two who had taken the stairs on the seventh floor. Equally obviously, they weren't a couple. They walked with a small space between them, their steps measured, their posture alert.

Both of them had dark hair. The woman's longer hair was pulled back in high ponytail. Both were wearing dark, form-fitting athletic gear, as if they'd just come from the gym—which was on the second floor, so it was plausible. They also carried small gym bags, the kind that looked like they'd pack easily.

And would hide a gun just as easily.

We watched as the two of them passed what would have been Bittner's room if they'd been on his floor. Neither of them glanced at it, or paused. Why were we watching this?

Which was just my own frustration talking. I didn't say the words aloud. From the intent looks on the others' faces, this wasn't the first time they'd watched this sequence. And they were looking for something specific.

On the screen, the two we seemed to be following kept walking. They turned a corner, and were picked up by camera three as they walked at a steady pace down that hallway. Then camera four picked them up. And I watched as the two of them disappeared through the door to the stairs again.

What? They climbed from seven to sixteen—nine flights of stairs, only to take another set of stairs? "You think they're going down to Bittner's suite?" I said

"That's our guess," Cory said, freezing the screen for a moment.

I glanced at the time. Ten after six. Well within the range for Bittner's time of death.

"But without the cameras on fifteen, we can't prove anything," Cory added.

"If they didn't go to fifteen, they'd show up on camera on another floor," I said. "Do they?"

"No," he said.

"So the odds are they were headed for Bittner's floor," Marie said.

Then Cory hit some combination of keys, and the whole thing started over again.

This time, I moved so I could see my team's faces instead of the screen. There was no mistaking the intensity with which the three of them were examining every detail of the screen. Whatever they were looking for, it still wasn't obvious to me.

Then, as the screen switched from camera one to camera two on the second floor, Marie said, "There!"

Cory stopped the recording instantly.

"Good eye," Badger said as we all stared at the screen. It was probably the clearest shot of the two faces in the whole sequence.

"Can you enlarge it?" Marie asked.

Cory and Badger exchanged glances, and Cory's fingers flew. The faces on the screen enlarged and enlarged again, until finally they grew fuzzy. Cory backed it off, until the faces were as large and as clear as they were going to get.

Whoever they were, they'd known where the cameras were, so neither image was full-face.

"How did you find these two?" I said.

"It wasn't easy," Marie said. "We were looking at people who took the stairs during the time the cameras were out on the fifteenth floor. You'd be surprised how many people did that in two hours. Most of them just went up or down a couple of flights. Not like these two."

"Who are they?"

"No idea," Cory said. "This is the best shot of them we've found, but..."

"You have to know where to start," I said. "They look like they might have some military or martial arts training."

"Now that we've isolated the images, I'll see if I can match them," Badger said. "But with a search this generic, it could take a long time."

"Do you have footage of them leaving the building?" I asked.

Cory shook his head. "That's the weird part. According to everything we've found, they never did leave. Or at least not that night."

It figured. "Maybe they're guests with a really weird exercise routine that includes lots of stair climbing," I said with a straight face.

Marie laughed. Cory and Badger just looked at me. Not everyone appreciates my sense of humor.

"They could be guests," Marie said, leaning forward. "And stayed in the hotel that night."

"But they'd have to be staying on fifteen, or the cameras would have caught them leaving," Cory said. "And if they killed Bittner, sticking around afterwards is pretty dangerous, isn't it?"

"It is," I said. "What if they have very effective disguises in those bags of theirs? Would the software still recognize them?"

"No," Badger said. "There's stuff out there that would, but it's harder to get hold of. This program would be fooled by anything that would distort the cheekbones."

"Like putty inside their cheeks?" Cory said. "We tried some of that stuff in drama class once. It can make a big difference."

"Something like that," Badger said with a nod.

Cory looked pleased.

I was impressed that Badger hadn't made Cory feel bad about his—literally—high school analogy. It would have been easy to do.

But it seemed we were at a dead end with these these two possible killers unless Badger could find a way to identify them.

"Can you send a copy of that image to me as well," I said. "There are a few people I want to have a look at it."

Including Aiden Keller from Interpol. Whoever those two were, they could be local. But you never knew…

Cory nodded, and his fingers flew. "You'll have it now."

I checked my phone, nodded. "Thanks. So do you have a similar segment showing what Michael Gainer was up to after he left Bittner's room the first time?"

Cory nodded, and his fingers flew. While he brought the segment up on the big screen, I sent off a quick email with a copy of the photo of the two in black to Keller, asking if he could match either face against known contract killers. It was worth a shot.

"Okay," I said as I turned my attention back to the screen. Cory pressed play and the segment started.

It was strange watching someone I'd met from this perspective. Gainer moved casually, seeming unaware of the cameras, but he managed to keep his face turned away most of the time.

"How did you track him?" I asked as I watched. "I wouldn't have thought there was enough detail for the software to find him."

"Gainer seemed to have the same thought," Cory said with a grin. "But Badger has a few tricks that can make that system fly."

Of course she did. I kept watching as the cameras switched from one to two to three, just as they'd done in the previous montage.

Gainer had taken the elevator on the first floor—the camera had just caught him coming out of the Library Bar, a cozy place I loved on rainy days for its dark wood and comfortable chairs—and moving down the hall to the elevators. He was wearing the same silky looking grey suit he'd had on earlier.

I still didn't think Gainer had killed Bittner, but it was too soon to discount anything.

There seemed nowhere for him to hide a gun without destroying the lines of that suit. But I'd seen enough really good suits over the course of my career to know they could be tailored to hide almost anything, if you could afford to pay for good tailoring. Gainer could. And did.

He got off on eleven, and took the stairs. Presumably he emerged on fifteen, as he'd done earlier in the evening. He was still being cautious about being seen.

Was this one of the steps he took to conceal his affairs? Or was this something more?

There was a perspective jump, and I watched Gainer stride out of the stairwell at the other end of the eleventh floor half an hour later—and take the elevator down. What had happened in that half hour?

Gainer got off the elevator on the main floor, and went back to the bar. During the whole segment, the only time we saw his face was when he first got on the elevator from the bar.

Wait a minute. "Do we have footage of him leaving the bar later?" I asked.

Badger and Cory exchanged glances. "That didn't show up in our scan," Badger said. "We'll have to widen it. It's going to take awhile."

"Not a problem," I said. "And while you're at it, can you add in the footage of Gainer from earlier?" I was playing a hunch.

"You mean when the cameras on fifteen were still working? That footage?"

"Yes, but can you also track his movements to and from that visit? Just like you've done here."

"You want to follow him from the moment he enters the hotel until he leaves it," Cory said. He looked excited.

I nodded, hoping it was the challenge of the search he found exciting. "Just don't forget a man is dead," I said.

"And we don't want our client in jail," he said.

Apparently he had his priorities clear. "Exactly."

Cory and Badger put their heads together and talked quickly, with some waving of hands from Cory. "We can do it," he said after a moment. "It'll take longer, though."

"No matter. I could use a coffee," I said.

"And I'll go for a donut run," Marie said.

More donuts? I probably should have said no, but at the moment, donuts sounded about right. "Thanks," I said. "Just charge the office."

"I always do," she said with a cheeky grin.

She probably meant it. Which probably meant I should worry.

I didn't have the emotional energy left. Besides, I had a sneaking suspicion that she'd heard that particular lecture once too often. And this was her revenge.

Two could play at that game. "Get a couple of dozen while you're at it," I said. "Or maybe just order in."

"Pizza?" Cory said hopefully, looking up from whatever Badger was doing on the screen. She'd taken over the keyboard, and her fingers were flying with incomprehensible commands.

"Pizza it is," Marie said, looking smug. "I'll just whip down to that new place down the block."

The expensive new place. I'd heard about them. Their pizza was supposed to be amazing, as were their prices. Whatever game Marie and I were playing, she'd just won this round.

CHAPTER TWENTY-SEVEN

Marie had just returned with two boxes that smelled heavenly, and the three of us had gone through a full pot of coffee while Cory and Badger worked their magic, and I cleared some overdue paperwork off my desk.

"We've got it," Cory finally said, looking up from the screen.

"Perfect timing," I said. "More coffee, anyone?"

With a fresh cup in hand, I was ready to solve this case. Okay, so that was an exaggeration. I had my second wind, anyway. I'd take it.

We all grabbed pizza slices and napkins, then clustered around the monitor again, as Badger set the new recording running.

We watched Gainer come through the front doors at four thirty-eight, then take the elevator to the twelfth floor. He disappeared into the stairwell at the far end of the hall, the recording jumped, and I watched him emerge from the stairwell on fifteen.

"So taking the stairs and avoiding cameras was standard behavior for him," I said.

"The guy likes intrigue," Marie said. "So what are we looking for?"

"Just watch for any details that stand out for you," I said.

The power of suggestion can be an issue when it comes to subtle evidence. I didn't want to poison their judgement.

We watched in silence as cameras and camera angles switched from one to the next. Gainer went into 1517, then came out at five after five and took the stairs down. When he emerged from the stairwell on the main floor, he wasn't making much effort to avoid the camera.

We watched as he made his way to the Library Bar. An hour and a half later by the time stamp, Gainer came out of the bar and the segment we'd seen earlier played. He took the elevator to eleven, then the stairs, and disappeared from all cameras for half an hour.

Then he reappeared out of the stairwell on eleven and took the elevator back down to the bar.

Cory stopped the action for a moment. "Gainer has to have gone to Bittner's floor when he vanished then," he said. "It's the only place in the entire complex he could access via that stairwell that didn't have working cameras during that half hour."

"Good catch," Badger said.

And it might even be admissible in court, if needed. Though I'd have to have Marchant officially request the security footage from the hotel first.

Cory beamed, then restarted the recording.

This time, Gainer didn't come out of the bar again for two hours. Then various cameras followed him out to the street. After two fairly short meetings with Bittner, Gainer had spent most of his evening in that bar.

"I hope he took a cab," Cory said. "He's not walking quite straight this time. But I didn't see anything else."

"That didn't tell us much," Marie said.

I wasn't sure if I'd actually seen something or not. "Maybe it did. Play it again," I said.

Without comment, Cory did so.

"Watch how he moves," I said to them. What I was actually watching was the lines of his suit. It hung just a fraction differently in the second montage. Or was that just a trick of the light?

"His jacket hangs differently after he comes out of the bar the first time," Badger said.

"It does?" Cory said.

"I didn't notice that," Marie said. "But he's been drinking pretty hard. Look how he's walking—like he's deliberately placing his feet with every step."

I hadn't picked up on that. "Play it again."

We all watched it again. And again.

"He's carrying something the second time that he didn't have the first," Cory said. "And I think he's pretty drunk."

"Maybe the bartender can tell us how much he'd had that night?" Marie said.

Badger disconnected the big screen, then her fingers flew over her laptop. "He had three double scotches after the first time he visited Bittner," she said after a moment. "And the second time he's in the bar, he has another three doubles. That could hit him pretty hard."

There was no doubting the certainty in her voice. The hotel must have an automated inventory system linked to their point of sale records.

"He has to be a pretty hard drinker if he could drink that much in that short a period, and show it so little," Badger added.

Apparently Bittner wasn't the only one with problems. Which made sense. It's human nature to feel most comfortable with others who share our weaknesses. No wonder Gainer had ignored Bittner's issues for so long.

I wondered again what had happened in Vegas that had forced him to recognize Bittner's gambling problems.

"So what's he carrying?" Marie said. "It can't be heavy enough to be a gun, can it?"

"It's possible," I said. "He wears very well-cut suits. Those can hide quite a lot. And he's a criminal lawyer, who's spent years dealing with nasty clients. I'm wondering if he might have a carry permit."

And I knew just the person to ask about it, too.

"I'm wondering why he changed his shoes," Badger said. "And where?"

His shoes? Cory, Marie and I exchanged glances, and small head shakes. None of us had noticed his shoes.

"Run it again, please," I said.

She did.

This time we all stared at his feet. And Badger was right. In the first segments Gainer was wearing typical high-end business shoes —black, of course. When he left the bar at the end of the evening, he was wearing some type of black athletic shoe, cut to look like a business shoe at a casual glance. And you had to look really hard to spot it on a recording taken from above.

"How did he do that?" Marie asked. "Change his shoes like that?"

"And why?" Cory added

Good question. And I was going to find an answer. Fast. I still didn't think Gainer was our killer. But I've been wrong before.

"I don't suppose they have security cameras in their gym," I said.

"They do," Badger said. "Just not in the locker rooms."

That made sense. "Can you check and see if Gainer shows up…"

"He doesn't. I checked," Badger said.

Right. "Can you run it one more time before I pay a visit to the hotel?" I said.

Cory rolled his eyes. Badger looked amused.

This time the re-run showed us nothing new.

"Good work, all. Now go home," I said. "I'll ask a few questions and I'll see you all on Monday."

Cory seemed about to protest, but a look from Badger silenced him. "See you Monday," Marie said with a sly smile, and herded him out the door.

That smile had me worried until Badger glanced over at me. "We need to talk," she said softly.

Her expression drove everything else out of my mind.

CHAPTER TWENTY-EIGHT

Badger didn't say another word until the door had closed behind Marie and Cory. Then she waited another few moments, a slight frown wrinkled between her brows. Thinking? Listening?

Come to think of it, I wouldn't put it past Marie to be listening with her ear pressed against the door. One thing I'd learned in spades about my assistant—she hated to be left out of anything.

Apparently Badger had reached the same conclusion, and even faster than I had. She walked to the office door, opened it swiftly, and checked the hallway. I thought she was satisfied as she closed the door behind her. But no.

She went straight to the closet, and the hidden door to the adjoining suite. And how had she known about that?

Only after she'd made sure that was empty as well did she rejoin me.

I wasn't sure if it was her hacking skills that fed a caution that verged on paranoia, or the reverse. But either way that near-paranoia was a part of what made Badger, Badger.

"So?" I said as she sat back down at the table opposite me.

"A couple of things. I dug further into the Courtland Gallery's sales records."

Good. "And? Should Margaret be worried?"

"Probably not. Last time I checked, stupidity isn't illegal."

Stupidity. What? "So she's not being paid with dirty money?"

"No," Badger said. "By the time it gets to her, it's clean. Probably drug money originally, but these guys have made a point of making sure their transactions for art they're buying—and they're buying quite a bit of it—are all above board."

"So why are they buying so much art? And where does the stupidity come in?"

One side of Badger's mouth quirked up. "Same answer to both questions. These guys have figured out that some of the big international players use art as a kind of alternate currency to settle debts amongst themselves. Usually in those cases it's stolen art, and the paintings are by major artists, but that doesn't seem to have occurred to these idiots."

"So what are these guys using it for?"

"They seem to be using it the same way themselves, and as another form of investing. Kind of a portable bank account. But I gather none of them know anything about art."

"Then how are they valuing their purchases?" I asked, partly offended and partly intrigued.

Her smile widened. "They're going by whatever they paid the dealer for the piece."

"Which is what's driving up the prices on local art," I said. "Creating a kind of bubble."

She nodded. "Supply and demand. If they stop buying for some reason, then demand dries up…"

"And prices drop. And once they realize their portable bank accounts"—I cringed at the phrase, but it was apt—"have suddenly dropped in value…"

"They'll stop buying," she finished for me. "Margaret Courtland was right to worry. This won't continue. She seems like a pretty astute businesswoman. A good choice to handle your works."

My paintings. I hadn't thought about what this might mean for their value—and my artistic career.

What I was thinking must have shown on my face, because Badger actually patted my shoulder. "None of your paintings are affected. Everything was sold at the opening, and none of these guys"—her tone was beautifully dismissive—"were even invited."

It was a relief. Which I hadn't expected—given I'd been doubting I even wanted an artistic career ever since the show.

I tucked that thought away for later examination.

"Thanks, Badger," I said. "That's good work. I'll let Margaret know. She'll know what safeguards to put in place to protect her business."

Badger nodded. Leaned forward a little.

Uh oh.

"Bittner's death," she said. "And that couple in black. Something wrong there."

I wasn't too happy about them myself. At a glance they probably looked ordinary enough, but watching them on that video…

There was something in the way those two had walked—with a kind of focused intent, every muscle ready for action. They seemed out of place in a hotel hallway. They'd looked like the kind of people someone would send in to take care of a mess.

Like Bittner? Had he been killed because of his gambling, and not because of Justine's problems?

"We need to find out who those two are," I said. "And who they work for."

"With the quality of the images we have, it won't be easy," Badger said.

I knew that. "That's why I asked for copies. I have a few people I can send them to. Maybe between your searches and theirs, we'll get a lead. And we need a break on this case."

"Bittner's debts," Badger said.

"What about them?"

"They might be the break we need," she said. "As far as I can tell, Bittner's debt spiral seems to have been triggered by a trip he took to Vegas last spring."

"In March?"

"Yes."

The trip Gainer and Bittner had taken together. Gainer had said that was when he'd realized Bittner had a real problem. Had Bittner just hidden his addiction better before that trip? Or had something on that trip made it worse?

Maybe being in Vegas? Or trouble in their relationship?

"So what happened?" I asked her.

"From what I've found out so far, Bittner went on a major losing streak. He got in way too deep and maxed out his credit limits at three casinos—ended up cut off by all of them."

Cut off in Vegas? Not an easy thing to achieve. How much money had he lost, anyway?

"So then what happened?" I asked.

"He was back gambling at all three places the next day."

"What? How?"

She made a face. "I don't know."

"No money trail?"

She shook her head. "He must have re-established his credit, though. That money came from somewhere. Substantial amounts of it, too. And it wasn't from gambling."

"But Bittner still kept losing?" I guessed.

"Yeah."

"How bad?"

"Good question. But it was after he got back from Vegas that he took out the second mortgage on his condo. Then the third one a few months later. And that third mortgage looks shady—bad terms and terrible rates."

"Wait a minute. *After* he got back?" I said. How had that worked? And what lender had been stupid enough to allow it?

Although if Bittner had bought his condo long enough ago, Vancouver's astronomical rise in prices in the last dozen years would mean he was sitting on a lot of equity. But still, with his existing debts...

"There's a missing piece, somewhere," I said slowly, thinking it through. "By the time he died, Bittner's debt was out of control. I'd been assuming his debt had escalated over time, as his gambling problems grew worse. But you're saying the Vegas trip triggered it?"

She nodded. "He had a fair bit of debt before. And he used three of his fake identities to juggle money around. But he was making his payments on time. All of them. And he had more than a million dollars in equity in his condo."

"Wow," I said. "So how exactly how bad were Bittner's debts before he left for Vegas? And how much of it came after that trip?"

"I'll send you the details," she said. "I need to do a bit more digging."

"Thanks," I said. I was still thinking about Bittner being cut off by three casinos one day, and gambling again the next.

"After he got cut off," I said. "If he'd been using the equity in his condo as collateral with the casinos—he couldn't have remortgaged that fast. So he got money from somewhere else."

"And overnight, too," Badger said.

I nodded, still thinking hard. "How much would Bittner have needed to pay off the his accounts at those three casinos so he could keep gambling the next day?"

"A lot," Badger said. "More than half a million dollars."

"So where did it come from?" And what had Bittner done to get it?

"I don't know," she said. "I haven't been able to track that, either. If that money was a loan, it was a well-hidden one."

Badger hadn't been able to track it? Someone was good at hiding information. Really good.

And a windfall that big? That was interesting in itself. Any fool could see Bittner's debts were going to end in a downhill spiral, with him eventually unable to repay them.

Bittner was no fool, but he was a gambler with a problem. But what about whoever had given him that kind of cash? Why would they do so?

What did they have to gain?

It couldn't just be about the money. Not when Bittner was so obviously a bad risk at the time his half million dollar windfall had come through.

"Loan sharking?" I said, though I couldn't see why they'd bother. Something to do with the equity in his condo, maybe?

Badger raised a brow. "Possible. But it seems a pretty stupid way to go. He was clearly going to end up broke, and sooner rather than later. Plus he was on a losing streak, and in Vegas for another three days."

Exactly what I'd been thinking. "So who would give him the money? And why?"

She made a face. "I still can't answer that."

I'd never seen Badger frustrated before.

"There has to be a reason," I said. "But first we need to find out who these people are. Have you any leads at all on where the money came from?"

"No. There must be records somewhere, but I can't access them."

Given Badger's skills, that was saying something. "Maybe these records are kept on paper."

She gave me an annoyed look. "Who keeps paper records these days?"

"Someone who doesn't want you to track them?" I said with a grin.

For a moment Badger just looked at me. I could almost hear her thoughts whizzing by, she was concentrating so hard.

Then she smiled. "You're right. And if I can't find them online, we'll have to do it the old-fashioned way. Which means you need to go to Vegas."

Wait, what?

The trouble was, she was right. And we both knew it.

———

ON MY WAY HOME, I was so busy planning what I needed to pack, I nearly forgot about inviting Nick back for dinner. And if that wasn't a bad sign, I don't know what was. Luckily I remembered in time to order in.

And the sight of him at my door with a bottle of wine had my heart melting. Maybe there was hope for us.

He grinned. "Hey, there."

"Hey, yourself."

"How was your meeting?"

"Good. But I have to go to Vegas. Tonight," I said.

"Hypothetically?" he said, with a comically hopeful look.

"I'm afraid not."

He sighed a melodramatic sigh. "You think something happened when he was there?"

I do love a quick thinker. "That's it."

He nodded with that easy acceptance I was starting to accept. "How long will you be gone?"

"A couple of nights, probably. I don't know when we'll be able to fit in seeing the cottage house." Which was a relief. I'd had enough change for one month. Maybe for a year.

"Mrrrrt?"

We both looked at Cat, who was twining himself around my ankles. Uh oh. "And I'm going to need someone to feed him."

Nick burst out laughing. "You just figured that out?"

My mind was flipping through possibilities. Cory would probably do it for me. Or Andrea. Or…

"I'll look after him for you," Nick said with a twisted grin. "It'll be good practice."

Smart man. He didn't finish the thought so I couldn't challenge him on it.

What a prince. And for a change, I didn't mean it sarcastically. Maybe I'd get to keep him, after all.

And I felt like a fool when I realized I wasn't sure which him I was thinking about.

Maybe both of them.

CHAPTER TWENTY-NINE

Somehow luck had been with me, and I caught a last minute cancellation on an evening flight to Vegas. Even at that hour, I spent longer in the interminable lineups and the departure lounge at the airport than I did on the flight.

But at least it gave me time to nail down a few things. I sent a detailed email to Marie and a quick update to Margaret Courtland. I also had time for a long chat with Chelsea.

As my shuttle bus scuttled along the strip, I drank in the lights flashing and glittering everywhere—each one trying to outdo the next. "Look at me. Look at me."

I can never decide if I love or hate this city. Maybe a bit of both. It's such an addictive town on every level. Sights, sounds, smells, tastes—everything is designed to mesmerize. The entire place is set on stun.

I can't even choose just one phrase to describe it all—just think of every cliché you've ever heard. Lights. Glamor. Sex. Sin. That's Vegas.

And behind it all, money. Rivers and rivers of money. If you have enough of it when you get there, you own the town. Or they make you think you do.

What effect had this place had on David Bittner?

My brain was buzzing with a heady mixture of exhaustion and the adrenaline rush that is Vegas. Running through my head was the well-worn slogan, "What happens in Vegas, stays in Vegas."

Only in this case, it hadn't. Everything Badger had learned about Bittner's downhill slide pointed straight here. And my conversation with Gainer suggested the same thing—their relationship troubles as well as Bittner's money problems had escalated after their trip here in the spring.

Whatever had started in Vegas for David Bittner hadn't stayed here. And I was here to find out exactly what that had been.

———

I'D SCORED a last-minute booking at Paris Hotel and Casino— which I'd grabbed the second I saw it. I'm fond of the place, and it's pretty much in the center of the Strip.

I checked in, found my room. Then skimmed through my emails, zeroing in on the one Badger had sent me, with its three attached three data files.

The first file was a spreadsheet with the dates and amounts of Bittner's various loans. She'd even sorted it based on which of Bittner's various identities had taken out each loan.

The second was another spreadsheet showing the charges made on the Vegas trip against Bittner's various credit cards—all twenty-two of them. She'd sorted these in date order.

I spent some time reviewing the two files, and Badger had been right. Bittner had owed quite a bit of money before he went to Vegas last March. But it was in the week or so after his return that he'd completely buried himself in debt. Not before.

Shaking my head, I opened the third file Badger had sent. Through the magic of GPS, she'd provided me with the details of everywhere David Bittner had gone during the six days he'd spent here with Gainer.

I didn't ask any questions, just sent a quick text thanking her.

Then sat down at the desk and scanned through the list of where David Bittner had spent his time last March.

Apparently he'd spent a lot of his time right here at the Paris Hotel. Bonus.

Which was odd, because Gainer had booked himself "and guest" into the higher end Island Sun Casino and Resort. If Bittner was looking for big money gambling, that was the place to spend his time.

But he hadn't.

At least not to start with.

They'd arrived mid-day on a Sunday, and Gainer's conference ran Monday through Saturday. The first two days, Bittner had spent most of his days gambling at Paris and the linked Bally's casinos, eating in the multitude of restaurants and bars that the two establishments shared, a different one for each meal.

He seemed to have financed his gambling with whatever cash he'd had with him, and through cash advances on the five credit cards he held under one of his fake identities.

And while his five figure daily gambling tabs seemed exorbitant to me, my conversation with Chelsea told me they were pocket change to an addict like Bittner.

There was little or no spending on Bittner's cards on those two evenings—but he'd spent hours each night at Island Sun in various restaurants, presumably while he and Gainer were together. Probably Gainer had picked up the tab for their meals and entertainment as a business expense.

In the early hours of Tuesday morning, Bittner had cabbed it to the Paris casino and was gambling heavily. Every indication was that he was gambling alone. Had something gone wrong between the him and Gainer after dinner on Monday?

I suspected they'd had a blowout fight, and Bittner's gambling escalation reflected his stress and mental turmoil. In those circumstances, Vegas was the absolute worst place for him to be.

Because according to Badger's summary, he'd maxed out two of the credit cards he'd been using that night. Then he'd cabbed back to Island Sun and maxed out a third card. After which he set up a credit account with the casino.

He didn't use that account, though. Not then. Just went back to his and Gainer's room.

By mid-day Tuesday, Bittner was back at Paris, and spending more time eating than he was gambling. I wondered how much he'd drunk the night before.

Hangovers affect people differently. Some can't face even the smell of food. Others seem to use vast quantities of food to absorb and help burn off the alcohol. I was betting Bittner was the latter.

And maybe he was eating in an attempt to stay away from the poker and blackjack tables.

But Tuesday night was a repeat of the previous evening—dinner with Gainer, then gambling alone in the early hours, first at Paris, then at Island Sun. So much for togetherness.

Bittner was using advances on his credit card for gambling money again, though. He didn't draw on the casino credit he'd set up the previous night. Nor did he set up a credit account at Paris— he just drew heavily on two cards from a second identity.

Maybe juggling identities and credit card debt was how he'd managed his gambling sprees before he'd come to Vegas?

On Wednesday, Bittner spent an hour or so at Paris, but then broke his previous pattern. Mid-morning he showed up at Bellagio, opened a credit account with them—and started losing five figures. Then six figures. Until he exhausted that credit limit and they cut him off.

Then he took a cab down the Strip to the Wynn Casino, opened a credit account with them and kept gambling until he was cut off there, too.

By now it was early evening. Bittner took a cab back to the Island Sun, presumably in time for dinner with Gainer.

———

SOME HOURS AFTER DINNER, Bittner was back on the casino floor at Island Sun. Where he gambled until the very early hours of Thursday morning, until he'd used up his credit limit with them, too, and was cut off. Again.

He spent the next hour or so maxing out his cash advance limits on the five credit cards he had under his third identity. It must have been too little money to buy him out of his losing streak, though, because he didn't bother with any of his other credit cards.

Instead he spent the next three hours in the Russian Bar at the Island Sun. And no matter how drunk he was aiming to be, he couldn't have spent that much money on his own.

Someone—or more likely several someones, given the size of the bill—had to be with him, and he was buying rounds. Using his personal credit card.

It made no sense.

First off, spending that kind of money at a bar was totally out of character for Bittner. He didn't seem to drink much, and except for when he gambled, he was tight with his money.

Flights of high-end vodka presented in individual blocks of ice don't come cheap.

And Bittner didn't know anyone except Gainer in Vegas, as far as I knew. So who was he suddenly buying drinks for? And why?

Because later that same Thursday, after apparently catching a few hours of sleep in his and Gainer's hotel room, he was back gambling again, exactly as Badger had told me.

And there was nothing on Bittner's credit cards to account for it, and no draws against any of his bank accounts. But he spent hours on the casino floor in all three of the casinos that had cut him off the previous day—only in reverse order. He'd started at Island Sun. Then Wynn. Then Bellagio.

For a problem gambler like Bittner, spending that much time in casinos meant that he was gambling. Which he couldn't have done without paying off his previous debts and cleaning up his credit.

And he kept gambling, going from casino to casino in the same pattern for the next three days.

Wherever the money for Bittner's "windfall" had come from, it was hard not to assume it was from connections he'd made Wednesday night in the Russian Bar.

Which made the Russian Bar the logical place for me to start asking questions. Except I've learned the hard way on past cases that kind of assumption can lead an investigation astray.

So I'd be starting right where Bittner did, in the Paris casinos.

It's the questions you don't ask that cause the most problems. Especially the ones you didn't know enough to ask. Those are the ones that come back to bite you.

Just as I was about to head out to face the Vegas night life, I got a text from Nick. He'd attached two photos.

One was a selfie, which he'd titled "…and Cat". It showed Nick was reclining on my sofa, with a very contented Cat sprawled at his feet.

The second was a snap of the garden in back of the cottage he'd sent me that morning. He'd titled it "Cat's Jungle."

I had to laugh. Subtle Nick wasn't—but he went for humor every time. Gotta love that.

I sent him a photo of Vegas from my room and a virtual hug, then shut my phone off.

It was time to retrace Bittner's steps.

I left my carry-on beside the bed and headed out. Sleep could wait.

———

SEVERAL HOURS later I was questioning my strategy. Armed with a recent photo of Bittner that I'd got from Justine, I started with the servers at the Starry Nights restaurant. Bittner had eaten here several times, but no-one remembered him. Not surprising, after all this time.

I'd grabbed a quick—but very good—dinner at the buffet along the concourse that separated the Paris casino from the adjoining Bally. The meal was my reward for suffering through the flight, compounded by the meal the airline hadn't served.

Flying economy is a necessity in my business—at least at my level—but the actual experience seems to get worse every year. I swear the airlines are all playing a competitive game of "how many misguided souls can we cram in this time?"

I preferred casinos—the noise level wasn't much different, but it came with free drinks. And casinos are the world's best place to people watch.

After dinner, I headed straight for the Paris casino floor, which seemed to stretch the length of six football fields, and went looking for the blackjack tables. Bittner had been a poker player by choice, but from what Chelsea was able to tell me, he tended to start out at the blackjack tables, until he found a poker game with high enough stakes to suit him.

There were no major poker tournaments in Vegas during the week he was here—I checked. So he'd have talked to people until he found a private game. I needed to talk to the same people.

It wasn't as easy as it sounded.

None of the dealers at the blackjack tables remembered him. Again, not surprising—he hadn't been a big player here.

Ditto for the cashiers. Who probably couldn't have told me anything anyway, not and kept their jobs—even if they'd remembered one minor stakes player amongst the multitudes. But you never know when an innocuous question will shake something loose. As a P. I., it only hurts not to ask.

Then I methodically asked the same question at every restaurant and bar Bittner had spent money in, asking the same question. "Do you remember this man?"—showing them his photo. While they looked at the photo, I'd add—"He spent time here back in March."

By the nineteenth time I asked the question, and the nineteenth "No, sorry,"—some of them just glancing at Bittner's photo, others handing it back the instant I said March—I was feeling like an utter fool for wasting time like this.

And it had been a long day. Which promised to turn into an even longer night. I needed coffee.

Lots of coffee.

CHAPTER THIRTY

I headed for a small Parisian style café that Bittner had been to several times. Even in passing, their coffee smelled amazing. And being Vegas, I could be pretty sure of a bottomless cup. Gotta keep those gamblers awake.

I ordered the biggest espresso they had, then scrambled to find my wallet, which seemed to have vanished. I panicked a little before I finally found it—migrated to the bottom of my bag.

The server watched me with amusement—the place was practically empty, and she wasn't much older than eighteen. And probably bored. I handed her Bittner's photo. "Any chance you remember this guy?"

"He looks familiar," she said.

He did? "He was here in March," I said.

"Yeah, I remember him," she said. She tapped a couple of times on the counter. "His name was—David, that was it. Poor guy."

And that's why you never give up. "Poor guy?" I said.

"Uh huh. He came in one night, really late. There wasn't anyone here, and we talked a bit. His partner was caught up in some conference, had turned in early because of some meeting. David said he was a night owl, and couldn't sleep that early. He seemed lonely. And sad, y'know?"

I knew. "Did he tell you anything else?"

She shrugged. "Bits and pieces. Nothing important."

My gut told me there was something more here. "No?"

She smiled at that. "Well, maybe. But I'm studying to be a psychologist, and I try to practice the ethics that I'll need when I'm licensed. Confidences should be honored."

Impressive. I admired her commitment, and her ethics. And honesty deserved honesty.

"I'm a private investigator," I said, handing her my card. "I'm sorry to tell you that David was murdered last week. I'm assisting the police in finding the killer." Even if they didn't exactly know it yet.

Her eyes teared up. "Murdered? That lovely man?"

I nodded. "I'm afraid so."

"Is there any chance it was suicide?" she asked.

Which told me more about Bittner's state of mind last March than she'd probably intended. "No. He was shot."

"Oh, thank goodness." She bowed her head, took a few deep breaths. Wiped surreptitiously at her eyes.

"Look, can I buy you a coffee?" I said. "News like this is a shock for anyone."

"I'm not supposed to, but I could use a cup of tea."

I fought a grimace at the thought. She'd probably dump sugar in it too, for shock. Ugh.

"Ring it up along with my coffee, then," I said, authorizing the bill with a wave of my card. "And if it won't get you fired, you should probably sit down for a few minutes."

She gave me a look that said she saw right through me. "It's okay. I'll tell you what I know, if it'll help find whoever killed David. He didn't deserve to die."

No, he didn't. So I gave her the unvarnished truth. "Finding his killer is all anyone can do for David now."

"I guess so." She rang through the sales and started making my espresso with a hiss of steam. "Thanks for the tea. I'm Lauren, by the way."

"Barbara." I chose an inconspicuous table off to one side, where we both had a view of the passersby. I didn't want this conversation to be overheard. Nor did I want Lauren to risk being fired for helping me.

She joined me quickly, carrying a tray with my coffee and her tea, as well as two small creamers, two coffee spoons and a covered sugar bowl. The coffee smelled wonderful and the cream was fresh and thick. I savored a mouthful, trying not to watch as she dumped several teaspoons of sugar into the teacup, and added something that was too thin for cream.

"Two percent milk," she said with a quick smile, catching my look. "Anything else overpowers a good darjeeling."

"I'll take your word for it and stick to my coffee," I said. And waited.

I wanted badly to ask why she'd thought Bittner might commit suicide, but if I'd read her right, she'd respond better to patience than pushing. I didn't have to wait long. Lauren seemed as anxious to talk about David Bittner as I was to hear what she had to say.

"David struck me as troubled, and very stressed," she said. "He came in twice, and the second night he seemed even more tense than the first. I think he needed to talk, and I was happy to listen. And since I didn't even know his last name, and he was unlikely to see me ever again, I think talking to me felt safe."

"Which means you'll make a good psychologist," I said. "If people already feel safe opening up to you, you're ahead before you even start."

She looked pleased. "Thank you. I love to help people. And David—he seemed almost desperate for help."

"That doesn't surprise me."

"No? I guess you know something about his life, though, don't you? He didn't give me any background. I think he was trying to keep most of the details to himself. But he had to talk to someone."

———

LAUREN PAUSED, drank a little tea. "He told me he loved to gamble, but that he had to stay in control of it. I suspected he was a gambling addict. We see too many of those, even in this little café."

I didn't confirm her supposition, even though it was compassion rather than curiosity I sensed from her. But I didn't deny it, either. "This has to be a dangerous place for someone who loves gambling."

"Oh, I don't know. I've talked to lots of grandmothers and even great-grandmothers who love to come to Vegas to gamble a couple of times a year. They'll limit their spending to twenty dollars a day. Then if they can't sleep they get up in the middle of the night and spend another five dollars on the nickel slots."

She smiled. "Some of them can make that five last for hours. Then they'll come in here for a cup of tea and a chat."

"That wasn't David," I said.

"No. It wasn't. I think he was hoping his love for his partner—he called him Mike—would win out over his love for gambling, and keep him away from the tables. Especially the poker tables.

But whatever Mike was here for—some kind of conference I think—kept him busy most of the time. He and David would manage dinner and most of an evening together, and that was it."

"And it wasn't enough for David?"

She shook her head. "No. He was lonely, and I think scared about where the relationship was going. Or not going. Instead of love keeping his mind off of gambling, he was gambling to keep his mind off of love."

I wondered if that was an accurate reading, or if Lauren had a sentimental streak. Still, her read on the size of his gambling issues was accurate. "And the stakes had to be big enough to distract him," I said.

"Yes. The second night I saw him, I think it was the Wednesday —I remember because it was my last night before I went to Cancun for a week—he had that flushed, intent look that gamblers on a losing streak have. And he didn't even mention Mike.

It was all about the cards running against him. He told me he felt trapped, and he needed a way to get out of the life he'd built."

"That's why you were worried about suicide."

She nodded, her eyes moist. "The words he was using—they were textbook warning signs of suicide. I tried to talk to him, or to get him to talk to someone about what was troubling him, but he wouldn't. He said he could talk to me, and that was good enough."

She checked our cups, both empty, and got up to make refills without saying anything more. I waited.

When she came back with fresh drinks, she'd regained her composure. "I told David he needed to talk to Mike. He said Mike was too preoccupied to listen. I said it didn't matter. He said if Mike didn't want to talk about something, he'd just turn the discussion to David's gambling problems. Which made everything worse."

I could picture Michael Gainer—defense lawyer par excellence—doing exactly that. But I couldn't get a read on David Bittner.

"Did David ever say why he came to Vegas?"

"He said he and Mike needed time together. And that he'd needed to get away," she said.

"Did he say why?"

"No. But he muttered something about Mike's power games costing him too much. Including a friendship that mattered to him."

Justine's friendship, perhaps?

Justine had said herself she'd been preoccupied with the deal she was working on. Had David Bittner felt he was losing her friendship?

Or had Bittner done something he knew Justine would have found unforgivable? Leaked a few secrets, maybe?

"What kind of power games?" I asked.

Lauren sipped her tea before she spoke. "David never really

said. He was pretty careful not to identify much about Mike. But I have some theories, if you're interested?"

Why not? I didn't have much else. "Go ahead."

"If David's gambling was spiraling out of control, he might have been creating a story for himself where his relationship with Mike was the one thing that could save him from it. Whatever their relationship was originally, David wanted more.

I've heard it before—and from both sides. One partner or the other often ends up here, desperate to talk, to understand what had suddenly gone wrong with a relationship that had been "just fine" for a number of years."

It was possible. Lauren was observant—and she'd probably make a very good psychologist. I wasn't convinced David Bittner's relationship with Michael Gainer had anything to do with Bittner's murder, though.

And it was the murder that mattered now. "So Mike's power games?"

She stirred her tea. "This is just guesswork on my part, so don't read too much into it, okay?"

I nodded. I wanted to hear what she had to say.

"Mike might have been trying to keep the relationship as it was. David would see that as a dominance game, because he desperately needed it to become something else."

What wasn't she saying? "Or?"

She smiled a little. "You don't miss much either. Or, Mike could have been avoiding the conversation. Or promising David whatever would keep him in the relationship, but never delivering."

She was probably right about the tension between the two men —but it's always dangerous to guess what's going on in someone else's relationship. Especially when it's the kind of complex relationship Gainer and Bittner seemed to have had.

One thing was clear. Whatever was going on between the them, it had increased the stress on David Bittner.

"Thanks, that's interesting," I said. "What about the friendship he mentioned? Did he say anything else it?"

"No. David didn't say any more than that."

Interesting. "You said earlier he seemed unhappy with his life."

She nodded. "The life he'd built. Yes. He mentioned it more than once—and in those exact words. As if it was a series of choices he'd made, and he didn't like the result."

A series of choices. Lauren had a way with words.

I wondered what David Bittner's choices had been, and why he'd made them. Were they all about gambling? Or Gainer? Or had some of them related to Justine?

"He never said what those choices were?"

"No. He was only really specific about cards, and the bad hands he'd had that day."

"And about his lover?"

"Mike?" Lauren's eyes moved up and to the side as she dug into her memory. "He was more vague than specific, though he hinted a couple of times that Mike was the reason he regretted some of his choices."

"Including choices that could cost him a friendship."

"He only said that once," Lauren said. "But there was a lot of resentment and anger behind those words—once he'd said it, he looked a bit afraid, as if realizing he'd said too much. And he changed the subject immediately."

"Resentment and anger?" I said. "Against Mike?"

"I assume so," she said. "Since that's who he was talking about."

"And he didn't mention it again?"

"No."

"Were there other choices he said he'd made because of Mike that he did talk about again?"

Lauren nodded, sipped her sugary tea. "Other would-be lovers that he refused, I think. And times he could have ended the relationship and didn't. He called their relationship a dead-end in his life."

Had David Bittner believed his relationship with Michael Gainer could someday be more than it was? If so, he'd been deluding himself. The end of their affair had probably been inevitable from the beginning.

Maybe Bittner hadn't known that until they'd come to Vegas together.

Nothing good ever comes from hanging on to a doomed relationship, hoping it will one day change. I knew that from my own bitter experience, that long-ago relationship with Jayson.

Just like I knew how hard it was to admit a relationship was doomed, when everything in you wants it to work. You end up in a place where everyone can see the truth, except you.

Which hurts. And can lead to really, really stupid decisions—ones that just prolong the hurt. Those decisions can create a lot of damage in your life.

No wonder Lauren had felt sorry for David Bittner.

Exactly how bad had those decisions of his been? And had one of them had got him killed?

It was nearly one a.m. on Sunday by the time I made it the few hundred yards down the Strip to Bellagio. The main casino was more elegant than the one at Paris, with silk covered walls and multi-hued glass chandeliers like frozen jellyfish hanging upside-down from the paneled ceilings. But the feel was much the same.

Despite the elegance, it reeked of money and desperation.

There were no windows, so night felt like day, and vice versa. The rattle and clang of the machines was the same, too —though mostly the noise was for effect now, barely drowning out the croupier's call.

I strolled around the room, soaking it all in. The restrained elegance, the over-the-top accents, the lights, the noise, the buzz of a successful casino.

There was more money here than at Paris, you could feel it. Here and there I spotted the high-end gamblers with their attentive hostesses, making sure the money kept flowing.

How had Bittner spent his time here? And who could tell me?

Based on what Badger had dug up, he hadn't spent much money on anything except gambling here. Until he'd lost everything.

He probably hadn't been playing the slots. Blackjack? Roulette? I was betting he'd found a poker game.

As I glanced round the room, I pondered the problem of Bittner's relationship with Gainer. Had something gone wrong enough between the two of them to send David Bittner off on such a self-destructive binge?

Or had Gainer simply provided the excuse Bittner needed to prove to himself and everyone else that he could gamble his way out of all his debts? And where better to make a big strike than Vegas?

Chelsea had told me David Bittner hadn't hit bottom yet. That until he did so he'd never really accept that he had a problem that would only get worse the more he gambled. There was no jackpot big enough to fix the mess his life was in.

Had this trip been his attempt to prove that wasn't true?

So what had happened when Bittner gambled everything he could at three casinos, lost, and was cut off? Was that bottom for him?

Apparently not—since he kept gambling. How far had he been prepared to go to dig himself out of that mess?

And was that one of the things he'd regretted?

I went looking for the floor manager. If Bittner had been gambling big here, he'd probably have been assigned his own hostess. And I wanted to talk to her.

———

SHERRI C. WAS LOVELY—A tall, beautifully groomed blond with a bright smile and a bubbly manner. She was happy to talk to me—though she didn't seem to remember much. Until I told her David Bittner was dead, and that I had a few questions about his time here.

She paled a little. "Dead?"

"I'm afraid so."

Sherri sighed. "I hate it when I'm right."

"Right? About what?"

"I can always spot the self-destructive ones. There's always going to be winners and losers here…"

Especially losers. I hoped Sherri had more than clichés for me.

"But there are always a few that beat the odds. Some win more than the norm. Some lose more. And the ones who lose more—well, some of them seemed determined to keep losing," she said, redeeming herself. "Oh, they think they're chasing that big win. But they make bad judgement calls, and they keep making them. And they keep playing."

"Self-destructive?" I said, thinking of what Lauren had said.

Sherry nodded. "Yes, that's it exactly. They start out desperate and get worse. It almost feels—willed. Like they know they're going down in flames, and they just want to get it over with."

She paused for a moment, staring at a beautiful antique wall clock that didn't, of course, actually tell time. No point reminding gamblers how long they'd spent here.

"It's more than that, though," she said slowly. "It's like losing is the whole point. That's what they came to do."

She shook her sleekly coiffed head. "I hate working with them. I know that at some point they'll finally lose everything, and there will be nothing I can do for them. And I'm always afraid they'll end up killing themselves when they leave here."

"David Bittner didn't kill himself," I said.

She stared at me. "He didn't?"

"No."

"Oh, thank goodness," she breathed. "I always feel so guilty—as though I've been helping them kill themselves. But slowly, you know?"

I did know. Where does co-dependance start and stop?

I'd often wondered that over the years. Bars serve the drinks an alcoholic should avoid. Casinos—on and off-line—provide gamblers their drug of choice. And that's only the legal addictions.

But alcoholics can drink at home, just like gamblers can always find private games.

An alcoholic, a gambling addict—they can make another choice. Except when they can't. Because it's an illness, a bio-chemical dependance.

And the bartenders and the casino hostesses, they see that desperation. Probably recognize it—they've seen it hundreds of times before. I've cursed my share of bartenders for serving the whiskey my father craved, when it was so clear to me—and sometimes to him—that he shouldn't have been drinking at all.

But most of them need their jobs—and their sanity—too much to risk trying to help an addict who doesn't want to be helped. I'd never thought about the emotional cost that takes on them before.

"What happened to David?" Sherry asked, her eyes sad.

"He was murdered. I'm working on solving his murder."

"Oh, how awful. What can I do to help?" she said immediately.

I asked her to walk me through her interactions with David Bittner from the time she started working with him, as best she could remember. She did so, adding her own comments.

She didn't remember him well, though. Just another gambler—polite, she remembered that, preferred poker. Maybe a little more desperate than most.

"He lost a lot of money, fast," she said. "That I do remember. Then he came back over several days and lost more money, but slower. He took bigger risks as the week went on, and looked more and more strained."

Which wasn't much different from what Lauren had already told me—a desperate man, seemingly bent on self-destruction.

"Did he talk about himself?" I asked. "About his relationships, or what he was doing in Vegas."

"No," she said. "It was all about the games, and his bad luck. And making just one more bet. Until we finally it was all gone."

It was the same story on the casino floor at Wynn. And at Island Sun.

Until I talked to the hostess at the Russian Bar.

———

LOCATED at the far end of a corridor on the main floor of the Island Sun casino, the Russian Bar is linked to one of Vegas's best restaurants. The lighting is dim, the seating intimate. Small square tables with thick tops lit from within, that look like they've been carved from the blue ice at the heart of a glacier. Low, comfortable chairs. A hum of conversation.

For the decor alone, I'd have named it the Polar Bar. Except that it specializes in Russian vodkas, stocking every vodka you've ever heard of, and a lot you haven't. Well, I haven't, anyway. Especially the high end ones.

The hostess's name tag said she was Oksana V. and her strong features matched the Slavic sound of her name. With perfect makeup spotlighting high cheekbones and pouty lips, and a glittery silver dress showing off long legs and a perfect figure, she was dazzling.

Oksana was responsible for making reservations, recognizing the regulars, seating the bar patrons and keeping an eye out for trouble. She recognized Bittner's photo immediately, which surprised me. As the hostess, she'd have had little or no opportunity for conversation with Bittner.

Plus it had been six months, and as far as I could tell, Bittner had only been there once. Hardly a regular, even if he was throwing money around like one.

I asked her why she remembered him, out of the thousands of people that she saw every month.

"It was not him so much," she said. "I could not tell you his name, even though I made a point of learning it that night."

"So?"

"He was with one of my regulars. And it had clearly been pre-arranged. He asked for him immediately."

"One of your regulars? Which one?"

At which point she clammed up. Probably realizing she

shouldn't have said anything. And nothing—including a fairly hefty bribe—would get another word out of her.

But it was too late. I finally had the thread I'd been looking for.

Everything that happens in a Vegas casino is recorded. Everything. And all of it is for sale, too.

For a price.

I thanked Oksana, and went looking for someone in the hotel with access to those recordings. Someone with a very flexible conscience.

Several hours and quite a few bribes later, I had a name. Dominic Grassini.

And I knew there had been one other man at the Russian Bar with Grassini and Bittner that night.

But no-one seemed to know who that third man was. Not local, then. Or just not important?

I focused on Grassini—who was both local and important enough to do business regularly at the Russian Bar. I texted his name to Badger, asking her to see what she could find out. If anyone could unearth the man's connections—legal or illegal—it would be her.

Meanwhile, I headed back to the Russian Bar. Over the course of ordering and drinking a flight of vodka, I managed to grab a quick word with several of the servers who were working there. All of them were tall, blond and striking, with sensual accents and the same strong features as Oksana.

None of them recognized Bittner's photo. None of them would say a word about Grassini. And bribes didn't help.

Only one of the servers even reacted to Grassini's name, and she covered it quickly.

It was as if they were afraid to be caught talking about him. Which fit with the hints I'd been hearing elsewhere that Grassini had mob connections.

I still had no idea where Bittner's influx of money had come from. Could it have been mob money, with Grassini the middle man in some kind of deal? Or was it connected to the other man at the table that night? I had no idea.

I needed to find out who that third man was. And I was running out of ways to find out. I was also running out of steam.

I checked my watch. It was late. Or rather, early.

I'd chase the third man down after I'd had some sleep.

CHAPTER THIRTY-TWO

It was nearly eleven when I woke the next morning. My eyes were bleary and my head ached. It took a moment to realize where I was. And a longer moment to get over wishing I was somewhere else.

Then I rolled out of bed with a sigh, and strode to the window to stare out at the Strip, nearly unrecognizable under a burning sun. Waking up in Vegas late on a Sunday morning is a disorienting feeling. I nearly ordered room service, then realized it wasn't worth losing the chance to question someone else who might remember Bittner.

I set the in-room coffeepot—which included a decent blend of coffee—to brew while I showered. Then drank most of the fresh pot while I dressed, ran through my notes from the night before, and checked my email.

There was nothing new from Badger, which threw me a little. She's usually so quick, I'd begun to think of her as something of a miracle worker. Which was unfair to her. And dangerous for me to be relying on.

Badger would troll her online world for info on Dominic Grassini and get back to me eventually. Meanwhile, my priority for the day was to make sure I hadn't missed anything significant Bittner had done here.

And to find out where his influx of cash had come from.

Starting with digging up what I could on Grassini here in Vegas. As well as anything I could find on the third man who'd been with Bittner and Grassini at the Russian Bar.

Not knowing what the three men was doing at the table together was nagging at me like a sore tooth.

Maybe Bittner had met Grassini or the third man before they ended up at the Russian Bar together? I doubted such a meeting would have occurred at any of the places the frugal Bittner had spent his days.

No, my money was on Bittner's late night gambling at Island Sun, which didn't fit his previous pattern. Maybe Grassini or the third man was also a poker player, and had met Bittner on one of those solo late-night sprees?

All I could do was speculate. That had to change. I needed facts.

I'd just googled "Dominic Grassini" and "Vegas" when my phone rang. It figured that Badger would call now.

Except it wasn't Badger. It was Justine. And she wasn't happy.

"Barbara? Where are you? I'm at my wit's end. Everything is going wrong in the office without David to keep people on track. And the rumors are spreading in the design community about this deal that's supposed to be secret. Almost as fast as the rumors that my company is doomed. And that I'm done as a designer."

Rumors again. Where were they coming from? They were too consistent, and too detailed—judging by the emails Hughes Furniture International had sent to Justine—to be completely fabricated.

Those rumors had be to coming from a source who had access to at least some confidential information about those deals. A source who didn't wish Justine well. At all.

I tried to get a question in, but Justine wasn't listening. So I grabbed a pen and took notes while I waited for her to run out of breath.

"I can't figure out how the information is getting out," she said, her voice speeding up and going higher as she talked.

"But this is going to be the end of my company if it keeps up. And my career. I don't know where the leaks are coming from.

They know things no-one outside my company should know. And even things I'd have sworn only I knew. And my lawyer, of course."

It sounded like she had a mole in her company. "Go on," I said.

"It has to stop. But I don't know how to stop it. Can you help?"

This wasn't a problem I could solve from Vegas. And it was beyond my skill set anyway. But since I had a couple of computer magicians on payroll…

"I think so," I said. "Can you answer a few questions for me?"

"I'll try." She gave a shaky laugh. "At the moment, I'm not sure I have any answers left."

Not surprising, given the mess her life was suddenly in. "How secure are your computer systems?" I said.

"Well, we have a company intranet. And people who manage it, and are supposed to be providing high level security."

"Do your employees maintain your intranet and computer security? Or is it an outside firm?"

"It's a contract with an outside firm."

I wondered who was overseeing their work. Which was problem number one. "Is the information that's being leaked on the shared server?"

"No. It's only on my computer."

"And is your computer backed up to the server?"

All I heard was dead air. "Justine?"

"I don't know," she said. "I'm a designer—I can make a graphics program sing. But I have people to worry about this other stuff."

Of course she did. Shades of the Justine I remembered. "People?"

"David." The single word was a eulogy.

She'd lost far more than a valued employee with his murder.

She'd lost the colleague she trusted most. And the one who might have betrayed her.

I was going to find out what had really happened, if I had to drag myself to every casino in town. But first things needed fixing on Justine's side.

"You need to get your system looked at immediately, and any data leaks plugged," I said.

"I wouldn't know where to begin."

"I'll send someone." Cory would figure this out in no time.

"I don't want any of my people to know I don't trust them," she said. "Things are tense enough around here already."

I could understand that. But she had to be realistic. "Justine, someone is stealing that data. You have to be hardline with this until we find out who."

"If any of my people think they're being accused of something, they'll all quit. And I can't run this place on my own."

This wasn't an argument I could win. "I'll send my computer expert after hours, so that he doesn't run into any of your employees. Okay?"

"Yes. Thanks. When?"

I had no idea what Cory's schedule was. Other than that tomorrow was a school day. "Today if we can manage it. Tomorrow night at seven otherwise. Does that work?"

"That's good. By seven everyone else will be gone. And no-one works Sunday. Except me. And I work until nine most nights. I'll be doing that until I get this contract finalized." Her voice broke. "And replace David."

No wonder she was sounding so stressed. "I'll check with my expert and confirm that appointment later today."

I had no doubt Cory could handle this. And as long as he was home by nine-thirty, my sister shouldn't have a problem, either. I'd tell him to cab it, and put it on the office tab.

"My staff are going to ask questions about who this computer expert is," Justine said.

What had happened to the hard-headed business woman?

"That's why he's coming in after hours. They don't even have to know you've hired someone. After his initial visit, he can work remotely for whatever else needs to be done."

"Good."

She sounded a little calmer. Good thing. Justine under stress was bad enough. Justine hysterical, with me in Vegas? Problem. Big problem.

I made my tone matter of fact. "If anyone does spot Cory, he looks pretty harmless. You can make up something plausible. They won't suspect a thing. Trust me."

"I am trusting you. And your firm. You come highly recommended. But you're not making any progress. And it's getting worse."

Yes, it was.

"Calm down, Justine," I said. "We are making progress. You haven't been arrested yet, have you?"

She gave a brittle laugh. "I'm not so sure that's progress. If whoever is doing this to me manages to destroy my company, a jail cell might be all I can afford. At least I'd have food and shelter."

This was Justine talking? This case was taking a higher toll on her than I'd realized. "Leave it with me," I said.

And shot off an email to Marie, asking her to set up the meeting.

———

IT TOOK me a moment to put Justine's problems away and remember what I'd been working on. Right. Grassini and the mystery man.

I switched back to my Google search. And stared at the results.

Dominic Grassini was a lawyer. I clicked on the top link. With a specialty in criminal law. And what appeared, from his website, to be a thriving practice.

Which shouldn't have been all that surprising. A lot of people were lawyers. A lot of lawyers made a lot of money. Especially lawyers with mob connections.

Not that anyone I'd talked to last night had said outright that Grassini had mob connections. More like some of them had hinted at it.

But no-one had even hinted that he was a lawyer. Why was that? Maybe they thought it was obvious—everyone knew Grassini, the lawyer.

You know, the one who handled high-profile mob cases.

I suddenly wondered if Gainer knew Grassini. It was a long shot, but Gainer had been in town for a legal conference. Maybe Grassini was a big enough name locally to have been a presenter at the conference?

I checked my notes, but Gainer hadn't mentioned the name of his conference. I tried a Google search. Nothing. Not really surprising, given how broad my search parameters were. I glared at the screen for a moment, then gave in and texted Cory.

I'd given up on Badger, at least for now. Cory would probably have an answer for me before I finished my very late breakfast, anyway.

I closed the files I'd had open and made a few cryptic notes in my notebook, preparatory to locking my laptop in the room safe for the day. I glanced at Bittner's expenses before I closed the spreadsheet, and the charge from the Russian Bar caught my eye. And my attention.

Not just because it was astronomical. Because I now knew there had only been three of them. To spend that much, they'd probably been drinking the expensive vodka. A lot of it.

But still, there were only three of them. Either they'd drunk enough to send three normal men to the hospital. Or they'd both eaten and drunk very well. "Forget the cost, this one's on me," kind of very well.

Which made sense if Grassini—or the unknown third man—was paying the bill. In that scenario, they likely wanted something from Bittner. Or were trying to sell him on something.

But Bittner had paid that astronomical bill.

Bittner who had just lost everything at the tables. And then he'd turned around and spent this much entertaining Grassini and the unknown man?

I wasn't buying it. The one thing I'd learned yesterday was that Bittner was a contradiction—when he was gambling, money slid through his fingers. When he wasn't gambling, he was frugal. Very frugal.

Everywhere David Bittner had spent his money outside the casino floor, he'd chosen the cheapest options. Except for the Russian Bar.

I texted Marie, asked her to send me the info Badger and Cory had compiled on Bittner's finances asap. Minutes later I was scanning the document. I saw the same frugality there. Bittner's Yaletown condo was worth a lot of money in our current insane real estate market—but he'd bought into the area long before it was trendy.

His monthly expenses were low, especially compared to his salary. His clothes were good—he shopped at an exclusive men's boutique—but his wardrobe must have been carefully chosen, judging by how little he spent. And Bittner belonged to the local Y, not to an exclusive gym.

He'd made good money working for Justine, but he'd lived frugally. And he had no savings, no investments. Other than his condo. He'd never have spent the kind of money that was charged to his bill that night at the Russian Bar.

Which meant—he'd been too drunk to think straight?

Or one of the other two had given Bittner the cash for the bill, then Bittner had put the same amount on his Visa. For a gambler, that probably made sense. Sort of.

But why the subterfuge?

Unless someone didn't want a record that they'd been at that bar that night?

Who carried that kind of cash? Dominic Grassini, the lawyer? Or the third man, whoever he was?

And what did they want from Bittner?

———

I WAS JUST ABOUT to leave when I got an email for Marie. I opened it with some trepidation. Generally my assistant manages to surprise me. And not always in a good way.

This email was one of those. Before leaving Vancouver, I'd emailed her some items that needed follow up, including a request for Cory to check out the gym and change rooms at the Grand Pacific hotel. I still wanted to know how Gainer had managed to change clothes between his first and second visit with Bittner on the night the latter was murdered.

Apparently, instead of sending Cory, Marie had elected to take on the assignment herself. But her reasoning made sense. She might not be able to stroll into a men's locker room as easily as Cory could, but she was better in getting answers from people than he was. Especially males.

In fact, along with her new image, Marie seemed to have acquired a fairly devious set of skills for winkling information out of people. I was impressed.

But I was beginning to worry a little how far she was prepared to take what she'd explained to me as a kind of performance art. If she kept this up, she probably needed to start working on getting her P. I. license.

Marie with a license to detect? I shuddered.

But she had been proving herself lately. And she did seem to have a natural talent for certain aspects of investigations. Much as I hated to admit that.

I kept seeing the frantic woman with bad taste in spandex that I'd first met. And she was growing into something else.

I'm beginning to suspect that delegation isn't my strong point. Who, me? Though even I have to admit that trying to do every-thing myself would limit me in other ways.

Especially when I'm in Vegas and the things that need investigating are back in Vancouver.

I skimmed the rest of the email, then focused on the details. Marie had established that there was a very convenient set of stairs that gave access to the third floor gym from the second floor bar at the Grand Pacific. Those stairs emerged just outside the men's locker room. And that exit wasn't monitored by security cameras.

The hotel gym was designed for guests, so you needed an electronic key to get in. But they also sold annual memberships to locals who didn't mind paying their exorbitant fees. Those memberships came with permanent lockers. And Gainer was a member.

Marie didn't volunteer how she'd found all that out. And I wasn't going to ask. Not until I got back, anyway.

I closed the email, and grabbed another cup of coffee, my mind racing. What had Gainer kept in his locker? Athletic shoes, obviously—ones that looked almost like regular shoes. And maybe a gun that might, or might not, have slightly changed the line of his suit?

Which reminded me. I sent my buddy Jerry a quick email, following up on Gainer's gun license. Or lack of one.

And switched back to thinking about those shoes. Why would Gainer change from business shoes to athletic shoes? It wasn't like he was wearing four-inch heels, where every second was torture. Maybe he'd planned a quick run to relieve stress?

When I'm under pressure, I often sneak in an extra run. It helps me decompress, and clears my thinking. After a bitter lover's quarrel, a run might have helped.

But Gainer had also been drinking heavily. Running in that condition was beyond stupid. And Gainer wasn't stupid.

So why change his shoes after he went back to Bittner's room the second time?

Unless he'd had blood on them.

Don't tell me my instincts had led me astray and Gainer was the killer all along?

I needed to take another look at my assumptions about Gainer, and the role he'd played in all this. After I finished cursing, and wishing I was back in Vancouver so I could deal with this myself, I sent off another email to Marie.

Then very firmly focused on what I needed to accomplish here. Since I was in Vegas, and not Vancouver.

CHAPTER THIRTY-THREE

I was starving. Breakfast was way overdue. But as I rode the elevator downstairs and went looking for a cab, I was still speculating about that dinner at the Russian Bar, and what someone might want from Bittner.

Why him? And did he give them what they wanted?

I didn't have an answer by the time I arrived at the Island Sun's swankiest restaurant, the Star.

I looked around me. The restaurant was elegantly decorated, and clearly high-end. Bittner would never have paid to eat here. But he'd breakfasted here the first three mornings, and dined here four times, which suggested Gainer had been with him—and paying the bill.

This time the hostess didn't recognize Bittner's photo. But my server did. As he slid the immaculately prepared my order of Crab Benedict onto the table in front of me, I showed him the photo.

He nodded. Yes, he remembered him. "I always wondered what happened with those two," he said.

"Oh?"

"Yes. The first two mornings, they were a very happy couple—

wrapped up in each other, enjoying everything. One would think they'd never had breakfast together before."

They probably hadn't. "And then?"

"Well, then things were not so good. But please, madame. Enjoy your eggs while they are warm. I will be back with more coffee and the fruit and pastry tray in a little bit. We can talk then." And with a Gallic nod he swept quietly away.

Apparently I was going to enjoy a fruit plate with my breakfast. And more of this heavenly coffee. It was a good thing Justine had deep pockets.

When I'd finished my meal and was savoring the last of my coffee, my server returned, pushing a cart with a variety of fruit plates and pastries. "And for madame?" he asked, tongs at the ready.

I hate being called madame. But the food was so good here that I didn't care. I couldn't take my eyes off the offerings on the cart. It was past eleven—I'd just call this brunch. "I'll have the fresh strawberries with… is that creme fraiche?"

"But of course. And our chef has a special touch with it."

"Yes, please. And I'll have a slice of St. Honoré cake as well." I had to stop myself from ordering two. When I'm short of sleep, I seem to be hungrier than ever. I'd have to fit in an extra run when I got home to pay for it all.

He smiled as he transferred the two dishes to my table and refilled my cup with the strong, fragrant coffee. I glanced around us. The room was less than half-full now, and it looked like all of the other patrons were working on their main meal.

"Now, about this man," I said, and tapped Bittner's photo, which I'd left on the table as a not-so-subtle reminder. I slipped a couple of twenties under the used plate that he had yet to clear. "You said after the second morning it didn't go so well for him?"

He made slow work of clearing my plate. "I work the morning shift, so I didn't see them at dinner, of course," he said. "But one hears things. And the third morning, they were arguing over something. I didn't overhear, of course…"

Meaning Bittner and Gainer had stopped talking the minute he came near enough.

"…But the body language was very clear. The two of them didn't breakfast together again."

Which wasn't much information for the additional food he'd convinced me to order. Not that eating it would be any hardship. "That must have been awkward. They didn't leave for another four days."

"Ah. The other man, not this one," and he tapped the Bittner's photo. "He came back, and met others here. They were from the conference he was attending, I think."

My phone buzzed once against the table's surface. I had a text. I ignored it.

"You said earlier you'd heard things about their dinners. Do you know someone who worked the evening shift when they were here?"

His expression was suddenly neutral. "Oh, I wouldn't want to get anyone in trouble. Not when they're still working the same shift."

Good to know. I slipped another twenty under my coffee saucer. "I'll keep everything confidential."

He nodded, and refilled my coffee cup—palming the bribe at the same time in the smoothest move I'd seen yet. "Will there be anything else?"

"No, just the bill, thank you."

He handed it to me. "I trust that is satisfactory?"

I looked from the amount to the name he'd scrawled on a slip of paper and tucked on top of the bill. —Annette Y. How very discreet of him—"That's perfect. Thank-you."

With a nod, he moved off with his cart.

I checked my phone. I had a text from Nick and an email from Cory.

Nick had sent another listing—a surprisingly affordable two bedroom suite with an amazing ocean and mountain view. I was sold—until I saw the square footage. Six hundred and ten square feet. For the two of us? Nick tops six-two, and I'm five-ten. We'd be tripping over each other. No thanks.

"Great view. Too small. I'm not a gymnast." I sent back with the appropriate emoji.

He sent back a sad face emoji and one of a coupon that said Lessons. Now where had he found that?

I sent back an emoji rolling her eyes. But I was smiling as I opened Cory's email.

Cory had sent me the name of the legal conference Gainer had attended, and he'd also tracked down a link to the conference program. That would save me some time.

I texted him my thanks, and started reading. The conference was about changes in international law in an increasingly global world, and one track had focused on criminal law. I clicked through the program, but it didn't tell me much more. What I really needed was a list of registrants. Preferably with photos.

I texted Cory again, asked him to see what he could find. If there wasn't anything online, I'd see if I could track down the organizers of the conference. Somewhere there had to be a list.

Then I took the time to enjoy my cake and the strawberries, and finished off my coffee. As I did so, I watched the ebb and flow of customers, noting which ones had come from upstairs, and which ones from the casino floor.

Of the latter, it was easy to spot those who'd been losing. Most of them looked exhausted but defiant. A few looked devastated. Had Bittner been one of those, coming straight from the gaming floor to breakfast?

I paid my bill with a generous tip, then on my way out stopped at the hostess station. I spun her a story about a previous visit here where I'd had exceptional service. And left with a booking for that night, in Annette Y's section.

I'd be back for dinner. And I planned to enjoy every undoubtedly delectable morsel.

While grilling Annette for everything she knew about Bittner.

————

WHICH GAVE me nearly eight hours to figure out where Bittner's influx of cash had come from. As I strolled through the busy lobby, headed for the Strip, I considered my options.

I could stick to my original schedule, and keep following in Bittner's tracks. Which felt like an exercise in futility. Because the day after the meeting in the Russian Bar, Bittner had started gambling here, at the Island Sun. From what little Badger had been able to dig out, he'd won there. And won again.

But he played too long, and started losing.

He repeated the pattern at Bellagio. And again at Wynn.

None of which was likely to get me closer to the mystery man. Or to where Bittner's windfall had come from.

The more I thought about that windfall, the more I wanted to know who the third man was, and how he fit in. He felt like the missing piece.

Who was he? And why had he been at the Russian Bar that night?

My phone pinged and I pulled it out. An email with a photo attachment. From an anonymous account. One of my contacts from the previous night had come through.

I stopped just outside the hotel doors, and off to one side, out of the pedestrian walkways. Shaded by the roof overhang, I clicked on the attachment.

It was a photo of Grassini, Bittner and another man. The background was the Russian Bar. I zoomed in and studied it.

Three men, all wearing dark suits, clustered around a table cluttered with glasses and stacked empty plates. No wonder the bill for the evening had been so high.

Two of them, Grassini and the third man—leaned in a little. Bittner sat back, his hands on the table, as if he were going to leap up at any moment. None of the men were full face, but their expressions were clear enough.

Grassini looked slightly amused, but he was sitting between

Bittner and the door. A big man, heavily muscled in a way even his very well-cut suit couldn't hide, his body language said he wasn't going anywhere. Except for the quality of the suit—and that hint of amusement—I would have taken him for hired muscle. At first glance, any way.

The unnamed third man wore an ordinary dark business suit, and looked intense. Thin and wiry, his features were unmemorable, but his facial muscles were tight, his eyes focused on Bittner.

Bittner looked cornered, like some small animal that's been brought to a standstill by hunters bigger and wilier than he was. That wasn't the look of someone handed an offer of endless cash. Or a gambler handed a way out of his almost overwhelming debts. What was going on here?

All thought of following in Bittner's footsteps gone, I grabbed a cab back to my hotel. From the relative privacy of my room, I sent copies of the photo to Badger and to Marie, with a quick note asking them to use any methods available to them to identify the third man. And to text me as soon as they had anything.

Then I used a photo editor on my laptop to isolate each of the three men and crop out any identifying background. I emailed the results to the photo place near my hotel, asked for half a dozen copies of each image within the hour.

The sooner I could figure out where the third man fit into this mess, the better.

CHAPTER THIRTY-FOUR

I was on my way to the Bellagio casino, still trying to figure out where the third man fit in, when I my phone buzzed. I had a message. I glanced at the screen—Cory.

With the sun hot on my back, I paused in front of the fountains to listen to water magic while I looked at what he'd sent me. Which turned out to be a link to the handout for participants at Gainer's legal conference. Yes!

I clicked through to the section listing attendees—and it included photos of all the participants. I skimmed through the first few pages of very boring looking men and women in suits. They all looked ready to stand in front of a judge and argue their respective cases. Probably they were.

I wondered what kind of personal lives hid behind those oh so professional photos as I skipped forward to the G's.

And there he was. Dominic Grassini. Nice to have that connection confirmed. But I had a few questions for Michael Gainer when I got home.

I was considering paging through the entire thing on the off chance that the third man had also been an attendee. But I needed my laptop. Phones are not meant for skimming long documents.

I'd just headed back to the hotel to collect my computer when a second text came in. That was quick. I glanced down, expecting it to be from Badger. Wrong again.

I read Marie's text. She'd scanned the photo I'd sent her into the database she'd been building for the case. Then she'd done the same for the photos of everyone registered from the legal conference. And run a search for the third man's image against the whole database.

The third man had been at the same legal conference as Gainer and Grassini. And he'd also been at the Grand Pacific Hotel the night Bittner died.

I hadn't seen that one coming. But at least I hadn't written the third man off as unimportant in favor of Grassini who was, on the surface, the much likelier connection. Maybe there was hope for my instincts after all.

I kept reading. Marie had attached a link, which took me to the conference attendees listing, and the third man's photo and information. I glanced at the man in the photo—a dead ringer for the third man at the Russian Bar—and started reading.

The third man was an American, Robert Bingham. He was a lawyer too. For TML Corporation, a firm I'd never heard of.

I texted back. "Thanks. Find out everything you can about Bingham's firm. Get Cory to help if you like."

I was pretty sure Marie could handle digging out what I needed on Bingham's firm on her own, anyway, given what she'd just done here. She'd really taken the initiative, and the result was pretty impressive. And on a Sunday, too.

I'd definitely need to talk to her about studying for her P. I. license.

Then I shook my head. What was I thinking? My small firm was doing well, but we'd never have that kind of business. And trying to manage Marie the P. I.—even Marie the apprentice P. I.?

It wouldn't be pretty. But she did have good instincts…

———

I TURNED to watch the dance of water in the fountains in front of me for a moment, as the lights played over them in time with the music. And thought through the puzzle at hand—Bingham, Grassini and Bittner. And what I still needed to know about the three of them.

It irritated me that I hadn't heard back from Badger. Her ability to dig out well-hidden data—especially financial data—had proved invaluable on previous cases. And I still had the feeling there was something key I was missing on this one.

I was starting to worry about her, too. This long silence wasn't like her. What was going on there?

I sent Marie a quick text, asking her if she knew why I hadn't heard from Badger since Saturday. I got a quick reply. "Badger's been busy. She'll be in touch soon."

Which implied that Marie was in contact with Badger, while telling me nothing at all. Interesting. But not very helpful.

I thought about texting Badger again—which I knew would be a waste of time—but luckily I was interrupted by another text from Marie. "Cory meeting with Justine this afternoon, instead of tomorrow."

Good. We needed to put an end to the rumor mill that seemed to be coming out of Justine's office.

And speaking of rumor mills… "Thanks. Keep me posted," I texted, then headed into the casino. I had some very different questions to ask this time. I wasn't looking forward to it.

As I crossed the casino floor, I dodged a very motivated senior with her eyes fixed on the nickel slots. If I had more time, I was tempted to join her—sometimes watching those wheels spin helps me sort out my thinking. And after the feast masquerading as my breakfast, I couldn't face any more coffee.

———

A COUPLE OF HOURS LATER, I got a text from Cory. He'd made it to Justine's office, no problem, and was starting work on her computer.

Which prompted another panicked call from Justine. "I'm worried about multi-million dollar losses, and you send over your nephew? Really?"

I'd finished my interviews and was half-way across the casino floor at Bellagio, and I could barely hear her. Her frustration came through loud and clear though.

I shot a quick glance around then headed for the nearest exit. The last thing Justine needed was to hear the artificial clanging and ringing of the slot machines all through this call.

"Calm down, Justine," I said. "If he were a few years older, he'd be working for me full time. He's that good."

"He's sixteen! Barbara, I don't think you're taking me seriously, or you'd have come yourself."

I'd found a semi private niche in one of the hallways leading to the rooms, and leaned back against the wall. "Justine, Cory is so much better with computer systems than I am that it embarrasses me."

"Are you really that bad?"

"No, he's that good."

She wasn't listening. "Or are you seeing this as a chance to get even with me for whatever petty thing I might have done at art school all those years ago?"

Here we go. This was no time for the old Justine to show up.

"Justine? Calm down. Look, I know this is tough. But Cory will figure out what's going on with your systems. And if he finds something really nasty, I have a high-priced specialist on retainer who will work with him on fixing whatever it is."

She sighed. "I'm sorry. I don't know what's wrong with me."

I did. Too many shocks in too short a time. "Just let Cory do his thing."

"He is. I am."

Wait a minute. If Cory was in her office, where was she calling from? The noise from the casino had hidden a weird humming sound that was coming from her end. "Justine, where are you?"

"The staff lunchroom. Your nephew's in my office, doing—something—with my computer and muttering to himself."

I'd been hearing a dishwasher—the cleaning service must work on Sundays. I bit back a laugh. That wouldn't help things.

"Okay, that's good. Just let Cory do his thing—he'll let me know what he finds, and what needs to be done about it. And I'll give you a full report."

"Good. But I don't need a written report—not right now. I just need to know what's going on."

"I'll call you and let you know as soon as I hear anything," I said. "For now, just make yourself a cup of tea or something. Then go help Cory with any questions he has."

She muttered something. I caught "hate computers" but not much else.

I could sympathize. Sixteen year-old prodigies weren't easy to take. Before I could respond, she surprised me.

"Where are you?" she said sharply.

Apparently I hadn't been fast enough getting out of the casino. "Vegas," I said, and braced myself for her reaction.

But she surprised me. Again. "You think something happened there on David's visit last March. And it relates to his death," she said.

Even too many shocks couldn't keep that sharp mind of hers down for long. "Yes. I'm following up on what happened while he was here."

"And? Are you getting anywhere?"

"Yes, we're starting to make real progress," I said firmly. Which was true, even if I hadn't figured out how it all fit together yet.

"But how could his gambling relate to the threats against my business?" she said. Hearing her own words seemed to trigger connections she'd never made before.

"Ohhhh," she said. "No. Not David. He wouldn't betray me."

But there was fear and an awful kind of knowledge in her tone.

I had discounted Marie's rumor that Bittner was selling Justine's secrets when Badger hadn't been able to confirm it. The secrets that were still being leaked from Justine's company after Bittner's murder seemed to refute the rumor, also. And to answer the question I'd hoped I wouldn't have to ask Justine.

But I wasn't prepared to be definite on anything. Not yet. Especially given what Lauren said David had hinted at.

And the facts I'd been gathering still didn't form a picture that made sense to me. Until they did…

"It's one possibility," I said. "But there are a number of others. We don't know anything for sure yet."

"But how could he?" she said, as if she was talking to herself.

Had she even heard me? "He might not have. But David Bittner was a gambler," I said bluntly. "It's a disease."

"I knew he gambled, but… I never thought it was that bad."

Again, I could hear the doubt as clearly as the denial.

"Worse," I said. I nearly told her to talk to her niece, but that would be betraying a confidence. "But I've found nothing to tie his gambling to your business problems." *Yet* hovered unspoken across the miles between us.

"I'll wait for your report," she said abruptly, and hung up.

Justine was a strong woman, but this case was coming close to breaking her. And I was no closer to naming the killer.

I had to solve it, and fast. For everyone's sake.

CHAPTER THIRTY-FIVE

By seven p.m. and time for my dinner reservation, I'd worked through every conceivable connection for Grassini, Bingham and Bittner. Plus a few inconceivable ones.

And I'd continued to try to find someone who remembered seeing the three of them together. No luck.

Finding anyone who remembered Robert Bingham wasn't much better. He did have a rather unmemorable face. But maybe he wasn't a gambler. Though in that case, why had he chosen to attend a conference in Vegas, of all places?

I got no further with questions about Bittner. That is, nothing beyond the answers I'd already got the night before.

Grassini was the easy one—everyone recognized him. And no-one would say a word about him.

It hadn't occurred to me to ask if anyone had seen Gainer, Grassini and Bingham together. Not until Annie Y. came to take my dinner order that night at the Island Sun's Star.

I'd laid the photos out in front of me as soon as I was seated. They'd given me a slightly better table than that morning, I noted. Maybe Annie Y. rated a better section.

Annie introduced herself as my server for the evening, ran

through the list of specials, then glanced at the four photos I had laid out on the table. Her expression remained professionally neutral, though I thought I saw a flash of recognition.

"Know any of them?" I said.

She nodded thoughtfully. "These two dined here quite awhile ago," she said, tapping the photos of Gainer and Bittner. "Not very happily."

"Oh?" I said neutrally as I slipped a twenty under my saucer. "They must have been memorable. It's been nearly six months."

"Hmmm," she said. And waited.

I added a second twenty.

"It was typical stuff," she said, pitching her tone so only I could hear it. Clearly she'd had a lot of practice.

"*He* thought he gambled too much. He thought *he* worked too much. Nothing got resolved, and nothing probably ever would." Annie pointed from Gainer to Bittner, then from Bittner to Gainer as she spoke.

"No details?"

"No. It sounded like an old argument, one they both knew only too well. So they were fighting bitterly, in their own very civilized shorthand."

I knew exactly the kind of argument she was talking about. I'd run across them on what I called my "follow the errant spouse" cases. It's why I avoid those cases as much as possible.

"Now these three," she said thoughtfully, tapping Gainer's photo, then Grassini's and Bingham's.

"You've seen them together?"

She nodded.

Well, they were all at the same conference, so it shouldn't have been that surprising. I'm not sure why it was.

"Just the three of them?" I asked as I slid another twenty beside the others.

"That time," she said, giving me a significant look.

"Oh?" I said. And slid her another bill, making it an even hundred.

She gave me a slight smile and a little nod. Apparently I'd found her price. "The first two had dinner together, just them, a few times, I think."

Gainer and Bittner. "Go on."

"I think I saw these three at dinner one evening," she tapped Gainer's photo, then Bingham's, then Grassini's.

While I was still gaping over that one, she dropped her bombshell.

"Then all four of them had dinner on Wednesday night," Annie said. "I remember because none of them ordered the special, which is always lobster on a Wednesday. Most people order Wednesday's special. In fact one of them was allergic, I think…"

She hovered over the photos for a second, then tapped Bittner's photo. "Seafood allergy, I'm pretty sure."

Wednesday—the night of the Russian Bar.

O. M. G.—as Cory's sister would say. "Just that one night?"

She nodded. "Yes. And I think these three," and she tapped Gainer, Grassini and Bingham's photos, "Had dinner again the following night."

I wondered who had instigated those threesome dinners. Gainer? Somehow I doubted it. I couldn't see him setting up his lover.

But then I didn't think he was the murderer, either. I could be wrong on all counts. There was still the unanswered problem of why he'd changed his shoes.

Had Gainer known whatever it was the other two were up to? Or was there some innocent reason for these dinners that I was missing?

Suddenly I wondered why Gainer had invited Bittner to Vegas. It had seemed out of character for someone who likes to keep his various affairs very, very quiet.

And why had Bittner agreed to go? He had to have known it would be hard, if not impossible for him not to gamble to excess, surely? Unless he thought Vegas was the place he could finally make that big score?

"Then, on the last night, the lovers had dinner together," Annie was saying, tapping Gainer and Bittner's photos. She seemed determined to give her money's worth.

"*He* seemed sad, as if he'd lost everything that mattered." And she tapped Bittner's photo again.

She probably wasn't far wrong.

———

I WAS TOO stunned by what I'd just learned to choose food, so at Annie's suggestion I ordered the Chef's Choice. I was served an amazing four course meal, with Annie bringing me one exquisite dish after another.

I remember savoring every course, but not what the dishes were. I was too focused on trying to figure out what the information Annie had given me meant.

What if they'd all been in it together? Gainer, Grassini, Bingham and Bittner. Or maybe just Gainer, Grassini and Bingham? Or had Bingham and Grassini wanted something from Bittner, and used Gainer to get to Bittner?

That last seemed to me the most plausible.

I mentally ran through everything I knew—or thought I did—about David Bittner. And everything I'd learned in Vegas. By the time the dessert course came, my head was spinning.

I took a bite—I think it was some kind of chocolate torte—washed down with their terrific coffee. But my brain wouldn't let go of the puzzle that this case had become.

How did the pieces fit together?

A soft ding from my phone. I grabbed it, to see a short text from Badger. No explanation for the texts she hadn't responded to, just a few brief words. But they were explosive.

Robert Bingham's firm, TML Corporation was a privately held multinational firm which owned majority stakes in companies all over the world. Including Hughes Furniture International, the company that was doing the furniture deal with Justine.

What?

Had this been about Justine and her company all along, and not about Bittner's gambling addiction?

Suddenly all those meetings, and David Bittner's Vegas windfall raised some very different questions. And all my speculations about mob loans or some convoluted money laundering scheme looked like I'd been chasing a red herring.

That huge windfall could have been offered to Bittner by TML as some kind of loan, a Trojan Horse designed to play on the man's weaknesses?

Or it could have been an outright payment—a bribe—for something they wanted from him? Like insider secrets, maybe—the kind that had started those rumors?

As I considered the second option—windfall as bribe—I could almost hear the pieces clicking into place.

Or was I still missing something?

I checked my watch. Cory would still be meeting with Justine now. I wondered how that was going, and what secrets he'd be able to uncover. Someone was betraying Justine.

Had David Bittner, her best friend, been part of that?

He'd had access to all her company information, anything that TML Corporation might have wanted. Had he agreed to give it to them?

Or did they have to use his inevitable gambling losses as leverage?

Had Grassini played a role in all of this? Did he have something to do with the amount of credit three major casinos had extended to Bittner—a man even the casino hosts could see was floundering.

I needed to know more about that conference. It had brought Gainer to Vegas, and given Grassini and Bingham access to him. And to Bittner.

Who had organized it? How long ago? And where had the funding come from?

Wait a minute. I pulled up the conference welcome package.

And there it was, emblazoned on the very first page. "With thanks to our sponsors."

And the first listing? TML Corporation.

I felt like doing one of those exaggerated movie slap-to-the-forehead routines. I'm sure my fellow diners would have been impressed.

I flipped to the listings page. There was an entire track of lectures and talks on "trademarks and licensing in the international world." Of course there was.

I ate the last delicious bite of whatever-it-was, finished my coffee and signaled for the bill.

I needed to get back to my hotel. I had a few calls to make.

CHAPTER THIRTY-SIX

The insistent ringing of the phone woke me the next morning. I answered groggily, half aware that it was still dark out. It felt like I'd had no sleep at all.

I glanced at the clock. One a.m. I'd only been asleep for an hour.

"Barbara, it's me." Marie's voice sounded tight, and had a note I hadn't heard since her sister was kidnapped.

"Marie. What is it?"

"Barbara, there were two more murders."

My breath hitched. Cory had been helping Justine yesterday. "Not Cory? Justine?"

"No, no. They're both fine," Marie said quickly. Her breathing wasn't quite steady.

"Then who?"

"No-one you know. And the murders aren't recent."

"Start at the beginning, Marie. And take a deep breath first."

While she was doing that, I grabbed my robe and a bottle of water from the mini-fridge. I sank into the club chair by the window, and stared out at the glittering lights and improbable structures stretching out to the horizon while I waited for her to get her thoughts in order.

"You know I've been looking into Justine's stalker," she said in a rush. "And why Justine didn't finish her degree, and anything I could find out about the other student, Ethan Walker, the one who committed suicide."

"Go on," I said, taking a slow sip of water.

"Well, I finally tracked down his sister. Walker's sister, I mean. She's in Australia. Perth. I just talked to her."

"That's good work. But how does that relate to the murders?"

"She told me about the murders. One a year ago, one two and a half years ago. Both unsolved."

"Where?"

"In Perth."

"How does this tie in to Bittner's murder?"

"The victims were both former schoolmates of Walker's. He did his schooling in Australia, then came to Vancouver on an exchange scholarship. His body was sent home to Australia for burial."

Too much information. She needed to focus. "Have the police linked the murders to Walker?"

"The sister—her name's Maddison Harris—she says not. But she's sure it's connected."

"Why?"

"Because someone has been sending her notes. It sounds like Justine's stalker. I've just emailed them to you."

I opened my laptop, found the email and read through the two notes—both 'written' using letters and words cut out of a newspaper and pasted haphazardly on a page. Someone—presumably the sister—had scanned the result a little crookedly, adding to the amateurish feel.

One note read "Ethan was murdered. They need to pay so he can rest in peace," and the other "The scales are balancing. Ethan rests easier"

"Did she send them to the police?" I asked.

"Yes. The sister—Ms. Harris—says they didn't believe her. They did look, but didn't find anything to connect the notes with the murders. And there was nothing that would identify the sender, either."

Something was missing here. "Why are you so worried, then?"

"She just got another note," Marie said. "And this one had a clipping from the Vancouver Sun about David Bittner's murder. Her scanner died just as she was about to send it, so she read it to me."

It only needed that. "There were no clippings with the first two notes?"

"No."

"What did this note say?"

"Almost done now. Soon Ethan can sleep," Marie said with a catch in her breath.

"The same cutout and pasted on letters?"

"Yes," Marie said.

"Did Ms. Harris take this note to the police?" I asked urgently.

"Not yet. She just got it this afternoon. It was mailed to her."

"Call her back. Now. Ask her to take all three notes into the police department there, and to have them send copies to the Vancouver police."

"I'm on it," she said. No indecision now.

"Justine's going to need protection. I'll set that up from here. And I'll talk to Cory. And Badger. Can you open the office early tomorrow—I mean this morning?"

"I'll do that."

"And if you see Badger before I talk to her, have her call me, will you?"

"Sure thing."

"Thanks, Marie. Call me if you need me," I said, and disconnected.

It sounded like this case was about to blow wide open. In a completely unexpected direction. Had I been wrong about why Bittner had died all along?

I needed to get home. But I had a couple of things to do here first.

———

I WAS TOO WIRED for sleep. But there wasn't much I could do at one-fifteen a.m. Except head back to the casinos, and I wasn't going to find my answers there.

But it was four-fifteen in the afternoon in Perth. And they had two unsolved murders on their books.

I didn't have any police contacts in Australia, and on this case, I didn't like my chances if I called them without a professional introduction. But I did have a contact at Interpol. And it was ten-thirty a.m. at Interpol headquarters in Lyon.

I put on a pot of coffee. While it brewed, I had a quick shower and got dressed—a bathrobe wasn't going to cut it for these calls. Coffee in hand, I picked up the phone.

I'd worked with Adrien Keller of Interpol on a previous case, one that had ended well for both of us. He was happy to take my call.

"I need a favor," I said bluntly when he answered.

"You've earned a few," Keller said. "What can I do for you? I received your email about money laundering the other day. Can I assume this call is related?"

"Well, yes and no," I said, which surprised a laugh out of him. "I'm in Vegas right now, following up on the gambling angle, and the case has just taken an unexpected turn. Now it seems that the money might not be about laundering, but about industrial theft."

"That isn't exactly Interpol's jurisdiction," he said.

"It is when it's intellectual property, right?"

"Go on." Now he sounded somewhat intrigued. "What kind of intellectual property?"

"Design—high end furniture and accessory design. And there are at least two more murders involved, which also relate to the same designer's work. Plus accusations of trademark infringement. Still not interested?"

"I could use a few details," he said in his driest tone.

I would have laughed, but it wasn't even two a.m. I'd had about five hours sleep in the last forty-eight hours.

And I desperately needed to get out ahead of this case before there was another murder. This time of someone I knew and cared about.

I filled him in on the case so far, but kept Justine's name out of it.

"So from what you're saying, there's really two cases here?" he said. "One is a company that's supposed to be leasing this designer's works, but may be bribing her employees to steal her intellectual property instead.

And the second is an individual who's accusing the designer herself of stealing a different intellectual property a number of years ago. And this individual is claiming that he's murdered three people over the last two years in retaliation. Including one of the designer's key employees—who is one of the people the first company was bribing. Have I got that right?"

I had to remind myself that it was a reasonable hour of the morning where he was. Because he'd just made more sense of my case in five minutes than my tired brain had managed in the week I'd been working on it.

"That summarizes the case so far," I said ruefully. Draining my mug, I walked from my desk to the in-room coffee maker to pour another cup.

My mind was still turning over his summary. Two cases? Both involving Justine and her designs? Something was wrong with that theory.

I didn't have a better one, though, and I needed his help. For now, I'd go with the notion of two cases.

"Much as I'd enjoy working with you again," Keller said, "I wouldn't be the logical choice for this one. And it would be a stretch for Interpol to get involved at this point, anyway. I'm sorry."

"It's okay, I knew that," I said. "It still isn't clear enough to me what's really going on with all of this. But there do seem to be three related murders—which gives us a serial killer. And the timeframe between the murders is getting shorter."

"Go on," he said.

"If this is real, this individual has killed in two countries, Australia and Canada, which makes any investigation difficult. And he's been stalking my client for the last six months, and his threats keep escalating. I'm afraid for my client's safety."

"I'm still not sure what we can do for you?"

"I need to make sure the authorities in Perth are talking to their counterparts in Vancouver. I have contacts on the Vancouver force. But I don't know who to talk to on the Perth force. And I need them to take me seriously."

"You need a contact on the Perth force?" Keller said. "That I can do."

"Preferably one who's been dealing with these two cold cases," I said. "And I need an introduction, so I'm not just some unknown P. I. with a far-fetched theory."

"I'll make the call myself," Keller said. "I'm happy to tell them just how accurate your far-fetched theories can be."

"Thanks. I think."

"Don't mention it." I could hear the grin in his voice. "I'll email you the name and number as soon as I've talked to the police in Perth," he said.

"I appreciate it. And I've just sent you what information I have on the two murders in Perth," I said, suiting action to words. "I'll wait for your email."

CHAPTER THIRTY-SEVEN

My call to the detective who was handling the two murders in Perth went far better than I had any right to expect. Especially since the two previous murders had both gone cold.

Apparently Keller had sung my praises, while convincing the officer that I was both reliable and trustworthy. Not an easy feat when you're talking about the relationship between the police and private investigators. A few P. I.s with questionable ethics have given the rest of us a bad name.

"We had a couple of suspects, but we couldn't prove anything," Inspector Keith Anderson of the Western Australia Crime Investigation and Intelligence Services said. "So the case went cold. When Walker's sister brought in the original notes, we thought it was some dipstick wanting attention. We did look, but we never found any connection between our suspects and Walker or his suicide. This latest murder changes things."

"So Walker's sister brought in the latest threat?" I asked him.

"She left just before your Interpol fellow called. It was good timing."

Bless Marie for calling me so quickly. And for persuading Ms.

Harris to act immediately. "So you'll call Vancouver about your cases?"

"If you give me the officers' names, I'll get right on that."

"I'll email them to you," I said. "But with the time difference, they won't be in for another six hours or so."

"I'll email everything to them, then, along with my cell number," Anderson said. "We'll sort it out quick enough. We've got a serial killer running around. I want this guy caught."

I could hear it in his voice. Good. Justine wasn't going to be safe until this guy was behind bars.

"I'll send you the names of the two detectives assigned to the case and another Homicide detective. I haven't had a chance to update them yet—I've been running down leads in Vegas—but I will make sure to brief at least one of the detectives before you talk to him."

Jerry was not going to be impressed, but at least he'd listen to me, even over the phone. Detectives Aaron and Singh I wasn't so sure about. And I didn't have time to waste.

"I'm going to suggest we work with Interpol as well," Anderson said. "Just to make sure we aren't missing anything. We probably need their databases, anyway. Keller passed on a contact name on their end."

"Perfect," I said, and made a note to find out where TML Corp was headquartered. "Thank you."

"No, Ms. O'Grady. Thank you. If we do end up catching this guy, the drinks are on me if you ever make it to Perth."

"It's Barbara," I said. "And same goes. Whoever this is has been making my client's life a misery. I want them stopped, and soon."

"Keith," he said. "And that makes two of us."

There wasn't much more to say after that, so he gave me his email address, and we exchanged cell phone numbers.

"Feel free to call anytime if you need info or if you learn anything more," he said.

"I do have one question," I said. "What calibre of bullets did your killer use?"

"22's," he said. "That a match to your guy?"

"It is indeed," I said with quiet satisfaction. Marchant had managed to get that information from somewhere and had passed it on.

I thanked Keith and disconnected, then sent off the information I'd promised him.

———

I CHECKED MY WATCH. Just after two. It was much too early to call Jerry, or the security firm I use. But it was way too late to go back to bed.

I put together an email updating Jerry on the situation, and asking him to a) call me on my cell as soon as he got this and b) brief the officers responsible for the case, plus anyone else they needed to bring in. I sent Nick a quick outline of the same—"fyi"—with a promise to call soon.

I shook the tension out of my fingers, drank some more coffee, and sent an email to a security firm I've worked with in the past, explaining the situation, and requesting they a) call me asap and b) assign bodyguards for Justine and Cory.

I left an email for Justine, and a text for Cory. Both said the same—call me as soon as you get this. No way I was telling them their lives might be in danger via email.

Then I checked that my cell was fully charged, and reached for the room service menu. I was going to need a lot of fuel to get through this day.

———

THE FIRST CALL came in just as I was finishing my plate of bacon, pancakes and eggs. It was my security firm. I glanced at the time. Two forty-five a.m.

Good to know they monitored emails, even in the middle of the night.

It was a brief call. The guy on the other end, Robert Ng, was someone I'd worked with before, which made the explanations easier. I filled him in, and asked him to put a watch outside both Justine and Cory's homes.

"Hold off on anything more until you hear from me," I said. "I'll need to talk to these two, then I'll get back to you."

He gave me his cell number, and we disconnected.

———

I'D JUST CLEARED my plate and poured another cup of coffee when my phone rang again. I glanced at the ID.

"Cory? What are you doing up at three a.m.?"

"Aunt Barbara? I saw your email. And I have stuff to tell you about Justine's computer systems, too. What's up?"

He'd evaded my question, but that could wait. I filled him in on what Marie had found. To my amazement, he laughed. Quietly, because he was probably in his basement bedroom, and he wouldn't want to wake his mom, my sister.

Neither of us would ever hear the end of that one.

"You think I might be in danger because I was helping Justine with the problems at her firm?" Cory said. "There's no way. She's in so much trouble."

"What do you mean? What kind of trouble? And why didn't you text me?"

I reined myself in. They were valid questions, but I was sounding more like a worried aunt than I was a seasoned P. I.

"I'm still working on her systems," Cory said.

My stomach clenched. "Tell me you're not still at her offices."

"Of course not," he sounded offended. "I'm at yours. I needed the screen here."

"Alone? At this time of night." That couldn't be safe. "And where does your mom think you are?"

I heard the sigh over the phone. "Take a breath, Aunt B.," he said. "I'm studying. With a friend."

I used my laptop to send a quick text to Robert Ng, asking him to redirect the security from Cory's home to my offices.

"You lied to your mother," I said. Half-horrified at the words coming out of my mouth. None of my filters seemed to be working, and I was way more worried about Cory than I'd admitted to myself.

"No, I really am studying with a friend," he said. "Badger's here. We're doing a deep dive in the Grayson Design systems. They're a total mess. You wouldn't believe what we're finding."

He must have put me on speaker phone because I suddenly heard Badger's voice in the background. "Tell her about the office security," she said.

"Oh. Yeah. When we saw what we had here, we made some changes to your office security systems. Badger insisted. We're safe here. And Marie's here too," he added. "So you don't have to worry about her, either."

When had they had time to make security changes? And why hadn't Marie told me where she was calling from? "You've been there all night? All three of you?"

"Sure. Since after I met with Justine yesterday. There's a lot here to do. And it couldn't wait."

"I'm assigning someone to watch the building anyway," I told him.

This time Badger's voice was louder. She must have moved closer to the phone. "That isn't necessary. They won't come after Cory."

"How do you know?"

"Because he didn't leave any tracks in Justine's system. As soon as he saw what was going on, he got all the login codes from her and called me. I met him here."

"So no-one is looking for him? What about the digging around in the Grayson Design systems you're doing now?"

"We're good. Cory and I upgraded the security here last night, so it's close to impossible for anyone to track anything using your servers online," Badger said. "Basically, Barbara O'Grady Investigations now has invisible computers as far as the internet is concerned."

Okay, then. I gulped some coffee. "What are you finding?"

———

WHAT WEREN'T THEY FINDING?

There were data leaks everywhere. The original security for Grayson Design's computer system had so many back doors built in that it was practically transparent. In addition, there were several viruses on various employee's computers—including Justine's—that gave total access to whoever was holding the reigns of that particular virus.

Justine's receptionist and one of her designers were both skimming information off the server and sending it to an anonymous address somewhere in Europe. The *same* anonymous address.

And someone had added a senior user with access to nearly everything—only that user was outside the firm. The path for that senior user bounced from server to server all over the world. Badger had finally tracked it back through a series of trapdoors to an anonymous user at TML Corporation.

And whoever had set that senior user account up, they had administrative access to the Grayson Design systems. Was that what TML had bribed Bittner to do?

Or had they just attempted to bribe him to do it?

Just listening to the catalog of problems was giving me a headache. I couldn't imagine how Badger and Cory were feeling.

Or how Justine was going to feel when I told her. It sounded like she'd been betrayed at every turn. By employees she trusted, even thought of as family.

But where was all this coming from? There was too much of it for this to be a random attack. Or even a series of random attacks. And the connection to TML Badger had found argued very strongly that it wasn't.

But who was behind it all? Robert Bingham? Or was he a front for someone else?

I thanked the three of them, and extracted a promise that they'd call me with regular updates. Cory was the one who agreed—I suspected after some behind the scenes nudging from Badger and Marie. I also suspected that we had different definitions of "regular."

Just as I was about to disconnect, Badger spoke up again. "I'm still looking into TML," she said. "They're a very *interesting* company."

Which probably translated as 'they're a collection of robbers and thieves who will stop at nothing to make more and more money.' Or maybe something worse.

I couldn't wait.

CHAPTER THIRTY-EIGHT

I was making notes from my conversations with Perth, John Ng, Cory and Badger, and comparing them to the scenario I'd started to put together from what I'd learned in Vegas.

Something was starting to emerge from this mess of data, but the outlines were blurry, and I wasn't quite sure how everything fit together.

But I was sure that it did. This wasn't two cases. This was one huge, ugly mess of a case. And it was all aimed at Justine.

Whoever was behind this was focused, organized, highly intelligent—they had to be, to keep all these parts moving—most likely some flavor of sociopath. And vindictive as hell.

I wasn't sure yet if greed was the real motive behind all of it, or if it was revenge. But whatever the motivator, Justine had pissed someone off, and they intended to make her pay for it.

———

I WAS STARING at my notes and wishing for a whiteboard when my cell rang. Again.

As I grabbed it, I glanced at the time. Quarter to four. Wasn't anyone sleeping this morning?

"Justine? Why are you up at this hour?"

"I'm always up at four. What's wrong now, Barbara?" She sounded torn between resignation and panic. "And why are there security people in my hall?"

Bless John Ng. I wasn't sure how he'd got his people into Justine's secured building—or why she'd spotted them—but I was glad they were there.

"It's going to be okay," I told her. "My computer gurus are sorting out your computer systems and closing off the leaks." Or at least, I assumed they were closing them off. They hadn't actually said they were.

I firmly put that distraction away. Computer leaks were the least of Justine's worries at the moment.

"Look, Justine. I have some bad news," I said. "We've just received information that may have linked David Bittner's death to two unsolved murders that occurred in Australia over the last two years."

"Australia?" Justine's voice was ice. "Ethan Walker was from Perth. This whole thing is related, isn't it?"

"I think so."

"And I'm next? That's what you're trying to tell me? That's why the security?"

Her voice had risen, cracked. "This is all my fault."

She was on the verge of hysteria. And I was stuck in Vegas.

"No, it isn't your fault." I said firmly. "Snap out of it, Justine. This is the work of a serial killer, who has some invented reason for killing people. And the police are going to catch him."

"How? You don't even know who's doing this."

"Whoever it is has left electronic clues every where. My team is getting close. And the killer has started sending notes to Walker's sister," I told her.

"Whoever this is wants to be caught, Justine. And we'll catch him. You just have to stay safe until we do."

Something clicked in my brain as I tried to reassure her, and some of the facts I'd been collecting began to realign.

"Why should I get to be safe, when David was killed because of me?" Justine was saying.

"David was killed because we're dealing with a serial killer. Someone whose world works according to rules only he understands," I said, thinking hard as I did so.

My only answer was a sob.

"Justine?"

Silence. Oh no.

"Justine!"

I used my laptop to send a text to Chelsea—hoping she'd set a ringtone loud enough to wake her—with the message that her aunt needed her. Now.

Moments later I heard Chelsea's voice in the background, and let out a breath of relief.

Next thing I knew Chelsea was on the line. I briefed her on what was happening, asked her to stay with Justine. "Of course," she said.

"Call me if you need anything," I said. "I'll let you know when anything changes."

"Good, thanks," Chelsea said. "And we'll be fine."

I hoped that was true.

———

AS SOON AS I'd disconnected, I pulled up the registrant's list from the international legal conference that had been held in Vegas in March. And I searched for Maddison Harris. Ethan Walker's sister.

To my not-quite surprise, I found her.

Maddison Harris was forty-one. She was blond, tanned, very fit, and wearing a suit that clearly cost more than my entire wardrobe. Including the shoes.

She had a lovely smile, and looked far too vulnerable for her very senior position. Except for her eyes—the barracuda peered through in her pale blue eyes.

And Maddison Harris worked for TML Corporation. She and Bingham were colleagues.

My totally off-the-wall intuitive leap had been right.

But I needed to be absolutely sure. I called my office.

As I'd expected, Marie answered. She really was going above and beyond on this case. It was time I told her so.

"Marie—thank you for being there," I said.

"Barbara?" she sounded worried. "Are you all right?"

Note to self—never give compliments on too little sleep. It comes out all wrong.

"I'm fine," I said briskly. "But I need everything you have or can dig out in the next twenty minutes on Walker's sister."

"On Ms. Harris? But why?" Now she sounded like the one who'd got too little sleep. Which was probably also true.

"I'll explain later. But I need to know where she was when the three murders took place."

"You're kidding me, right? She's the victim's *sister*." I could hear the astonishment in Marie's voice. She'd seen where I was going with this.

"Exactly," I said. "His big sister. And have you found anyone else still grieving Walker's suicide?"

There was a pause. "Well, no," Marie said.

"It's a long shot," I said.

Though less of one now. Which I wasn't about to tell Marie. "But have a look anyway. And I need it for a phone call with the cops in Perth in twenty-five minutes. Can you do it?"

Or have Badger do it. I suspected getting access to Maddison Harris's travel schedules would be a walk in the park for Badger.

Which apparently didn't need saying—someone was already triaging the assignments I'd given all three of them, and figuring out who was the best person to handle each one. I couldn't figure out if it was Badger or Marie who was in charge of it. Or some weird combination of both of them.

The only thing I was sure of was that it wasn't me.

Which was something that should probably worry me, and maybe it would. Tomorrow.

Or whenever their system stopped working, and I stopped getting the data I needed, when I needed it.

"Of course," Marie said. "I'll get it to you shortly."

I was counting on it.

"Thanks," I said. "And if Badger has anything on TML Corporation, send me that too."

———

MARIE CAME through with the information. I skimmed through the email and both attachments. Then I read all of it again, slowly.

And spent the next ten minutes reviewing the data points she and Badger had sent, comparing them against everything I already had, and moving the puzzle pieces around.

All of which would have worked much better if I was in the office with the team—and several large whiteboards. I wished I'd flown home last night, but I had one last thing to do here. As soon the business offices at Island Sun opened this morning.

Not all of Vegas is open 24/7.

I slotted several more pieces in place. Looked at what I had, and put in a call to Keith in Perth.

I didn't quite have everything sorted yet, but this was too big to wait until I did.

My call went to voice mail.

Seconds later, the phone rang and I pounced on it. I'd expected it to be Keith, but it was Jerry. Which was probably just as well— Jerry would have more patience while I laid out this theory than someone I'd never worked with before. He could be the sounding board I needed.

Then he could sell it to everyone else.

"What is all this, O'Grady?" he asked.

Normally I would have given him a bad time about being up so early. These weren't normal times.

"The Justine Grayson case. Or rather, the David Bittner murder."

"I figured that much out," he growled.

Jerry's never been a morning person, so I ignored that. "I've been working on Justine Grayson's issues with an anonymous stalker, which seem to be escalating."

"That should be a police matter."

"I agree. But at the moment, your guys are more interested in whether Justine killed her friend."

"Bittner?"

"Yeah."

He sighed. "Okay. I got it. Now what's this about murders in Australia and this being a serial killer here too? What's the connection?"

It was all in the email, but I knew how Jerry worked. He liked to hear cases laid out for him if possible.

"The stalker. Whoever that is, he's been clear he blames Justine for the suicide of a fellow student—Ethan Walker— more than a decade ago. Says Justine stole the student's ideas, which drove him to suicide."

"So? That was a long time ago."

"Turns out that student, Walker, was originally from Australia— he was in Canada on an exchange scholarship. And the two murders there, both still unsolved—Walker's sister has been getting newspaper-cutout-type letters from someone claiming to be the killer."

"How were they killed?"

"Both shot," I said. "Same calibre bullet as Bittner."

"I'm not even going to ask how you know that," Jerry said. "So what? A lot of murderers use .22's. So what do these letters have to do with anything?"

"The letters claim the murders were avenging Walker, the student. No details, though. The police confirmed that the two victims were former classmates of Walker's, but were never able to make a connection to the murders, or find the sender."

"Go on." Jerry sounded totally awake now. Good.

"Walker's sister just got another letter, with clippings from the *Vancouver Sun* on Bittner's murder. Same claims as before—avenging Walker's death. And making it clear there will be more murders."

"You think Justine Grayson is in danger?"

"That's my fear. I've got security keeping an eye on her. But..."

"We need to move on this, and fast. If any of this is true. But the same student, this Walker, being linked in all three cases, and in two countries? Gives those letters more weight."

"That was my thinking."

"Your email says you talked to the investigator in Perth?"

"Keith Anderson. Yes. He seems on the ball. And very interested in Bittner's murder."

"He would be. The last Perth murder was a year ago?"

"Yes."

"His cold case just went hot," Jerry said. "If this is true. Okay, I'll brief Aaron and Singh. They'll connect with Perth, take it from there. If they need to bring you in...?"

"I'm in Vegas," I said. True enough. No need to tell him I expected to be home by tonight. Not yet, anyway. "But you have my cell."

"Vegas? Never mind. Okay, you can count on a call from them."

"Jerry. There's one more thing. I have a call in to Keith Anderson, but I haven't been able to reach him yet. So I'll tell you first. I haven't been able to make all the connections on this one yet, so it's still mostly theory."

He muttered something under his breath.

"What was that?" I asked. With a grin I was glad he couldn't see.

"I'm listening," he said

"Walker's older sister," I said. "Maddison Harris. She's a high-flying corporate lawyer on the fast track. She works internationally, and she travels a lot. She was in Vancouver the week Bittner was killed. And in Perth when each of the others was murdered."

My long shot had come in when Badger had confirmed those travel dates. Much to Marie's amazement. And even to mine, a little.

"The sister? The one who's been receiving the letters from the killer? You saying you think she's a suspect?"

"Yes, that's exactly what I think. Justine Grayson is dealing with industrial espionage as well as being a suspect in Bittner's murder. I suspect there's a stone cold killer with a very devious mind behind all of it.

"One trained to consider all the angles, and to pay attention to detail—and that part fits Maddison Harris to a T. I also think Harris had motive and opportunity for all three murders."

There was a brief silence on Jerry's end. Outside my room, I could hear a room service cart, and the blare of traffic. Vegas was starting to wake up.

"You're going to pass this notion to Keith Anderson in Perth?"

"Yes. As soon as he gets back to me. "

"Did they look at Harris in the initial investigation?"

"No. They had no reason to. And if what I suspect is true, she knows exactly how to present herself, and how to manipulate people."

"You think we're dealing with a sociopath."

"Don't you?"

"Too few details to draw that conclusion," he said automatically. But I could practically hear his mind working.

"I think it would be worth looking into what she was up to when she was in town for Bittner's murder," I said.

"That's up to Singh and Aaron. But we'll see what Perth has to say."

Uh huh. "I'll see how persuasive I can be," I said.

Meanwhile I'd get Badger to look into what Maddison Harris had been up to in Vancouver. It couldn't hurt.

I didn't share that thought with Jerry. Not yet.

Because I no longer thought Harris would kill Justine. Not right away. First she'd destroy Justine's business and reputation, and leave her sitting in the smoking ruins of her life

Then she'd kill her.

And I was determined to stop her.

But first I'd have to unravel the complex and devious plan Harris had put in place.

CHAPTER THIRTY-NINE

No sooner had Jerry disconnected than my phone rang again. This time it was Keith Anderson in Perth.

"Sorry I missed your call earlier," he said. "I just got out of a meeting."

I had to remind myself of the time difference. It was seven in the evening there. "Oh?" I said.

"Yup. Just met with Maddison Harris."

I felt a cold chill down my spine. "How did that go?"

"She brought in the clippings and the letter you told me about. You were right. The three cases looks connected. But the letters make it hard to take seriously."

I didn't like the sound of that. "Why do you say that?"

"Well, frankly, they're amateurish—raggedly pasted on a page, mis-spellings. And the threats sound empty. Not the kind of thing someone capable of carrying off three murders on two continents would do."

"Maybe they were designed to sound that way," I said.

"Funny, that's what Ms. Harris said, too," he said. "She was very persuasive."

What kind of game was she playing? I had to go carefully here. I needed Keith on my side—not the killer's—unknowingly or not.

"So are you persuaded?" I asked him.

"Leaning that way," he said. "We're going to re-open the investigation, anyway. I'm just waiting for the call from your guys in Vancouver."

"I've spoken with Detective Jerry Haworth. But they may want to check a few things before they talk with you. You should be hearing from them in two or three hours."

"Good," he said. "If there's something in this, we want to get going on it before it gets any colder."

"I can imagine," I said. "At least Maddison Harris came to you right away, so there was no time lost there."

"I sensed some frustration from her, because we didn't take her seriously the last time."

Which would be her ostensible reason for being so open with Marie when she'd called. I wondered what her real reason was.

"It must be hard for her to be getting those letters," I said carefully.

"Guess so," he said. He didn't sound sold on the idea. What was that about?

"It helps when you can interview someone in person," I said, probing carefully. "What's your impression of Harris? Is she over-reacting to these letters?"

"No, she really believes there are three murders related to her brother's suicide. And she's—you end up wanting to make things easier for her. So she doesn't have to be upset," he said. And waited.

Interesting choice of phrasing. It sounded like Keith was a pretty experienced officer. Maybe one who'd been burned by a skilled manipulator before? "Sounds like something about that is bothering you?" I said.

"Maybe. She's a lawyer—you'd think she'd know more about how we work here."

Had he picked up on something off about Harris? That would be helpful. "She's not a criminal lawyer though," I said.

"Guess not."

He'd shut down again. He must have picked up on something—but he wasn't about to put it into words. Not unless I did so first. Time to take another risk.

"I took a look at Maddison Harris's resume," I said. "And she's a pretty high-powered corporate attorney. Not someone who usually waits around for someone else to solve her problems for her."

"Huh."

"There's one other thing," I said. "My team has dug up a bit more information about her. Maddison Harris works internationally, and she travels a lot. I found it interesting that she was actually in Vancouver the week our dead guy was murdered. And in Perth when each of the others was murdered."

"She lives here." His words sounded automatic.

"She doesn't live here. And it was her brother who committed suicide."

I let a small silence hang between us. "I thought it might be interesting to take a harder look at her."

"Huh," he said. "I might just do that from this end. And Barbara? Keep me posted, would you?"

"Sure thing," I said. "And right back at'cha."

He chuckled, and hung up.

———

WELL. I sat staring out the window as the sun began to rise golden over Vegas. That was unexpected.

I'd actually got more support from Keith in Perth than I had from Jerry.

But I knew Jerry. He'd heard me, he'd look into it. And he'd come around.

I just wished I was sure Detectives Singh and Aaron would do so. Maybe they wouldn't call.

My phone rang, and I cursed under my breath.

But it was an anonymous number. Badger. Had to be.

I don't think I'd ever talked to her on the phone before, though. Texts were her usual style. Saved time. I could just hear her saying it. So I answered more cautiously than I might have.

"Barbara O'Grady."

"Keep your nose out of our business," a deep, hoarse voice said. "And get out of Vegas, if you know what's good for you. You won't be warned again."

The line clicked as he—or she?—disconnected, leaving me staring at the phone.

I was getting close, obviously. But to whom? Or to what?

I'd have assumed it was Maddison Harris. Except that as far as I knew, she didn't know I existed. How could she have my phone number?

Not that many people even knew I was in Vegas.

Just when I thought I had a handle on this case, it took another twist. Each one stranger than the last.

Leaving this town was a good idea, though. I glanced at my watch. Nearly five a.m. I made a few quick calculations, then went online and booked my flight home.

It was time to put Vegas behind me.

———

BY EIGHT I was packed and had arranged for a late checkout, leaving my laptop in the room safe. I'd gone back to the La Village buffet in the concourse between the Paris and Bally casinos for a second breakfast. Lashings of coffee and some seriously good pastries had gone a long way to convincing my tired body and brain that it could make it through the rest of the day.

By nine I was walking into the grand office of the woman responsible for the Island Sun Casino's compliance with state gambling regulations. She had a fancier title, but that's what it meant. I'd had Marie book the appointment from Vancouver an hour ago.

"Don't accept a no," I'd told her. "Tell them I'm flying out later this morning, and it's in their best interests to hear what I have to say."

I wasn't sure it would work, but Marie had pulled it off.

The Director rose from behind her massive desk to shake my hand. "Ms. O'Grady? Please have a seat. What can I do for you this morning?"

Her suit was at least as expensive as the one Maddison Harris wore in the photo I had. And her demeanor was all business.

"Thank you for making the time to see me," I said. "As I believe my colleague told you, I'm a P. I., here on a case, and I've spent a great deal of time in your casino. Based on what I've seen, I have some questions and a few concerns."

"I see," she said. "Go on."

"One of the things I've been looking into was a visit made to Vegas, and to your casino, last March, by one David Bittner, since deceased."

I leaned forward a little, met her eyes. "Mr. Bittner had a gambling problem, and he lost a great deal of money at several casinos in town. Including yours. All based on the overly generous credit limits extended to him by the casinos.

Eventually his credit ran out, and he was cut off, but oddly enough he was able to gamble again at Island Sun the following day."

She hadn't moved, but she was watching me steadily. I couldn't read anything from her face or her body language. I'd bet she was a hell of a poker player.

"I know for a fact that Mr. Bittner didn't have additional funds available to him at home," I said. "Nor any legal sources of additional money. Yet somehow he was able to continue gambling—and losing, I might add—for another three days.

For obvious reasons, your main office have been reluctant to tell me how Mr. Bittner paid the moneys he owed to reestablish his credit so quickly."

"What do you mean, *how* he paid them?"

"Was it cash? A bank line of credit? What form did the funds take? And from what source?"

"Your concern, then, is that he may have been laundering money, and that the appropriate questions weren't asked," she said briskly.

"That's a very succinct summary," I said.

And exactly what I'd hoped she'd think I was fishing for. Really, I wanted to know who had funded Bittner, and what the source of those funds had been—and ideally what bank it had been drawn on.

I was guessing it was TML Corporation, as part of whatever deal had been arranged with Bittner during that meeting at the Russian Bar. But it would be handy if I could prove that, given that no-one was likely to believe me.

But she'd never tell me if I asked directly.

"Why did you come to me?" Her tone was neutral, but she'd begun to look at me like a particularly nasty species of bug.

"Well, I could have gone straight to the gambling commission and reported my concerns that your casino might be—inadvertently, I'm sure—laundering money. But I always prefer to extend professional courtesy where I can," I said.

I sat back. It was her move.

"I'm glad you came to me," she said, with a lovely smile. And a nasty look in her eye that she probably thought I couldn't see. "Let me see how I can help you."

She picked up her phone, pushed two keys, and spoke softly into.

CHAPTER FORTY

As the private jet I'd hired cleared the Vegas tarmac, I sat back in the luxurious leather seats and sipped a glass of water. Once the safety lights went out, they'd be serving me lunch. I was still in overdrive, too hyped up from my unfolding case and lack of sleep to be tired. But I was really hungry.

As we gained altitude, I looked out at the sprawl of the city in the valley below me. Even from up here, it didn't look quite real. In the far distance I could see the beginning of the raw mountain ranges we'd fly over on our way home.

I couldn't quite believe I was traveling by P.J., as Justine had insisted on calling the private jet when I called her to clear the expense. Her niece had worked miracles in calming her down—and Justine's own strong leadership instincts had come to the fore. The call from Jerry had apparently helped too.

The Vancouver and Perth forces were marshaling behind the notion of a serial killer who was now targeting Justine. And they were looking very hard indeed at Maddison Harris.

Once Justine's enemy was named—and Harris had proven herself an enemy indeed—Justine was ready for a fight, using any tool at her command.

Apparently P.J.'s—I grinned at the term—were one of those tools.

"Get used to it, Barbara," she'd told me. "You can't run an international business without them. It just takes too long to run the gauntlet of commercial airlines these days. And time is money."

I wanted to remind her that I don't run an international business. But she spoke before I could. She seemed to have read my mind.

"And you do run an international business," she said. "You just don't know it yet."

When Justine isn't panicking, talking to her makes my head hurt.

———

THINGS UNFOLDED QUICKLY once I got home. I'd texted the information I'd got from the Island Sun's Compliance Director to the team. They'd already been doing a deep dive on TML Corporation, even before I'd confirmed that's who was behind Bittner's sudden windfall.

By the time I got into the office, they had almost everything pulled together. I didn't ask who had dug up which pieces. There was no time now.

And I'm not sure I wanted to know—then or ever. What mattered was that Marie, Cody and Badger had worked as a seamless team, even under increasing pressure. And apparently on very little sleep.

Pulling together, they'd unearthed the information we needed to close this case.

That information made it very clear exactly what forces had been directed at Justine. And they were impressive.

The two dark-clothed operatives that the team had been following on the video feeds when I left for Vegas? Once we had TML Corporation's name, Badger had—somehow, and I wasn't asking—got her hands on the employee databases, including photos. Marie had done the rest. Those two worked security for TML.

We still hadn't quite worked out how Maddison Harris had justified their presence and their actions that night. Badger had worked through several layers of bureaucratic paperwork online to find Harris's signature on the original orders that had sent them there.

They weren't the killers, though.

Maddison Harris was one of the guests registered on the fifteenth floor of the Grand Pacific Hotel the night Bittner was murdered. She hadn't even used an assumed name. Why would she? She was there on legitimate business.

And no-one was looking at her.

In fact, Robert Bingham was staying at the Grand Pacific too, though he was staying on a different floor. Maddison Harris herself was staying on the fifteenth floor, the same as Bittner.

And Bittner knew her. She was one of the people Gainer had introduced him to. He probably wouldn't have hesitated to let her in when she showed up outside his room.

I'd found all that out just before I flew home. Once I learned that Harris had been at that international legal conference, I'd taken the photo of Harris from that conference and headed for the Island Sun's Star, showing the photo to my server from the previous day's brunch. He'd immediately recognized Harris as one of the people Gainer and Bittner had breakfasted with.

I still didn't know if Gainer had been complicit in any of this. Probably Harris had snowed him, too. It fit the picture I'd been building of her.

And that she'd want to do the killings herself.

Harris had hidden in plain sight. And she had to be one hell of an actress. Or con-woman. She had that ability to blend, to make people like her—and not see her as any kind of threat—that the most prolific of serial killers seem to have.

The perfect sociopath.

And a brilliant one. The traps she'd set up to destroy Justine? Impressively devious. And flawlessly executed.

She'd been the stalker, of course—using layers of anonymity that were well beyond my computer knowledge. And she had used the prototype of a worm developed by a particularly capable computer tech at one of TML's subsidiaries to sneak into all of Justine's online systems.

Then she'd set it up to look like Justine had been betrayed from the inside, by her own people. And put the computer equivalent of tripwires everywhere, so she'd be alerted the instant anyone dug deep enough.

Even Badger had been impressed.

Badger was more impressed with Cory. Who had somehow spotted one of the tripwires before he'd triggered anything, and called her in immediately. Apparently that should have been impossible.

I'd known Cory was good, but it sounded like everyone had been seriously underestimating him. He was looking a bit too cocky for his own good, though. This was going to need careful handling.

The look Badger gave me at this point in their story told me she'd seen it too. And that there was a conversation the two of us needed to have, as soon as this was all over.

For someone who doesn't talk much, Badger says a lot.

Harris had also engineered most the problems Justine had been having with Hughes Furniture International. While Hughes was supposed to be partnering with her, Harris had been working behind the scenes, with the access she had to Justine's computers, to steal Justine's designs and her ideas for the line.

Then, in a move worthy of Paul Newman in *The Sting*, Harris had set it up so that it looked like Justine had stolen her own ideas from yet another subsidiary of TML Corp.

Badger had copies of a series of emails where Harris had provided date stamped documents and drawings to "prove" to the heads of Hughes International that Justine was trying to sell them copyrighted designs that belonged to someone else. Plans were well underway to sue Grayson Design for everything Justine had, as well as to blacken her name and her brand internationally.

There would have been no way for Justine to recover from an attack this massive and this well coordinated. No-one would believe her.

And it would take a hacker as good as Badger to find the truth.

And Badger was expensive. Justine wouldn't have been able to afford her. Or someone like her. Not after Harris was done with her.

Probably once Justine's life was destroyed, Harris would have moved in for the kill.

But Maddison Harris would never get that chance. As soon as we had this documentation together, I'd be sending copies to both the Vancouver and Perth police forces. And to Interpol.

Once I'd realized just how many countries Harris had been operating in, Keith and I had looped in the Interpol guy.

I was also sending copies to Justine herself.

When we were finished, TML Corp wasn't going to know what hit them. Maddison Harris had broken so many laws in their name, and committed so many injustices against Justine and her company, it was hard to know where to start.

TML was also vulnerable because of their own lack of checks and balances, which had allowed Harris to create all the havoc she had.

Justine was going to be able to sue them from so many angles... She and Brian Stewart were meeting now, putting together their strategy based on the outline I'd sent her from the plane.

And Maddison Harris?

She was already in custody—though she didn't know it. Keith Anderson in Perth had texted me a few hours ago that they had her in interview. She was 'helping' with the investigation.

From what I'd learned about her since I discovered she existed —was it only this morning?—I suspected Maddison Harris wouldn't be able to resist being so close to the investigation. It would feed her feeling of superiority, that they didn't even suspect her.

It wouldn't be long before three police forces were arguing about who got to arrest her. And on which charges.

CHAPTER FORTY-ONE

I didn't get to see the ending of the case. Maddison Harris was arrested in Australia, and as I'd predicted, they were still sorting out charges and jurisdictional issues. But once the police started looking at her, the evidence in all three murders started to accumulate.

And I was still amused by the reaction to the data files I'd sent them.

I didn't hear anything from Jerry, Keith or the Interpol guy I hadn't met. Adrien Keller, however, had called me fifteen minutes after I'd sent the file.

"Holy cripes, Barbara," he'd said when I answered. "I thought your expertise was the art world, like mine. How'd you pull this one off?"

"It took a lot of research," I said. "And I have a good team."

"You must have. Any of them want to work for Interpol?"

I tried to picture Badger working for Interpol, and failed. I grinned. "You can always ask them."

"Somehow I don't think it would be the same."

"Probably not," I said.

————

BY THE TIME I got home, it was very late, and I was so tired my brain felt like it had shut down. I unlocked the door, and smelled fresh coffee. What the…

The hall light was on, and I spotted a fresh pot of coffee on the kitchen counter, with two mugs beside it. Probably not a burglar, then.

Cat came padding out to meet me, and to sniff at my boots. Then he sat down and gave me his patented, "Tuna. Now!" look. He didn't look at all nervous or upset.

There was a muffled thud from the living room, and Nick came padding out behind Cat.

"How…?" I began.

Nick held up his phone. "Marie," he said.

She just didn't know when to stop organizing things, did she? But for once, I was grateful. "Sorry. I should have let you know."

He stuck his phone on the counter and hugged me. "I know how it goes. And it sounds like you were pretty busy, right down to the wire."

I nodded, sank into his embrace. It felt good.

Several minutes later, he said, "Want some coffee?"

"Please."

Something in my tone must have told him how tired I was, because he pulled back a little and examined my face.

"When did you last sleep?"

"Ummm. I got about an hour this morning. And I napped on the plane." A little. Sort of.

"Uh huh. Bedtime for you."

"Coffee first."

"You won't sleep."

"Oh, I'll sleep."

And I did. After he'd properly welcomed me home.

CHAPTER FORTY-TWO

Over the next few weeks, the last details of the case unfolded. Some of it was horrific, some of it was sad. And some of it was almost amusing.

Almost because three people were dead who shouldn't have been. And a good woman's life had nearly been destroyed.

The athletic shoes I'd been so worried about, the ones Michael Gainer had changed into after he'd gone upstairs a second time the night David Bittner was killed? Gainer had drunk too much to drive safely, so he'd decided to walk home, and had changed his shoes to do so.

Gainer had finally told me what really happened that night. He'd gone upstairs to see Bittner again—but it had been an even shorter meeting than the first. Bittner was adamant that they were done—and that it was to protect Gainer himself from the "ticking time bomb" Bittner said his life had become.

One thing Bittner had finally told Gainer was that someone— he'd refused to say who—had been pressuring him to betray Justine's business secrets, and that he'd refused to do so.

But he'd then accepted a bribe from these people, so that he could keep gambling and win everything back.

Which explained a lot of what was going on in Vegas.

According to Gainer, Bittner's plan was that once he'd hit that jackpot, he'd return their money and tell them to go to hell.

Except that he'd lost, of course. Again and again.

Once back in Vancouver, Bittner had taken out the additional mortgages and borrowed money from everywhere he could, legal and illegal. He'd put himself hopelessly in debt—and potentially in danger, given some of those loans—but he'd paid back that bribe.

Which put him front and center on Maddison Harris's hit list.

Bittner's resistance to the effort to bribe him seems to have played a large role in why Harris chose him as her next victim. Or maybe it was that he accepted the bribe, then backed out.

Though in Bittner's version, as told by Gainer, it wasn't a bribe, it was a trap disguised as a loan.

Harris hadn't actually admitted to any of it, but she'd been dropping hints during her interrogations. Apparently she still thought she could outthink everyone around her.

But Harris was a sociopathic killer and Bittner was dead, so likely we'll never know.

As for Gainer himself? His appointment as a judge has just been confirmed. I still wasn't entirely easy about his role in introducing Bittner to Bingham, Grassini and Harris.

But who knows how long Harris had been plotting her revenge against Justine. Probably for years, to develop that complex scheme with its interconnecting details.

Did Bittner figure in those plans even before Harris met him in Vegas? Or did she see an opportunity and grab it?

It was possible Harris was pulling Gainer's strings along with everyone else's. Or not.

I'd just have to live with not knowing.

And Justine? The next time I saw her, Justine didn't say much. Which I understood. Her entire life—everything that mattered to her—had been infiltrated and attacked.

I made sure she knew that David Bittner had never betrayed

her, though. Even at such a high cost, when his own world was falling apart, he'd protected her.

She'd thanked me in a broken voice, then hugged me hard.

And my bill was paid promptly, including a very generous bonus—which I'd shared with the team. It was enough.

Or so I thought.

———

I WALKED up the stairs to my office on a crisp, sunny Tuesday morning a few weeks later. Nick and I had taken a long weekend, and I was feeling refreshed. The only thing on my mind was another cup of coffee.

It wasn't quite eight, so I didn't expect the whole team to be standing there when I walked in. Which they were.

Cory and even Badger wore expectant looks. And Marie was beaming at me. I knew that look. I didn't trust it.

It meant she'd been messing with my life again.

I glanced around. Everything looked the same, but it also looked different. It took me a moment to figure out what was wrong. Then I got it.

"Where's my desk?" I'd grown fond of the eggplant monstrosity, which really did work as well as Justine had promised. The meeting table was gone, too. "What is this, a mutiny?"

Cory laughed. I was glad to see him so happy—and a little worried.

"You need a ship for a mutiny," he said. "This is an office."

"So you say," I looked around suspiciously. All the furniture had moved around. "But it's not the same office I left on Thursday."

Marie grinned, and grabbed my hand. "Come with me."

I allowed myself to be dragged back out into the hallway. They'd earned a bit of latitude, so I'd go along with the joke. For now.

Until Marie came to a stop in front of the office she'd tried to convince me to rent. The one that now bore a very elegant door with a sign reading "Barbara O'Grady Investigations, International" in fancy black lettering, shaded in gold.

Oh no. What had she done now?

Marie flung the door open, and pushed me through. Four voices chorused, "Surprise!"

Four voices?

As I stared at a completely redone space, Justine Grayson stepped out from behind the door.

"I never thanked you properly," she said.

I should have known the minute I saw that sign, but the surprise rendered me speechless. Which was probably just as well.

Justine waved her hand around the space. "This is just the beginning. I still plan to work with you on your branding, but you needed a base if you're going to grow."

"This door," Marie leaped forward gleefully and flung it wide. "Leads into the rest of the office. And everything's been painted to match"

It was. I stared at the connecting door—it looked bigger now. Maybe it was the frosted glass. And it didn't open into a closet anymore.

I hoped that didn't mean we didn't have any storage. That would be bad.

I walked slowly into the new office space, with Cory and Badger crowding behind me. My eyes took in a meeting room, the two offices—one of which held my eggplant desk—a reception station. Everything Marie and I had discussed that day, including all the changes I'd mentioned to her original plan.

My gaze stopped on a counter beside the receptionist—a beverage counter. With one of those coffee or tea pod machines, a small fridge—and a top of the line espresso machine. A cupboard above it held mugs, a tea pot, plates. Even creamer and sugar dishes.

I blinked.

"I have someone in mind for the position," Marie said, waving at the receptionist chair. "If you approve of her, of course. She'll be your assistant, too. And she's a whiz with that espresso machine. Perfect cappuccinos every time."

My mind stalled. What position? Assistant? Marie was going back to school full-time, and she hadn't told me?

"Don't worry, I'll be here too," Marie said.

I guess she'd reached the same conclusion I had—it was time for her to train as a private investigator. So why was I feeling relieved?

"I'm going to be your Office Manager," Marie said. "So you don't have to worry about the stuff you hate doing anyway. I'll just take care of it. Which means you'll still have time to paint in the mornings. We can talk about my salary later—after I've proved that I'm worth what you're going to pay me." She stopped for breath, watching me carefully.

Since I wasn't arguing—yet—she kept going. "But I don't want an office. I'll work in the other room, with Cory and Badger. Don't worry, they think it's a great idea. And it works better if we can toss ideas back and forth with each other."

So that's what had happened while I was out of the office. I was right about the triaging. And it had been Marie doing it.

"It worked while I was in Vegas. And in the middle of a crisis. We'll try it for a month. Then we can talk about it," I said calmly.

Inside I was wondering what on earth I was doing.

Cory was watching me, his grin impossibly wide. "You look like you need a coffee. I'm pretty good on this thing," he said.

And the next thing I knew the office smelled richly of coffee and Cory was handing me a fresh cup with just the right amount of cream. In one of the new mugs.

"Americano," he said confidently. "Cappuccinos take longer."

I drank some coffee. Looked around me again. Found my voice. "Justine. Can I talk to you a moment? In private?"

She shook her head. "I know what you're going to say."

I doubted that. She was still looking pleased with her surprise. Me? Not so much.

Then she surprised me again.

Opening her hands wide, as if to embrace the entire office, and all that it stood for, Justine said, "You and your team, you gave me my life back. And my business. If it hadn't been for the work all of you put in… I don't know. I just don't."

Marie patted her on the shoulder, and Cory handed her the second cup of coffee he'd just made. She smiled at them both.

"I wanted to do something for you, but for them as well," Justine said. "I talked to your team, and this is what they wanted. They wanted to work for you and your company as it grows. All of us see the opportunity here, even if you don't."

I'd been about to blast her for her presumption in making decisions for me, but how could I do that now?

I glanced around me. It was an amazing thing they'd all done for me, but I have to live in reality. Given what this had cost? Plus the additional rent. And additional salaries…

I'd be struggling to make ends meet in a year, max.

Justine seemed to be reading my mind. Or maybe my expression, though I tried to keep it neutral. She held up a hand. "Just listen for a moment, will you?"

It was a plea, not a demand, so I nodded.

"With everything you and your team uncovered, my negotiations with Hughes International and TML Corporation went amazingly quickly. I think poor Brian is still recovering from the shock."

She smiled. "But they were more worried about their reputation than the money, and we had all the documentation. So they made an offer and I settled. It's a very generous settlement, since it takes all of the damages into account. My business will be stronger than ever."

"I'm glad," I said. And I was. She deserved it, after everything she'd been through.

"All due to you and your team. You were amazing—and your business deserves to flourish too. So this is something I can do in return, as a small thank-you for saving me."

"You've already paid our bill,"—including all the expenses for Vegas—"plus a generous bonus," I said. "That's more than enough."

Justine ignored me. "I've already paid all the bills for the reno‑ vations, the furniture and the equipment. Together with the ongoing branding consulting—at no cost to you—those are one part of it. The other part is that I've arranged and paid for a fifteen-year lease on these premises and your old ones next door. To give your firm a cushion, and the time to grow and flourish."

I felt like the floor had just fallen out from under me. All of this already paid for? And no rental payments for fifteen years?

For what I'd been paying on rent, I could hire Badger. And a receptionist, too. Suddenly the expansion everyone seemed to have been pushing really looked possible.

"Justine, it's too much," I said. "The renos and the furniture— that I'll accept with thanks." Since they were already a *fait accompli*. "But paying our lease is just too much to accept."

"And the branding consulting, don't forget. You'll need it," she said, her sharp eyes considering me. "Barbara, you have no idea how much TML's transgressions are worth, do you? Everything here, including the lease costs, is a small fraction of that amount— no more than I'm paying my legal team. You've earned it."

I glanced at Badger, who was nodding. It figures that she'd have found that out.

And Justine's legal team had made that much? Maybe I was in the wrong business.

I glanced around me and knew that was wrong. This was the right business—for me, and apparently for my team. And the future was only going to get brighter.

Then I got a text from Nick. With yet another townhouse list- ing. This one was in White Rock, on the other side of the tunnel— making it an hour out of town. On a good traffic day.

Oh no. Surely he wasn't serious.

I was still staring at it when his next text came in.

He'd sent me a photo of a watermelon. With a bright red bow on it. I could just hear his deep chuckle.

I burst out laughing.

ACKNOWLEDGMENTS

Many thanks to everyone who was there for me at a particularly difficult time. Particular thanks go to Linda Roggeveen for an amazing copy edit and Colleen Cross for great feedback on the beta version. Any errors or omissions are, of course, mine.

www.ingramcontent.com/pod-product-compliance
Lightning Source LLC
Chambersburg PA
CBHW061602190726

48288CB00007B/2135